LADY SARAH
AND THE DUNG-CART
KNIGHT

KINGFISHER
An imprint of Kingfisher Publications Plc
New Penderel House, 283-288 High Holborn
London WC1V 7HZ
www.kingfisherpub.com

First published in the United Kingdom by Kingfisher 2006
2 4 6 8 10 9 7 5 3 1

Text copyright © Gerald Morris 2004
Published by special arrangement with
Houghton Mifflin Company.

A CIP catalogue record for this book
is available from the British Library.

ISBN-13: 978 0 7534 1337 1
ISBN-10: 0 7534 1337 X

Printed in India
1TR/0506/THOM/SCHOY/80SSH/C

LADY SARAH
AND THE DUNG-CART KNIGHT

GERALD MORRIS

KINGFISHER

"But listen, gentlemen; to bring things down
To a conclusion, would you like a tale?
Now as I've drunk a draught of corn-ripe ale,
By God it stands to reason I can strike
On some good story that you all will like.
For though I am a coarse and wayward man
Don't think I can't tell moral tales. I can!"

> *Chaucer's "Pardoner", in the prologue to*
> *his story in* The Canterbury Tales

CONTENTS

For Grace,
her own princess

I

SARAH

Sarah was almost certain that the big knight on the grey horse wasn't the one she was looking for, but she followed him anyway. The knight of the fires had seemed smaller, but that could have been because he was farther away from her that night in February. If this knight would just say something, she was sure she would know from his voice, but the chattering lady at his side wasn't giving him a chance.

Happily for Sarah, the knight and the lady were riding at a ridiculously slow pace, and Sarah was able to keep up with them on foot, even while taking pains to be quiet. Occasionally, Sarah heard snatches of the lady's monologue: ". . . a most lovely shade of pink, but how she thought she could wear it with her yellow hair . . . So nothing would do for him but to fasten her token to his helmet, where *of course* it looked utterly like a purple pigtail, so that we were all obliged to hide our smiles . . . If Gareth hadn't married her, I don't know who . . ." It sounded like a great deal of nothing to Sarah, which may have been why the big knight was silent.

At last the knight and lady came to a small clearing, and the knight stopped his horse and said, "Shall we take a rest here, my lady?"

"Already?" The lady sounded astonished.

"I want to check my horse's hooves," the knight said calmly. "He seems to be favouring the right side." He dismounted and stepped around his horse's neck, and Sarah saw his face clearly. It was not the knight of the fires. She sighed softly and sat behind a bush to wait for them to move on. The knight glanced briefly at his horse's hooves, then strolled over to the tree beside Sarah's bush, removed his long sword from his side, and sat down. "May as well rest a moment while we're stopped," he said.

"Why, my dear brother, I believe you must be getting old," the lady said. "Tired after barely an hour's riding!" She dismounted and then glanced mischievously at the knight. "Is your rheumatism acting up? Shall I brew you a hot posset?"

The knight laid his sword on the grass beside him and leaned against the tree. "The day I see your ladyship brewing a hot anything is the day I shall truly know I'm getting old."

The lady laughed and sat beside the knight, resuming her cheerful monologue about fashions and knights and ladies and courtly nothings, but Sarah no longer listened. Her attention had been caught by the knight's sword. It looked awfully large up close, and Sarah wasn't at all sure she could use it even if she had it, but it was impossible to pass up. For months she had been wishing for a weapon, and here one was, not five feet away. Cautiously, she inched

2

forwards, making no sound as she crept around the bush. When she was right behind the tree where the knight sat, she reached around the trunk until her hand was just above the sword's hilt.

Then came a crushing pain from her forearm, and she felt herself jerked roughly forwards into the tree trunk. Her face smacked the tree, then scraped along the bark as the knight, who had grabbed her arm, dragged her around the trunk and threw her sprawling into the middle of the clearing. She scrambled to her feet and clenched her hands into tiny fists.

The lady was staring at her, open-mouthed but silent, but the knight only regarded her placidly. "That's *my* sword," he said.

"Don't come near me," Sarah said fiercely, "or I'll make you regret it."

The knight's face relaxed, and his lips seemed less stern. "Indeed, I did not know that this forest harboured such ferocious creatures. Stay near me, my lady. I shall try to protect you if we're attacked."

"Fie on you, Kai!" the woman said. " 'Tis but a child! What have you done to her?" Sarah looked sharply at the knight. Was this the same Sir Kai that Mordecai had spoken of?

The knight answered the lady without looking away from Sarah's face. "This child, my lady, was trying to steal my sword, doubtless to cut our throats and rob our corpses."

"No!" Sarah exclaimed, appalled. "I never would have!"

The woman rose to her feet. "Of course you wouldn't," she said soothingly. "Why would a noble young lady like you want to steal a sword?"

Sarah eyed the lady warily, and the knight said, "Noble, you say? Now how might you know that, my lady? She looks like an extraordinarily dirty village urchin to me."

"Perhaps she *could* use a wash," the lady admitted, "but the dress she is wearing beneath that old cloak is of Norwich silk, or I'm a fishwife!"

Sarah blinked with surprise. She wasn't sure if even Mordecai could have identified the quality of her dress so unerringly, considering that no more than two inches of mud-spattered silk showed beneath her coarse woollen cloak.

"Don't bother denying it, child," the knight said to Sarah. He still sat in the grass, leaning against the tree. "My lady here is never wrong about such matters. Nevertheless, whether you're gently born or not, you *were* trying to steal my sword."

"Don't be ridiculous, Kai!"

"Weren't you?"

Sarah lifted her chin. "Yes, I was. But not to kill you with it!"

The knight's thick eyebrows arched. "Then why, child?"

Sarah thought about saying that she only wanted to see it because she'd never seen a sword up close before, but the stern look on the knight's face reminded her strongly of the disapproving frown that Mordecai used to give her when she told a lie. She said clearly, "I wanted it so I could kill my enemies, sir."

The lady grew pale. "No, my child, I beg you. Unsay those words and put aside such thoughts. They will only bring you pain and distress." Sarah set her lips and said nothing, and the lady turned to the knight. "Kai, tell her

4

she's being foolish."

"Is she?" the knight asked. "Killing enemies is what a sword is for, is it not?" In one smooth motion, surprisingly quick for one of his size, the knight rose to his feet and took a step closer to Sarah. "Do you indeed have enemies that deserve killing?"

Sarah felt her eyes burning, and her throat grew tight. She nodded.

"And you wish to be the one who does this?"

"Yes," Sarah whispered.

The knight looked into her eyes for several seconds, his own eyes dark and unreadable beneath his heavy black brows. Then he nodded to himself. "Why then, my child, you should have a weapon, but this broadsword of mine is not for one of your years. How old are you?"

"Thirteen, sir."

"Small for your age, too." The knight walked across to his horse and began untying a bundle behind the saddle.

"What are you doing, Kai?"

"I'm giving the lady a sword. She has need of one."

"No, Kai, not to a young lady. Not to one of her birth."

"I don't know the circumstances of her birth any more than – I beg your pardon, my lady – any more than you do. But much has happened in this child's life since then, I would think. By the by," he called over his shoulder to Sarah, "what's your name?"

Sarah hesitated, then said quietly, "Sarah."

The knight looked back at her, and his eyes narrowed. "Is it, then?" He started to speak, then stopped. At last he bowed his head and said, "A very great pleasure, I'm sure. I am called Sir Kai." Sir Kai untied one last thong and produced a slender sword in a black leather scabbard. Sarah's eyes widened, and without thinking she stepped forwards, hands outstretched.

"Kai, that sword was made for your son! Will you truly give it away to a chance-met stranger in a wood?"

"Trebuchet can make another," Sir Kai replied.

Sarah stopped, and she looked searchingly at Sir Kai's face. "I can't take your son's sword."

Sir Kai chuckled. "You have curious scruples, Sarah. Were you not willing to take my own sword not ten minutes ago?" Sarah looked at the ground and reddened. "Nay, my child. It is no great thing. My son is but two years old and barely walking. This was to be a gift many years hence. You, I feel sure, will need it before he does."

The lady tried once more. "What are you doing, Kai? You can't give such a sword away! Especially to a girl! She should be at home with her mother, sewing samplers and learning to dance!" Sarah's jaw tightened, and her eyes grew hot again.

"T'sh, child," Sir Kai murmured softly. His black eyes rested on her as he brought her the sword. "Think not of it." He threw the belt over her head and left arm, then adjusted the scabbard and stepped back. "It could have been made for you."

Sarah tried to understand what was going on, but her mind only groped helplessly for explanations. Why was this knight giving her a sword? "Thank you, sir . . . Sir Kai. You are too kind. I . . . but I must be going now." She began to back away, fearing that he would change his mind and take the sword back.

Sir Kai shook his head. "Nay, my child. I give no one a

sword unless I may teach how to use it. 'Tis not a toy. First, you must learn to hold it. Draw your sword now."

"What?" the lady gasped. "Do you mean to . . . are you going to give this little girl lessons in swordplay?"

"Just so, my lady."

"And what, pray, am I to do while you do so?"

"You could brew me a hot posset," Sir Kai replied seriously. "For my rheumatism, you know."

Sarah was small, but she had always been wiry, and her life the past three months had given her strength and quickness. She first learned to draw the sword – not at all as easy as one might think, especially when wearing a dress. Sir Kai made her draw the sword again and again, for over an hour, telling her, "Anyone you face is likely to be stronger than you; you'd best be faster than he." After that he showed her how to hold the sword defensively. Then Sir Kai replaced the sword with a stout wooden staff, and taught her how to attack. He said to always hold the sword with two hands. "It will limit your range of motion somewhat, but it will make you faster and give you more control."

"Do you use two hands when you fight?"

"Yes. Occasionally I'll shift it to one hand or the other, but I'm four times your size and much stronger. If I were fighting with that lighter sword, now, I'd use only one hand and rely on speed."

"You *do* have very quick hands," Sarah admitted, rubbing her forearm.

"Sorry about that, Sarah. I wasn't sure if you were a man or a woman. It was hard to tell through the bushes."

"You saw me through the trees?" Sarah asked.

"While we were riding," Sir Kai explained. "Why do you think I stopped? I wanted a better look at you."

"But no one ever sees me when I creep through the brush!" Sarah exclaimed. Her ability to move through the woods without being seen was what had kept her alive since February. She couldn't believe that this knight had seen her.

"Mayhap I have quick eyes, too," Sir Kai said. "Now, pretend I'm coming at you from your right. Position! No, no, child. Look at your feet! One little shove, like this, and you're flat on your . . . you're sitting down. Here, let me show you."

Sir Kai continued teaching Sarah swordplay through the morning, while the lady leaned against the tree and watched. Despite her early complaints about having nothing to do, she showed no boredom. Indeed, she watched the lessons with a growing smile. At last, when the sun was high overhead, the lady interrupted the teacher and the pupil. "Forgive me," she said politely, "but I grow hungry for luncheon. Mistress Sarah, would you honour us with your company for a meal? Are you hungry?"

Sarah was always hungry. Trying not to betray too much eagerness, she thanked the lady and swept a curtsy. Unfortunately, she still held her sword, and when she lifted her skirts she nearly jabbed the lady with the point. "Oh, dear. I'm so sorry," she said. "I'm afraid I don't know how to curtsy with a sword in my hand. Sir Kai, how do you do it?"

The lady burst into laughter, and even Sir Kai grinned. "That, my dear, you'll have to work out on your own."

Together they walked back to the tree, where the lady

had emptied one of the packs from the horses' saddles and had laid out bread, cheese, and some cooked meat. "I may not have brewed you a posset, Kai," she said cheerfully, "but you see that I've been domestic. Mistress Sarah, would you care for some water?"

Sarah nodded vehemently and turned her attention to the offered water bag. Swordplay was thirsty work, and she drank greedily until Sir Kai stopped her. "Not too much at once," he said. "Have some food now."

Sarah took some of everything, trying not to wolf it down. "Thank you, madam," she said, remembering her manners.

The lady glanced at Sir Kai. "See what I mean? Listen to her speech! I'm sure she's gently born!"

Sir Kai was watching her acutely. "A real princess," he said. Sarah glanced at him sharply, but his face was expressionless. Sarah ate hungrily until all the bread and cheese and venison was gone. It was the first time in months that she had felt full. She reached for the water bag and drained it, then looked up guiltily. "I'm sorry," she said. "I've emptied your water bag." She leaped to her feet. "I'll refill it for you. There's a spring just through that copse. I'll be right back." She adjusted her sword, picked up the water bag, and hurried away through the trees. She had no trouble locating the spring – by now she knew every source of fresh water in the forest – and in no time she had refilled the bag and was nearly back to camp. As she drew close, she heard the lady speaking.

". . . had told me five years ago that I'd watch the great Sir Kai spend a whole morning teaching a girl, I'd have thought them mad. Now admit that you've changed!"

"Nay, my lady. You can't say I've changed. I've never been asked to teach a girl swordplay before."

Sarah slowed and listened. "Perhaps," the lady replied. "But you were so patient an instructor! Indeed, your marriage to Connoire has wrought a marvellous work in you."

"Connoire is a marvellous woman," Sir Kai replied. "But I doubt I should have spent so much time on a girl had I not reasons of my own. Her name – Sarah – it is not a common name. I must find out more about our little princess."

Sarah stopped entirely. "Such as?" the lady asked.

"Where are her parents? What brings a girl like her out into the woods so far from any town? And whatever could have happened to inspire a tender child like her with such a depth of hatred?"

"Hatred?"

"Not for us, but for someone. And again, there's her name. It means 'princess', and she knows it. When she returns, I must ask her about an old friend of – Who's this?" This last was spoken sharply, and, peering around the bush, Sarah saw Sir Kai leap to his feet, his sword in his hand. At the other side of the little clearing was a knight sitting on a great white horse. Her hands went immediately to her own sword, and she leaned forwards to see the knight's face, but the visor on his helm was down. The strange knight held a long lance, and without a word he pointed it at Sir Kai's chest and booted his great horse into a run.

Sir Kai waited until the knight was close, then leaped to one side. The knight must have been expecting this, because his lance moved also, following Sir Kai's jump. It missed Sir

Kai's chest but struck him solidly on his right hip. Sir Kai went sprawling, spattering the grass with blood and losing his grip on his sword. The strange knight leaped from his horse, drawing his own blade, and rushed towards Sir Kai. Sir Kai tried to stand, then crumpled, and then the knight's sword was at his throat.

"Do you yield?" the knight asked hoarsely. Sir Kai glared balefully at the knight and said nothing.

The knight raised his sword for a blow, and the lady shrieked, "He yields! We yield!"

The knight slowly lowered his sword and then turned to face the lady. "Do you indeed yield to me, my love?" The lady stared at the knight blankly and did not reply. The knight continued, "Oh, yes, I know you, your highness. Did you think I came upon you by accident? I have waited many years for the day when I should be able to make you mine."

"Who are you?" she whispered.

"All in good time, my dear. You shall learn to know me well – indeed, to love me – as we grow old together in my castle."

"I shall do no such thing. I am already married."

The knight laughed harshly. "Just as you were when Lancelot was still at court. You are not famous for your faithfulness to your husband, you know. I think you will grow to love me as well. Now that Lancelot is gone, *I* am the greatest knight in England. But you will see. For now, you will come with me."

The lady blushed a fiery red at this speech but said, "I will not."

"Then I shall truss you like a pig and sling you over your

11

horse's back. It might even be fun." He turned back to Sir Kai, whose face was grey with pain, and raised his sword again. "Goodbye, Sir Kai."

Sarah reached for her sword, but before she could unsheath it the lady screamed, "Wait!" The knight hesitated, and the lady hurriedly continued, "I will go with you without a struggle, but on one condition: you must bring Sir Kai with us, and when we reach your home, he must see a doctor."

"No, Gwen," Sir Kai said, trying again to stand and failing.

The knight paused, then lowered his sword. "All right, but not because I care whether I bring you home bound or free. I let him live only because you must learn to love me, and it might complicate matters if I begin by killing your husband's brother."

Sarah let go of her sword and shrank behind the bushes. If she thought she could have killed the strange knight, she might have tried to attack him from behind, but he wore armour, and she realized that she didn't even know where to strike. The knight removed Sir Kai's armour and threw it into the shrubbery, keeping his sword, and then, with the lady's help, bound up Sir Kai's bleeding wound and hoisted him onto his horse. By the time they were done, Sir Kai looked about ready to faint, but then he sat up straight and said in an abnormally loud voice, "Your villainy will not go unpunished! When word gets to King Arthur at Camelot that his queen, Queen Guinevere, has been taken prisoner, you shall be hunted down like a dog!"

The strange knight laughed. "And how do you expect this news to get to Arthur? Do you think the field mice carry tales? No, when the two of you fail to appear at the court, Arthur will no doubt suppose that his wife has run off with another lover." He laughed again, harder this time. "But how delicious, dear Guinevere! He'll believe that you betrayed him with his own brother! Yes, it's a very good notion not to leave Sir Kai's body to be found by Arthur's men. Come along!"

Sir Kai only said, "Camelot, by the way, is south of Bristol."

This made the knight shake his head slowly. "I know where it is, Sir Kai. Are you delirious?" Then he led the way through the trees, back in the direction from which he'd come.

Sarah watched them go. So that was the Queen of England. Sarah's life in Mordecai's little wagon had seldom brought her into contact with knights and ladies, but even she knew of King Arthur and Queen Guinevere. It looked as if she was going to find out more about knights now, because there was no doubt in her mind that Sir Kai had just sent her to Camelot.

In the years before the fires, as Sarah and her mother had travelled around England with Mordecai, Purveyor of Fine Cloth, they had been to Bristol at least once, but in those days Sarah had never paid any attention to roads or directions. She had developed her sense of direction considerably since February, but her ability to find her way through the woods surrounding the hamlet of Milrick was not enough to guide her to Camelot. If Sir Kai had only pointed in the direction of the court, she thought, she could have found her way, but telling her that it was south of Bristol was no help at all.

She had to have directions, which was more difficult than it sounded since she trusted no one in the neighbourhood. In fact, she had stolen food from most of the villagers, which might make it awkward to ask them for help. The only person she could approach, Sarah decided, was the old woman of the woods.

Sarah had discovered the old woman in February, after dark on her third night alone in the forest. Finding the old woman had saved her life, in fact. By that time, Sarah was faint from hunger and frozen to the bone. Creeping through the icy forest, Sarah had seen a light and, investigating, had come upon a small cottage hidden away in a dense part of the woods. In a small yard in front of the cottage, an aged woman and a cat sat by a large fire, eating bread and meat. As Sarah watched, the crone stood up, stretched, and said, "Time for bed, Jeffrey. Shall we leave the rest of this food out here for our forest friends?"

The woman and the cat retreated into the cottage and shut the door, leaving half a loaf of bread and a slab of meat on a flat rock by the fire. Sarah waited for what seemed like an hour but was probably only a few minutes, then dashed out, grabbed the food, and retreated into the shadows. No one came out, and after waiting another few minutes Sarah slipped out of the woods again and warmed herself by the still burning fire.

The next night the woman left a whole loaf of bread and a wedge of cheese, but of far greater importance was her second offering, a thick old woollen cloak that she left hanging on a branch outside. The crone wore a different cloak, so this was obviously her spare. She didn't need it, and Sarah most definitely did, so she took it. The cloak had undoubtedly kept her alive through the winter, but nevertheless it was the only one of Sarah's foraging raids that bothered her conscience. She had no compunction about stealing from the villagers: they had stolen her mother and guardian from her, after all. But the old woman was not from the village and had not been by the fires that horrible night, and now that spring had come, Sarah had been thinking about returning the cloak anyway.

It took Sarah a little over an hour to get to the crone's cottage, frustrating for Sarah in that she suspected that time was precious. The sooner she delivered her message to King Arthur, the sooner he could send his knights to save Sir Kai and the queen. When she came to the cottage, though, she hesitated. After three months, avoiding all human contact was a hard habit to overcome. At last, taking a deep breath, she stepped into the yard before the old house and called out, "Hello?"

There was no answer. Sarah called again, then crossed the yard to the cottage and gently tapped on the door. She looked in the window, and finally went inside. No one was home. Sarah sat disgustedly on a rock by the outdoor fire pit and waited, while the strange knight was no doubt leading his captives miles away, or perhaps hiding them somewhere where they'd never be found. To pass the time and vent her frustration, Sarah drew her sword and practised long, level swings just at neck level.

"I never thought I'd see that cloak again," came a crackly old woman's voice from behind her.

Sarah whirled around, suddenly self-conscious of the sword in her hand, but the crone paid no attention to it.

"I'm sorry," Sarah said, panting from her exercise. "I didn't see you coming." She quickly sheathed the sword and removed the cloak. "I've come to return the cloak to you, ma'am. I know I shouldn't have taken it, but I was so very cold, and you left it—"

"I left it for you, dear. Along with the food."

"Oh!" Sarah exclaimed. "Then you saw me?" First Sir Kai, now this old beldam. Evidently Sarah wasn't as quiet in the forest as she had thought.

"Only that first night," the old woman assured her. "After that, I never saw you at all. The only way I knew you had been near was when the food I left out for you was taken. By the by, dear, have you been eating enough? You haven't taken as much recently."

"Yes, ma'am," Sarah said politely. Then, mindful of her errand, she said, "Thank you so much for the cloak. It was most thoughtful of you to leave it for me. But that isn't the only reason I've come. I need help."

The old woman nodded. "I will do what I can, little princess."

Sarah swallowed, momentarily distracted. "Why did you call me that?"

"That silk dress, of course," the old woman replied. "It's fit for a princess, isn't it?"

It was what Mordecai had said when he gave it to her, and Sarah set her jaw grimly. "What I need," she said resolutely, "is directions to Camelot."

The old woman frowned. "No, child. That won't do the trick at all."

"I must see King Arthur as soon as possible."

"But what do you think he will be able to do for you?" the

16

crone said, shaking her head slowly. "He has to stay within the rule of law. Is that what you want?"

Sarah was confused. What was the old lady talking about? Did she already know about Sir Kai and Queen Guinevere? "He can send knights! Surely that won't be against the law."

"The king cannot deal vengeance," the crone replied. "It's a pity, but there it is."

Sarah frowned at the woman in consternation. "You're saying he can't even rescue his own queen?"

The old woman's head jerked up, and for a second her wrinkles and loose skin seem to fade, and Sarah could almost see the beautiful woman that she must have been years before. "What's that? Guinevere?"

"Yes, and Sir Kai."

"What's happened to her?" the crone demanded sharply.

"That's what I've been talking about! What did you think I meant?"

The old woman hesitated. "I assumed you had some grievance to take to the king. That's what most people want from him. But go on! What of the queen?"

"She and Sir Kai were passing through the forest this morning when a knight came on them, drove a spear through Sir Kai's leg, and took them both away."

The old woman's face grew hard, and again for a second seemed less ancient. Then she said, "You'd better tell me from the beginning, every detail."

"But shouldn't we hurry?" Sarah protested. "So that the king's men can get on the road at once?"

"You're three days from Camelot, child. It is already too

17

late for a pursuit. All that is left is a search, and for that we must know everything that happened. Tell me, and don't leave anything out. We'll leave at first light tomorrow."

"And then we'll have to walk for three days?" Sarah asked with dismay.

"Walk? No. That would take a week. Tomorrow I'll take you to a castle where you may get a horse and an escort, and you'll ride the rest of the way. Now tell me what happened, from the beginning."

So Sarah did.

II

BELREPEIRE AND CAMELOT

"There it is – Belrepeire," the old woman announced, stopping at the top of a small hill. "We've made better time than I'd hoped."

Sarah struggled up the hill and sank gratefully to the ground at the crone's feet, too weary to cast more than a cursory glance at the castle in the valley before her.

"You're not tired, are you?" the old woman asked mockingly. "I was so afraid that I'd slow you down."

Sarah didn't bother to reply. She had long since regretted her self-important words that morning – was it only that morning? – when she had suggested that the old lady should just give her directions and let her go on alone, because Sarah could make better time without having to wait for an old woman. The woman had laughed and said nothing, but from the moment they left Sarah had been scrambling to keep up with the crone's long, mile-eating stride. That whole long day she had walked behind the woman, sometimes having to break into a run just to stay within twenty yards.

"Now," the crone said, after a moment, "let me know when you catch your breath. I have some final instructions for you." Sarah inhaled deeply once, then met the old woman's gaze and nodded. "That's right," the woman said approvingly. "Now, listen. Belrepeire is the home of Sir Parsifal, one of King Arthur's most loyal knights. He will give you a horse and, doubtless, escort you himself to Camelot. You will tell him everything that happened to Kai and the queen, but – listen to this, child – tell no one but Sir Parsifal himself. You must speak with him privately."

"Why don't you tell him? He's more likely to listen to an adult anyway."

"I'm not going with you, child. I have other matters to attend to."

"You're leaving me?"

"Don't worry. Parsifal will take care of you."

"I'm not worried, and I can take care of myself," Sarah replied automatically. "But what if Sir Parsifal won't see me?" It was hard for Sarah to imagine that a great knight would give a private audience to a homeless girl in a ragged cloak arriving alone at his castle.

"Tell him that the sister of the enchantress sent you. He will do whatever you ask."

Sarah's eyes widened. "Your sister is an enchantress?"

"*Was* an enchantress," the crone replied. "She's dead now, or so we all hope. Do you understand what you must do?" Sarah repeated her instructions, and the old woman nodded. "Very well. Mind that you speak to no one at Belrepeire except Parsifal himself. And at Camelot, tell only the king. No one else. Now, do you have any questions?"

Sarah shook her head. "Thank you," she said suddenly. "I don't know if I'll see you again, but—"

"You'll see me again, princess," the woman said confidently, and then she strode briskly away, heading north.

Sarah gathered her aching legs beneath her and stood, adjusting her sword under her cloak as she rose, then walked down the hill towards the castle. She wished that the old woman had stayed with her long enough to present her to this Sir Parsifal, but she reminded herself that when she had set out on this journey she had expected to go alone to the gates of Camelot itself, and that would have been even harder. As she neared the castle, the great portcullis at the castle gate began to descend. "Wait!" Sarah cried out, breaking into a weary run. "Let me in before you close that!"

The portcullis stopped, and a helmeted head appeared from the front gate, looking around. Catching sight of her, a castle guard stepped out. "Good evening, miss," he said. His gruff, irritable voice belied the civility of his words. "What do you want?"

"I must see Sir Parsifal at once!" Sarah said with as much dignity as she could muster.

"Well, you can't," the guard replied.

"Tell him that I was sent by—"

"It don't make no matter of difference who you was sent by," the guard said. "The master's not here."

"Oh."

The guard turned back to the portcullis chain, saying, "And I can't tell you when he'll be back, neither."

"Why not?" Sarah demanded.

"Don't know." The guard resumed lowering the gate, and on impulse Sarah ran forwards and threw herself into the castle just as the metal spikes of the portcullis came down.

"Here now!" came the guard's voice. Sarah scrambled to her feet and whirled to see the guard approaching her, anger in his face. At once she threw back her cloak and drew her sword. It came out quickly and smoothly.

"Stay where you are!" she commanded. She held the sword two-handed, as Sir Kai had shown her, and pointed it at the guard's nose.

He didn't seem frightened. Smiling unpleasantly, the guard stepped back to the gate and took up a long, wicked-looking spear with a thick shaft and a pointed axe at the top. "Now, miss, you wouldn't want to hurt someone with that skinny sword of yours, would you?" He planted the butt of the spear on the ground and leaned on it as a shepherd might lean on his staff. "Would you?" he repeated menacingly.

At the soldier's insolent tone, Sarah boiled inside and her eyes grew hot. Without a word, she swung the sword with all her strength at the spear, just below the man's hands. She intended merely to shake the spear and let the man see that she was serious, but to her surprise the sword cut through the stout shaft as if it were a twig, and the knight, overbalanced, stumbled and fell at her feet, still clutching the top half of the spear. Sarah put the point of her sword at the guard's throat, much as the strange knight had done to Sir Kai only the day before.

"I need a horse," Sarah said. "And I need a sack full of food and a water bag, and – oh, yes – I need directions to Camelot. Call out now and tell someone to get them ready for me."

The knight didn't seem able to speak, but it wasn't

necessary. Other guards must have been watching, and a minute later Sarah was surrounded by armed soldiers, each with a spear pointed at her. She kept the sword at her captive's throat and repeated her demands, but none of the guards moved. Finally, one said to another, "What do we do?"

"Get me what I want!" Sarah replied, irritated.

There was a shuffling pause, and then one of the guards suggested, "Go get the smith's boy?" Another guard nodded and hurried away.

"I don't want a smith's apprentice!" Sarah snapped in exasperation. "I want someone who can make a decision and give me what I need! I'm in a hurry."

But nothing she said could move them, and she began to wonder if she had done the right thing by holding the guard hostage. She had no intention of killing him, of course, both because it was wrong and because she knew that if she did she would have to face the anger of all the others, but now she was committed to her bluff.

Footsteps approached from across the courtyard, and a firm voice called out, "Move aside, men." The guards made way to reveal a tall, muscular young man in a leather apron. "Good evening, my lady," the young man said, sweeping a courtly bow. "I understand you have a, ah, request to make of us. May I help?"

"I have to get to Camelot at once," Sarah said shortly. "I need a horse, provisions, and—"

The young man suddenly stiffened and interrupted her. "How came you by that sword?" he demanded.

"It's mine!" Sarah snapped back.

The young man looked into her eyes. "What has happened to Sir Kai?" he asked softly.

23

Sarah looked at him wonderingly, but did not answer.

The young man frowned for a moment, then said to the guards, "Leave us. Go back to your quarters at once."

The soldiers backed away, and the guard on the ground, finding a voice, or at any rate a whisper, said hoarsely, "Miss? I'm to go back to my quarters now, if it please you."

Sarah hesitated, then moved her sword point away from the knight's throat. He pushed himself away slowly, then scrambled to his feet and backed away.

"Durnard's been needing a trimming anyway," the smith's boy said lightly, watching the guard. "Altogether too surly, by half. Parsifal's had to remind him several times to speak politely to visitors. Perhaps this will cure him."

"Is Sir Parsifal really away?" Sarah asked.

"He is. Were you seeking him?" the young man replied.

"Yes. The ... I was sent here and told that Sir Parsifal would give me an escort to Camelot. I have to speak to the king."

"Are Sir Kai and the queen all right?" the young man asked. His eyes looked keenly into hers.

"I . . ." Sarah stopped herself. "What do you mean, sir?"

"Piers. Just call me Piers," the young man answered. "It's your sword, you see. My father made that sword. I sharpened it myself and placed it in Sir Kai's hands just four days ago. If you have it, that can only mean that something has happened to him."

"Sir Kai gave it to me before it happened, though," Sarah said hurriedly.

"Before what happened?" Piers asked.

Sarah swallowed. "I was told not to tell anyone but Sir Parsifal."

"By whom?" he asked.

"The . . . the enchantress's sister," Sarah replied.

Piers didn't look as if he knew who this was, but he must have been satisfied, because he said only, "I see. Or rather I don't, but I see you can't tell me. And you need to take your message to Arthur?"

Sarah nodded. "Sir Kai asked me to."

"Can you at least tell me if they are alive?" Piers asked gently.

"They were when I last saw them," Sarah said, after a brief pause. "But Sir Kai is badly hurt."

"We'll leave at once," the young man said. He shouted a summons, and when a servant appeared he gave instructions for two horses and food to be readied and various other preparations to be made. This blacksmith's apprentice appeared to have an uncommon amount of authority in the castle. Other servants appeared and began to scurry about the darkening castle, and a tall lady in a beautiful gown stepped out of the central keep and approached them.

"What is to do, my Piers?" the woman asked.

"This girl has an urgent message for King Arthur, Mother," Piers replied. "We must leave at once."

"But you must do no such thing," the lady replied calmly. She turned to Sarah. "Have you eaten, *ma chérie*?"

"Not since this morning," Sarah admitted. "I've been walking since then."

"Come with me," the lady replied.

"Mother—" Piers said.

"You must forgive my son," the lady said to Sarah gently. "Please believe that he was taught manners, but sadly he

25

grows more like his father every day."

"Mother—" Piers said again.

"*Pas de raisonnements, Pierre!* This girl will most certainly not ride all night with you. You are two days from Camelot, *n'est-ce pas?* When will you sleep? During the day? *Bah! Va t'-en!* You will sleep here tonight and leave at daybreak. The lady and I shall dine in my rooms, I believe."

Clearly defeated, Piers swept a bow and said, "It shall be as you wish, Mother."

"But of course it shall be," the lady replied, her eyes dancing. "You must make preparations for the morning now, yes?" And then she swept Sarah into the castle.

Sarah had never been inside a castle before. Riding across England in Mordecai's pedlar's wagon, she had seen many, but from the outside they had always seemed fierce and unhospitable places, bristling and spikey like angry boars. Thus it was with some trepidation that she stepped across the stone threshold behind the lady and followed her down the gloomy hallways to the lady's room. Once in the room, though, Sarah was surprised to find an inviting, homey, warmly lit chamber. The dark stone walls were softened by bright tapestries and small lamps glowing in sconces, and a fire in a hearth spread its warmth through the room, right into Sarah's bones. The lady guided Sarah to an upholstered chair before the fire and swept Sarah's old cloak off her.

"But what a lovely dress, my dear!" the lady said approvingly. "I am Lady Marie, chief lady-in-waiting to Queen Conduiramour, the mistress of this castle. You sit here, and we shall have dinner brought to you directly."

"You're a queen's lady?" Sarah asked with awe. It seemed

unspeakably grand to be in the room of a real queen's lady-in-waiting. Of course, just two days before she had eaten a meal with the Queen of All England, but that didn't count, because Sarah hadn't known her name at the time. Another thought came to her. "So that's why Piers acted so important, ordering people around: because his mother is a grand lady."

Tiny dimples appeared on Lady Marie's cheeks, but she only replied, "Who can say why a man thinks he is important? They all do, for one reason or another. It is best to allow them to think so, you know, or they become quite unmanageable." She leaned over Sarah's dress and scrutinized it. "My dear, your dress is of the loveliest silk, but it has been roughly used, has it not?"

Sarah nodded and coloured, suddenly and acutely aware of the mud that caked the hem and the dozens of nicks and tears in the cloth.

"Would you permit me to provide you with a new gown?"

"You are very kind, ma'am," Sarah replied. "But this one . . . it was a gift, you see."

"But of course, and a gift fit for a queen it was. Indeed, with a wash and a few stitches it will be as good as new, and quite worthy of comparison with all the most splendid gowns that you will see at King Arthur's court. May I?"

She held out her hand invitingly, and Sarah – struck with the image that Lady Marie had suggested, of dozens of gorgeously clad ladies at Camelot critically examining her clothes – nodded. Together they removed Sarah's dress and underdress, and Sarah had just wrapped herself in a velvet robe that Lady Marie produced for her when Piers arrived, bringing with him a tray piled high with bread and roasted fowl.

"Fie, Piers!" Lady Marie exclaimed. "Do you know no better than to enter a lady's chamber without knocking?"

"I beg your pardon, ma'am," Piers said to Sarah. Then he added, to his mother, "I did not know you would be dressing."

"I am going to wash and mend our friend's gown this evening, so that she shall be *convenable* at the court."

"She isn't going to a ball, Mother," Piers said mildly. "I see no reason for you to do all that work."

"I am sure, myself, that you do not," Lady Marie replied. "But that does not mean that there is no reason, only that you are not enough clever to see it. Thank you for the food. Now, go away and tell the cook to begin warming water for a bath. I shall send for it within the hour. Go now."

Piers sighed. "I brought the food up myself because I wished to tell you that all is in readiness. I shall come back here at dawn."

"Yes, very well," Lady Marie said. "Take yourself off, now, and don't forget that bath water. Indeed, you would do well to have a bath yourself, as you will be riding with a lady." She shooed her son out of the room and brought the food to Sarah.

"Thank you, my lady," Sarah said.

"Eat now," Lady Marie said. "Then you shall have a bath, and then I think you should sleep, no?" Sarah nodded, already feeling the drowsiness that comes from tired muscles beside a warm fire. Lady Marie said, "I shall be in the next room only, washing your dress."

"Thank you, my lady," Sarah murmured again. Then Lady Marie was gone, and Sarah turned to her supper.

Sarah barely remembered the bath and didn't remember going to bed at all, but when Lady Marie woke her the next morning, Sarah found herself cocooned between a wonderfully soft bed and a thick layer of heavy blankets. Though she could feel the crispness of the May morning on her exposed cheeks, for the first time in months she was warm right down to the tips of her toes. She stretched once, then curled up again in her pocket of warmth.

"My dear, I am so sorry, but you must get up now. Your breakfast is growing cold, and Piers is already getting the horses."

Sarah climbed out of bed and the first thing she saw was her blue dress, as shimmeringly beautiful as it had ever been, laid out on a chair. "Oh, my lady!" Sarah said with a gasp. "It's perfect again!"

Lady Marie smiled with satisfaction. "It is a gown of the very finest. It was an honour to restore it to its glory." She helped Sarah put on her underdress and then the silk gown, still talking. "I thought to mend your old cloak as well, but I did not. I hope you are not offended, but it is that I thought you might be safer travelling in an old and ragged outer garment, so I brushed it only."

"Yes, indeed, ma'am," Sarah said.

"You will remove the cloak when you arrive at court, yes?"

Lady Marie sounded almost anxious, and Sarah realized suddenly that she was speaking from her own professional pride as a lady-in-waiting. She would not send a lady from her care to the royal court looking anything less than her best. "Yes, ma'am," Sarah said meekly.

Lady Marie nodded with satisfaction. "When I brushed your cloak," she said quietly, "a small bottle fell from the outer pocket. It seems to me to be of great value, and so I have returned it."

"Thank you," Sarah whispered. Then, not knowing exactly why, she added, "It was my mother's."

Sarah ate her breakfast quickly and, when she was done, put on her sword and cloak and hurried downstairs to where Piers was waiting. He helped Sarah onto a glossy, dark brown horse and then waited patiently while she settled herself in the odd saddle. She tried to sit the way she remembered Queen Guinevere doing as she rode, and after a moment found a position that was not too uncomfortable, although the sword hanging at her side was awkward. She turned back to Lady Marie. "Thank you, my lady, for all your care," Sarah said.

"You will be safe with Piers," Lady Marie said calmly. "He is more clever than he sometimes appears."

"Merci, Maman," Piers murmured, and then they were off.

Sarah managed not to fall off the horse when they started, and by holding on grimly she was able to ride out the castle gate with some dignity. Piers said nothing for twenty minutes or so, but when they were out of sight of the castle he slowed and rode close to Sarah. She watched him apprehensively.

"Don't be concerned," the tall young man said, smiling. "I've only come to ask a few questions." Sarah's lips tightened. "Questions that you may, of course, refuse to answer. But as we are to be riding together for the next two days, I thought it would be best for me to learn your name."

"Sarah."

"I am honoured, Mistress Sarah," Piers said, bowing gallantly in his saddle. "And, if I may be so bold, I don't suppose you've ever been on a horse before."

"I have too!" Piers raised his eyebrows slightly, and Sarah sighed. "But only on a cart horse pulling a wagon. I've never guided a horse or been on a saddle like this."

Piers eyed her speculatively, but he said only, "Then we will probably make better time if you let me have the reins of your horse. I'll lead, and you can concentrate on staying in the saddle." Sarah nodded, and they were silent while this exchange was completed and Piers tied the reins of Sarah's mount to his own saddle. Then Piers cleared his throat gently. "As for staying in the saddle, Mistress Sarah, I suspect that you will find it easier to do without your sword hanging at your side."

"Yes," Sarah said, conceding the point. "I can't find a comfortable way to adjust it."

"I am very much afraid that ladies' saddles were not designed to accommodate swords," Piers said.

Sarah nodded. "Like curtsies," she said.

"I beg your pardon?"

"It's hard to curtsy when you're holding a sword, too."

Piers appeared to be struck by this. "Why, yes, I can see how that might be difficult."

"I asked Sir Kai to show me how to do it, but he said I would have to figure it out myself."

Piers's eyes gleamed with pleasure. "You asked Sir Kai to . . . to teach you to curtsy?"

"With a sword, yes. I know how to do it without one."

Piers was silent for a moment, and when he spoke his

voice was unsteady. "It seems a most useful skill. Perhaps when you figure it out, you can show Sir Kai how it's done so that he'll know as well."

"If I see him again," Sarah said soberly.

"Yes," Piers said, his tone serious again. "I gather that you gave your word not to tell anyone but Parsifal and Arthur about what happened to them, and so I will not ask again, but can you tell me how you came to meet them? And how Sir Kai came to give you that sword?"

Sarah decided to ignore the first part of this question, as the answer might invite further questions as to why she was alone in the woods and where her parents were. She said, "It was supposed to be for his son, you know."

"Yes," Piers said, nodding gravely.

"But he said that his son was still young and that I'd probably need it before his son did."

"For what purpose?"

Sarah replied warily, "Don't you think that I might need one for protection on the journey to Camelot?" This wasn't a very good reply, Sarah knew, since she had already told Piers that Sir Kai had given her the sword before anything happened to send her on her journey. From Piers's furrowed brow, Sarah guessed he was about to point out this inconsistency, and she added quickly, "He said that someone . . . I forget the name . . . could make another one."

"Trebuchet?" Piers asked.

"That's it. Is that your father?" Piers nodded, and Sarah hurried on. "And you're his apprentice?"

"Yes," Piers said.

"But that seems very strange to me," Sarah commented, relieved to be talking about Piers instead of about herself.

32

"I mean that you don't sound at all like a blacksmith. Anyone who heard you talk would think you were a great noble. You sound so polite and educated."

"Ah, but my father *is* a great noble," Piers said. "In the land where he was born, a smith can be as great a noble as a knight. But as for my manner of speaking, you must remember that my mother is a lady-in-waiting. She taught me the manners and language of chivalry from birth. Indeed, when I was younger, I had thought to become a page."

Sarah looked speculatively at Piers's broad, muscular shoulders. "You don't look very much like a page," she commented.

"Yes. It is fortunate that I gave up that plan, isn't it?" Piers replied agreeably. "Now, that's my excuse. What's yours?"

"My . . . excuse?"

"Yes, Mistress Sarah. You also speak with gentility and courtesy – except of course when threatening castle guards at the point of a sword – and you wear a dress of the finest silk. You already know how to curtsy – except not with a sword – and yet you've never ridden in a lady's saddle. You even admit that you have ridden a cart horse pulling a wagon, an undignified position that no young noblewoman would have ever consented to. You are quite puzzling, too, you know."

Sarah chose her words with care. "I think . . . I believe that my mother was an educated woman. It was she who taught me how to speak. But something happened when I was a baby and she was without a home. She would never say what happened, but it must have been bad. She told me that we were alone, without food or shelter, when Mor . . . when a cloth pedlar came by in his wagon. He took care of us, and we just stayed. He's the one who gave me the cloth for this dress. So you see, I just look genteel because of this silk. I'm not really noble at all." Piers shook his head slightly, but to Sarah's immense relief he asked no other prying questions, not all that long day on horseback, or the next.

Sarah had expected travelling by horse to be easier than walking, but at the end of the first day her muscles ached horribly, not only in the obvious spots but also in places where she hadn't known she had muscles at all. By the end of the second day, Sarah felt that she would have given anything for the privilege of walking, but when Piers at last stopped his horse and said, "Nearly there, Mistress Sarah," she was able to summon the pride to sit straight and pretend that she had merely been for a trot around a park.

Half an hour later Piers led her through the open gates of a majestic castle, made even more magnificent by pennons and banners and flags of all sorts, and made most splendid of all by the richly clad courtiers and ladies who flitted about like butterflies in a field of flowers. Sarah quickly removed the old cloak and draped it behind her saddle, near the place that she and Piers had finally found to secure her sword. She glanced at her dress, making sure that Lady Marie would approve, then moved her horse closer to Piers's. "How are we ever going to speak privately to King Arthur in all this throng?" she asked.

"I've been wondering about that myself," Piers admitted. "Normally, we would go to the king's seneschal and request an audience."

"Why don't we do that?"

"The king's seneschal is Sir Kai," Piers replied.

"Oh."

"Someone must be acting in his place while he's away, but I don't know who. I think I know what to do, though. Hi! Hi there, boy!" Piers called suddenly, beckoning to a boy who was emptying a bucket of water outside the stables. The boy approached. "Boy, do you know Terence, Sir Gawain's squire?" The boy nodded, and Piers gave him a coin. "Could you find him and tell him that Piers is waiting for him here at the stables and needs to see him? Tell him that it's an urgent matter."

The boy snatched the coin and raced away, and Sarah frowned. "A squire?"

"You'll see," Piers said. "Come. Let us put up our horses while we wait." He took Sarah into the stables, found two stalls, and showed Sarah how to strip their gear from the horses and rub down their sweating sides. Sarah put her sword back on. It had long since occurred to her that among all the knights of Camelot she might very well find the knight of the fires.

They were just finishing when a voice said, "Piers, how wonderful to see you again!"

Sarah jumped. She had heard no one approach, but the voice came from barely three feet behind her. She whirled around, her hand on her sword's hilt, but Piers placed his hand on hers and said, "Terence. I'm glad you're at court. I didn't know who else to talk to."

This squire, Terence, was a slim man in simply cut clothes. It was hard to tell how old he was – his triangular face had an ageless quality – but Sarah knew she had nothing to fear from him. She shook her hand free from Piers's restraining hold and released her sword. The squire bowed to her. "My lady," he said, smiling in welcome.

"This is Mistress Sarah," Piers said. "She has an urgent message for King Arthur."

Terence looked at Sarah. "A message from whom?"

Sarah hesitated, glancing around at the busy stable, and Piers quickly said, "It is to be for Arthur's ears alone."

Terence nodded. "Come to Gawain's rooms. We can speak privately there. I'll check with Bedivere to see when the king will be free."

"No," Sarah said. "I must see him at once."

Terence looked into her eyes, and Sarah had the odd sensation that the squire's eyes were sifting her most private thoughts. At last Terence said in a soft voice, "Nearly all who come here say that their business is urgent. Can you show me that it will be urgent to the king as well?"

There were too many servants bustling through. Sarah dared not say even the names Sir Kai or Queen Guinevere. The crone had been so insistent that only King Arthur was to be told what had happened. She shook her head.

"I gather that Bedivere's acting as seneschal?" Piers asked suddenly. Terence glanced at Piers, one eyebrow raised. Piers continued, "You mentioned arranging an audience with the king through Bedivere. Of course, I already knew that Sir Kai wasn't at court." Piers's eyes flickered significantly at Sarah, and Terence took a sharp breath.

"Yes, that's right," Terence said slowly. "He's gone to escort a lady home from a visit." Terence looked at Sarah, and Sarah nodded quickly, trying to show that she knew exactly which lady it was. Terence said, "Go to Gawain's rooms. I'll fetch Arthur at once." Then he was gone.

Sarah's scalp prickled; she had never seen anyone move so silently. Shaking her head, she followed Piers as he walked briskly out of the stable, up a flight of stairs, and down a corridor to a heavy oaken door. Piers knocked, waited a moment, then pushed it open and went inside. This was the second castle room that Sarah had ever been in, and while it was as different from Lady Marie's warm bedchamber as it could be, it was still comfortable. Not the slightest gesture had been made towards decoration here: everything was functional, from the deeply cushioned chairs by the fire to the cabinet with a row of bottles and goblets and, of course, the neatly arranged armour and weaponry that lined one whole wall. "Whose room is this?" she asked.

"Sir Gawain's."

"Who is Sir Gawain?"

Piers stared at Sarah, then laughed reluctantly. "I suppose that travelling with a cloth merchant you would spend little time with the nobility, but I had thought everyone in England knew who Sir Gawain is."

"Mother didn't like to talk about knights," Sarah explained.

Piers's face was still. *"Didn't?"* he asked gently. Sarah flushed, angry that she had given herself away by speaking of her mother as one gone. Piers said, "Sir Gawain is the greatest of all the knights of the Round Table."

Grateful to Piers for asking no questions, Sarah said, "My guardian, the cloth merchant, mentioned Sir Kai once or twice, but he didn't talk about other knights. Once, though, I heard a minstrel at a market day, singing about King Arthur's court, and I remember that he said that

Sir … oh, I forget the name … Sir Laundry, or something like that, was the king's greatest knight."

"Sir Lancelot, I imagine," Piers said, smiling. "You must understand that every knight is the greatest knight in the land as long as the song about him lasts, but it is true that many consider Sir Lancelot the greatest knight of all. He left the court many years ago, though. That leaves Sir Gawain."

"And this Terence is his squire?" Piers nodded, and Sarah asked, "What sort of squire is it who goes off to 'fetch' the King of All England without a thought?"

Piers grinned. "A squire like no other, and that's all I know."

The door swung open, and Sarah looked up, into the kindest, weariest eyes she had ever seen. They were set in a youthful face that, incongruously, was framed by a grey beard. The man with the kind face wore clothes of red velvet, and Sarah knew it was the king. Instinctively, she dropped in a low curtsy, sensing Piers kneeling at her side.

"Rise, please," the king said, entering the room. Behind him came Squire Terence and two knights. The first was a huge man, as large as Sir Kai but with a red beard, and the other was more slender, with a brown beard streaked with grey. The brown-bearded man gently closed and bolted the door behind them.

"This is the lady, sire," Terence said. "Lady Sarah."

"I am honoured, my lady," the king said, bowing graciously. "Terence says that you have an urgent message for me?"

Sarah nodded, her mouth dry. "It is supposed to be only for you."

"These are my closest friends and most loyal knights. I would trust Sir Gawain, Sir Bedivere, Terence, and, yes, Piers here with my life. You may speak freely."

Sarah took a deep breath and let it out slowly. She didn't want to give bad news to a man with such a face, but she said, "Queen Guinevere has been captured by a knight and taken back to his castle."

The silence was like a fog in the room. At last King Arthur said, "And Sir Kai?"

"Wounded. Badly, I think. But the queen made the knight take him too and promise that he would take him to a doctor."

"Did you see this yourself?" the king asked.

Sarah nodded. "I was in the bushes nearby. I don't think the knight saw me."

"How did you know that the lady was Queen Guinevere?" the brown-bearded knight – Sir Bedivere, King Arthur had called him – asked quietly.

"They had shared their food with me just before the knight came. I had only been away for a moment."

"Did the queen tell you her name? Or did Sir Kai?" Sir Bedivere asked.

Sarah thought about this. "Not at first. Sir Kai told me his own name, but he called the queen only 'my lady'. When the knight came, he knew her, though. Then, after Sir Kai had been wounded, he told the knight that he'd be in trouble when King Arthur heard that his queen had been captured. He said that really loud, so that I could hear, and I knew he was sending me to tell you."

"It sounds right, Arthur," Sir Bedivere said.

The king turned to his left and looked at the squire.

"Terence?"

"The child's telling the truth, sire. Not a doubt."

The knight with the red beard spoke for the first time. "Where did this happen? How long ago? Did you see the knight's face?"

"Wait, Gawain," Arthur said softly, placing a restraining hand on the knight's arm. "Let the child tell the story." He gestured to a chair and said, "Please, my lady, sit down." Sarah timidly sat in one of the cushioned chairs, and the king sat in a chair across from her. "Start from the beginning, please."

Sarah nodded and began.

III

QUESTING

Telling the king and his knights what had happened proved to be ticklish at first, since Sarah had no intention of telling her own story – especially why she was alone in the forest or why she had followed Sir Kai and tried to steal his sword. But the king did not interrupt her to ask any probing questions, and his knights clearly took their lead from him. They did occasionally exchange glances, and Sarah found that she was better off if she didn't meet Terence's penetrating gaze, but as she moved along in the tale her nervousness faded. She told everything she could remember, right up through her trip with Piers and arrival at Camelot. When she was done, the king reached across and took Sarah's hand.

"I cannot tell you what I owe you, my child. I will not forget what you have done this week."

"Sire?" Terence asked softly. "May I ask Sarah a few questions?"

Sarah took a breath, but the king pressed her hand

reassuringly. "Only about the events of the past few days, I think," King Arthur replied. "We owe Lady Sarah her privacy, at least."

"Yes, sire." Terence looked at Sarah, and his face was grim. "This old woman who helped you. Did she say she was an enchantress's sister? Or *the* enchantress's sister?"

"She said *the*," Sarah replied. "As if she expected Parsifal to know who she was by that."

"Did she say anything else about this enchantress?"

"Yes, she did," Sarah said, remembering their conversation. "She said that her sister was dead, or at least everyone hoped so."

Terence's lips set, and his eyes looked through Sarah without seeing her. Sir Gawain turned his head sharply. "You don't think—"

"I don't know," Terence said. "I hope we meet this old woman as we travel."

King Arthur stood. "Shall we leave at dawn?"

Sir Bedivere shook his head sharply. "You can't go, Arthur."

"She's my queen."

"It would jeopardize the kingdom. There is more going on here than one discontented knight looking for ransom. What will the court think when you disappear?"

"I care not," the king said firmly.

Sir Gawain spoke. "Bedivere's right, sire. You have to stay here for the same reason that we sent Kai alone. You and the court must go on as if nothing were wrong. Terence and I will find her. Everyone knows I get restless at court, and no one will think anything about my disappearing. But you – and Bedivere, too – have to stay here and keep on ruling the land."

Piers spoke for the first time since the king and the others had come in the room. "What is the affair? What more is there to this that I don't know?"

King Arthur nodded and sat back in his chair, his eyes dark. After a moment, Sir Bedivere spoke. "For the past year or so, there have been rumblings of rebellion. Nothing certain, and no specific names, but hints of unrest and of gatherings of knights in places where there was no reason for them to gather. Some of our own knights began to disappear, and then there were incidents. Here a village was burned, there a rumour of a dragon or a plague, and always more talk of rebellion."

"Why would there be rebellion?" Piers asked. "The land is at peace for the first time in anyone's memory."

"Maybe that's why," Sir Gawain commented. "There's little chance for glory and conquest when all's peaceful. You're too young to remember, but before Arthur, it was a yearly tradition for kings to go out and try to enlarge their lands by force. The strong can grow rich in times of lawlessness."

"Anyway," Sir Bedivere continued, "things have seemed unsettled, but not serious until just recently. Last month a report came to Camelot of a fortuneteller who was predicting that the king would soon be overthrown."

"Yes," Piers said. "I heard that, too, but I thought nothing of it. Such stories come and go. Last year a hermit near Belrepeire predicted an earthquake that would destroy the castle before Christmas. We're still around."

"This rumour was odd, though," Sir Bedivere said. "You're right that there are always charlatans and madmen predicting ruin, but in general they stir up a small area for a while, then fade away. Everyone in England seems to have heard this rumour, though. Even stranger, when we quietly sent messengers out to find the fortuneteller, they could find no one who had actually seen the seer telling it. It was as if the rumour had no source. Then just two weeks ago the rumour resurfaced with a new twist. England would know that the revolt was at hand when Queen Guinevere was captured."

Sarah's eyes grew wide, and Piers let out a low whistle.

"It sounded like a threat, so we took steps to take care of the queen. At that time, Guinevere was visiting her father, so we thought to bring her home, where not only would she be safe but where everyone could see that she was. But we didn't want to look as though we gave any credit to the rumours, so instead of sending a company of soldiers as an escort, we sent Kai alone. Few outside of Camelot know the queen's face by sight, and we thought, incorrectly it seems, that no one would recognize her even if they were seen. They were going to travel by lesser-known roads and, except for a stop at Belrepeire, were planning to see no one."

King Arthur looked at Sarah. "That's why Kai never spoke the queen's name or called her 'your highness' in your presence, my dear."

"But the strange knight knew the queen," Sarah pointed out.

"It can't have been an accident," Terence replied. "He was sent for her. Your highness, this is a deeper plot than it seems. Bedivere's right. You have to stay here. Gawain and I will bring her back."

The king was silent, and, as Sarah watched, his face seemed to grow old. "You are right," he said at last. He looked up into Sir Gawain's eyes. "I could not trust anyone more. But," he added, "I should like to trust more than one. Piers?"

"Yes, my liege."

"Do you think you can find Parsifal and ask his help?"

Piers shook his head doubtfully. "He and Queen Connie and my father are at Munsalvaesche, Parsifal's other kingdom. One cannot just go there, as you know, but I shall do what I can. You may believe that, O king."

The king nodded, and Terence said, "Lady Sarah? Were you intending to go back to your village?"

"My village?"

"This village Milrick you spoke of."

"Oh, yes. Yes, I was."

"Then, if you would permit us to escort you, perhaps you could show Gawain and me the exact spot where the queen was taken, and the direction they took."

Sarah nodded gratefully. She hadn't been certain how she would find her way back to the village.

"And Gawain," the king said suddenly, "take care of Lady Sarah. I am much in her debt."

"Yes, my liege," Sir Gawain said.

Sarah set out the next morning with Sir Gawain and Terence. The king had provided a fresh horse for her, a beautiful grey mare, and she rode between Terence's dun-coloured horse and Sir Gawain's colossal black one. Piers was not with them, and after they were out of the castle gates, Sarah asked, "Wasn't Piers going to ride with us? I mean, aren't we going the same way?"

"He left last night," Terence said. "I suppose he went to find Parsifal, but I don't know which direction he took."

"Don't you know where this Muns—this other kingdom

kingdom of Sir Parsifal's is?"

Terence nodded. "Munsalvaesche. Yes, I do. But knowing where something is is not the same as knowing how to get there."

This made no sense, but many things were making no sense. "Who is Piers?" Sarah asked. "I mean, why is he so important?"

"What do you mean by 'important'?" Terence asked.

"He's a blacksmith's boy, but at Belrepeire the guards all acted as if he were king. Then, last night, when I was telling my story to King Arthur and you, Piers got to stay, too. The king even said that he trusted him."

"Arthur trusts Piers because Piers is trustworthy, not because he's important," Terence commented. "Two very different things."

"Few people are both, in fact," Sir Gawain added.

"But I understand your confusion," Terence continued, ignoring his master. "You wonder how an apprentice smith came to be so well known to the king. I should explain that Piers once meant to become a royal page."

"Yes, he told me that," Sarah replied. "I told him he didn't look like a page."

"He did at that time," Terence said, chuckling. "He wore a foppish red hat when he rode out on a quest with Gawain and me."

"Rode on a what?"

"A quest. That's what we're on. A journey to find something that is missing and must be restored. Anyway, Piers proved himself on the trip, and when it was over, he decided he'd rather join his father at the forge."

"Why?"

"Because he'd found what was missing and had restored it. Most people have something missing, actually. Perhaps even you do." Terence's tone was polite and cheerful and not at all inquisitive, but Sarah quickly cast about in her mind for another topic.

"What did Piers mean when he said that you can't just go to that place where Parsifal is, Munsalvaesche? Why can't you?"

Before answering, Terence glanced speculatively over her at Sir Gawain, who shrugged and said nothing. At last Terence said carefully, "There are those who say that there is another world beyond this one, a different sort of world. Munsalvaesche is a place in that world."

"What do you mean, a different world?"

Terence hesitated. "The World of Faeries. I suppose you've heard stories of faeries and elves and such creatures?"

"Faeries!" Sarah said scornfully. "I don't believe in faeries."

"Don't you?" Terence asked politely. His face was bland. "Why not?"

"Well, I've never seen one."

"Ah, yes, of course," Terence replied. "Like the man who doesn't believe in invisible dogs."

"What man?" Sarah demanded. She was growing confused.

"He says he doesn't believe in them because he's never seen one."

Sarah stared at Terence in incomprehension, but she saw his eyes crinkle at the corners and realized he was laughing at her. Flushing, she stared straight ahead and lifted her chin. "Besides, I was told to have nothing to do with magical things like faeries, because they were all part of witchcraft and sorcery and were wicked."

"Your mother told you this?" Terence asked.

"No . . . a friend." Sarah could still see Mordecai's face, glowing in the evening firelight, as he read aloud to her from his Book. Usually he read stories, which she loved, but there were those other nights, when he read about "abomination" this and "you shall not allow to live" that. She knew that witches were in there somewhere. "They are abominations," Sarah asserted.

Terence nodded slowly. "I see. You were told that there were no such things as faeries, but that they are abominations, to be avoided at all costs."

Sarah frowned. Put that way, it made Mordecai sound confused, which wasn't at all the case. "Perhaps he meant only for me not to have anything to do with the *stories* about faeries."

"Perhaps so," Terence said amiably. "Then I'll be brief. Munsalvaesche is in one of those stories about another world, the World of Faeries."

"But if it's in a story, how could anyone go there for real?" Sarah asked irritably.

Terence's eyes looked bright, but he replied solemnly, "You see Piers's difficulty, don't you? To fetch Parsifal from a place that doesn't exist – except in a story – and that is an abomination to boot . . . well, I imagine it would be quite a challenge."

Sarah scowled, concluding that Terence was hiding something. Munsalvaesche must be a secret fortress somewhere, whose location Terence was concealing. She didn't mind that, but she wished he had said, "I can't tell you that; it's a secret" instead of inventing a child's tale about a faery land. She lapsed into silence.

They rode steadily, covering the ground even more quickly than she and Piers had, and Sarah was pleased to realize that she was riding more easily. Her body seemed to have learned the rhythm of a trotting horse, and she found herself moving in time with the horse's motions instead of forever bracing herself against them. By afternoon, though, her already sore muscles were aching again, and she was glad when Sir Gawain called a halt at a place where a stream ran beside the road. "We'll rest here a bit," he said. "Don't want to have spent horses when we finally catch up with our abductor."

He dismounted and reached up to give Sarah a hand down, but Terence stayed in the saddle, looking across the meadow. "Who's this, milord?"

Sarah followed his eyes and perceived a man in black, vaguely religious-looking robes riding a large grey horse across the meadow towards them and leading a second horse. Sir Gawain grunted. "That's Sir Griflet's peacocky gelding he's riding," he said.

"Ay, milord," Terence said. "But that's not Sir Griflet."

A moment later the black-robed man had joined them. "Well met, Sir Knight!" he exclaimed brightly in a thin, goatlike voice. He was smooth-cheeked – not like a man who has shaved off his whiskers but like one who has never grown any – and he wore his golden hair brushed back from his face and tied with a ribbon. He dismounted and bowed deeply, like a courtier, then stood and began making the sign of the cross at them all. Sarah scowled at him, but he smiled beatifically back at her and continued gesturing.

"Pacifus cum pocus," he announced. "Peace be to you."

"Thank you, friend," Sir Gawain said. He was hiding a smile, but not very well.

"Friend indeed!" the man said, sweeping another courtly bow. "I am Adrian the Pardoner, and I have long been a friend of knights."

"You appear to have met at least one knight. That grey horse belongs to Sir Griflet of King Arthur's court."

"Belonged, you mean," Adrian said agreeably. "The good Sir Griflet gave me this horse not two days ago."

"Gave it to you?" Sir Gawain asked. "How did that come about?"

"Not five hours' journey from here is the home of the Millpond Knight, he who challenges all comers to a joust and, upon defeating them, throws them in a pond," Adrian said, cheerfully. "Sir Griflet was on his way there when we met, and I was able to give him some assistance towards his assured victory. In gratitude, he gave me his horse."

"What sort of assistance?" Sir Gawain asked, curiously.

Adrian smiled broadly. "I was hoping you would ask, because it may well be that I can render you the same assistance. You see, I am more than a mere pardoner. I not only have papal pardons here" – he patted the bags on the back of his spare horse – "but I also have certain extremely powerful holy relics."

"Good Gog," Sir Gawain said, his lips curling in distaste.

"Indeed, God is good to those who trust in his power. To Sir Griflet I gave a toe bone from Saint Christopher, guaranteed to protect him from being unhorsed in any joust!"

"And in return he gave you his horse?" Terence asked mildly. Adrian smiled and nodded. "It ought to work, then," Terence said.

"It always works," Adrian declared. He looked at Sir Gawain. "Would your worship be desirous of having such a charm as well? As it happens, I have more of Saint Christopher's toes."

"No," Sir Gawain said shortly. "I prefer to protect myself from being unhorsed by scoundrels and cheats." He turned away from the pardoner and knelt at the side of the stream to drink.

Sarah stared, aghast, at Adrian. Was this man truly selling magic charms and claiming that they were from God? Adrian caught her eye and smiled ingratiatingly at her. "How about you, my lady?"

"No!" she snapped. "Why would I want some dead fellow's toe bones?"

"Ah, of course you wouldn't. You don't joust. But I have many relics here with powers more suitable for ladies. How about a comb kissed by the tears of Saint Lucy?" He leaned forwards and lowered his voice. "It will make your hair irresistible to men. They will hardly be able to stop from throwing themselves at your feet."

"I don't want men at my feet!" Sarah exclaimed, revolted by the picture that Adrian had painted.

"I can help you there, too, my lady," Adrian said eagerly. He reached into his horse's pack and produced a small stone. "This stone is from the holy shrine of Our Lady of Anglesey." He raised it reverently in the air, as if it were made of gold. Behind his back, Sir Gawain and Terence exchanged amused glances, but Adrian pressed on. "It is a virginity stone."

51

Sarah stared at the pardoner, too shocked to speak.

"As long as you carry this stone on your body, you are safe from the advances of any man. Such stones are very rare, and very powerful."

Still Sarah could not make a sound, her face frozen in an expression of disgust.

"Ah, I see what you are thinking, though. Perhaps it is *too* powerful, no? One does not *always* want the Blessed Virgin watching over, does one? That is why I also have this." From the bag the pardoner produced a small square of black material. "Put the stone in this sack, and it is rendered blind and powerless until you are ready for it to come out again! Take it out, and you have your purity again, and no one the wiser!"

"You're mad," Sarah said softly.

"Indeed, I think so," Adrian said, still smiling ingratiatingly at her. "I would have to be mad to part with such a relic, so much trouble and expense I went through to get it, but there, we do not live only for ourselves, and as soon as I saw you, I knew that for such a beauty as you I would make even this sacrifice. I seek no profit; all I would ask is that you restore to me the amount that I spent to obtain this miraculous stone."

Sarah wondered what Mordecai would say to this cheerful huckster of holiness, what condemnations he would utter, but she could think of nothing to say. Looking past the pardoner at Sir Gawain, she said, "I'm ready to go again."

"I understand perfectly," he replied. His eyes held an approving look as they met Sarah's. "But come get a drink of water first while I refill our water bags."

Sarah shouldered past Adrian without looking at him, drank, and then let Sir Gawain help her back into her saddle. A minute later they were on their way, but to her dismay the pardoner rode with them. At least he seemed to have given up on Sarah and was trotting alongside Sir Gawain.

"I have to tell you how much respect I have for you great knights," he was saying. "Indeed, I feel sure that I should never have the courage to face death every day as you do. Have you thought, for instance, what would happen to you if – God forbid – you should be killed in battle?" Sir Gawain glanced at Adrian briefly, but he did not reply. "Why, you would die unconfessed!" Adrian said earnestly. He reached out his right hand and gripped Sir Gawain's left forearm in a gesture of concern. "This is why I do what I do," the pardoner said. "It is how I can help people like you. Look here." From a hidden pocket in his cloak he produced a roll of parchment. Untying it swiftly, he unrolled it and held it over for Sir Gawain to see.

"See this? This is the seal of the pope himself." Adrian crossed himself, bowed his head, and murmured, *"Pontius pilatus buttificus."* Looking up, Adrian continued. "This is a pardon for all your sins, up to the date that I write on it. But I see what you're thinking. You're wondering about all the sins you commit after the date on the pardon, aren't you?"

"Not exactly," Sir Gawain said, his voice almost a growl.

"That's why, for you alone, I will write simply the words 'this day' in the space for the date, and that way you will always be current." Sir Gawain ignored him, and Adrian said, "If you won't do it for yourself, do it for your loved ones. Think what agonies of grief you can relieve for them!

If it should happen that – God forbid – you were killed, they would know at once that you are in eternal bliss!" His voice became suddenly very sombre. "I don't like to think about where you might be if – God forbid – you should die without buying this pardon today. Sir Griflet bought one before going to meet the Millpond Knight."

Sir Gawain turned his head in amazement and said, "You sold Griflet a charm to protect him from harm, didn't you?"

"Yes, of course, the toe bone—"

"And you sold him a pardon to protect him if the charm didn't work, too?"

Adrian seemed suddenly to realize the inconsistency of this, and he drew himself up haughtily. "Sir Griflet is a man of great faith," he said. Then, putting on his earnest face, he reached out and grasped Sir Gawain's forearm again. "As I know you are also, my friend."

Sir Gawain reached behind him on his saddle with his right hand and drew a small black-handled dagger from a sheath. "You may have faith in this, sirrah. If you put your hand on my arm again, I will cut off your fingers and provide you with five more holy relics."

"Guaranteed to protect the faithful from frauds," Terence added from Sir Gawain's other side.

Adrian snatched his hand away and fell into silence. Glancing over his shoulder at Sarah, who had dropped behind slightly, he slowed down, evidently planning to ride beside her for a while, but Sarah touched her mare with her heel and rode up between Sir Gawain and Terence. The pardoner trailed along behind them, muttering to himself glumly but evidently intending to stay with them despite their lack of faith.

Adrian was nothing if not persistent. That night they made camp in a wooded area that provided shelter from the wind and hid their fire. Adrian made camp beside them – not exactly with them, but not really apart, either – and after eating dinner he slipped up to where Sarah leaned against a tree in the dark.

"Good evening, my lady," he said in a quiet voice, glancing over his shoulder at Sir Gawain as he sat beside her.

"Go away," Sarah said.

Adrian nodded. "I understand completely," he said. "You don't trust me."

"That's right."

"And why should a young woman like you trust any strange man?" he said. "Young as you are, I'm sure you've heard many a lie from men. Why, how could it be otherwise, when you are so beautiful?"

No one except Sarah's mother had ever called her beautiful, but even if Sarah had believed the compliment, she would not have understood why being beautiful should cause men to lie to her. She started to point this out, but Adrian was still talking.

"But will those men, so full of untruth themselves, believe you? Of course not. Ladies of such beauty as you are never believed!"

This made no sense. "I'm no beauty, but even if I were, what would that have to do with people believing me?" Sarah demanded.

"Not all people, but the lucky man you marry. You see, the man who has a precious pearl is all the more jealous of his prize," Adrian said smoothly. Sarah had a feeling he had given this particular speech before. "What man, if he should marry a woman of such surpassing beauty as you, could help but feel jealous and always be suspicious?"

"Why would a man marry a lady if he didn't trust her?"

Adrian looked as if he didn't understand the question. "Eh?"

"It seems foolish to me," Sarah said shortly, "but as I don't intend to marry, it won't matter."

"I understand your feelings entirely!" Adrian replied, smiling unpleasantly. "Why should you confine yourself to one man all your life? 'Twould hardly be fair to the rest of mankind, to deny such beauty to them!"

"That's not what I—"

"That's why I brought this with me," Adrian said, plunging his hand into a bag he had brought and producing a small bone with a bit of silvery metal fastened to one end. "This is a shoulder bone from Saint Anselm, who never spoke aught but truth. Just put this in a man's soup, and he cannot help but believe every word you tell him. So you may marry after all, and yet still be as free as you wish. If your husband asks prying questions, just serve him this soup and tell him what you will. He will believe you."

Sarah was silent for a moment, thinking about this. "So you're saying that I could lie all I want, but he would always believe me."

"If you use this bone, yes," Adrian said eagerly. "And for one such as you, I will reduce my price from—"

"How is it that a bone from a saint who never told a lie can be used to make lying easier?"

"Eh? What's that?"

"Go away from me," Sarah said.

"If you don't care for the bone, then what do you want? What is it that you need? Trust me, I have something for everyone. What is your deepest desire?"

"It doesn't matter," Sarah said, matter-of-factly. "I don't have any money." Adrian stared at her in disbelief. "Really," Sarah assured him. "Not a groat to my name. Look." Standing, she showed the pardoner the pockets of her cloak.

"What's that?" Adrian demanded suddenly.

Glancing down, Sarah saw her mother's crystal bottle in her pocket. She closed her pocket at once and said, "Nothing. Just a bottle."

"That was genuine crystal, that was!" Adrian exclaimed eagerly. At once, though, his expression of interest disappeared, and he added, "Probably a fraud, though."

"Well, you would know," Sarah said.

"However, it looked as if it's a fair imitation, and although I would surely lose in the bargain, I would be willing to exchange this valuable bone for that little trifle."

"What would you want with this bottle?" Sarah asked.

"I might be able to sell it for some pennies to some lady somewhere."

"And tell her it's a magic potion to make her beautiful or something, I suppose," Sarah said with a sneer. A flicker in the pardoner's eyes confirmed her guess, and she leaned close. "Actually, it contains a poison that kills liars. Bring me some food and I'll let you try it."

The pardoner glared at her. "There's no cause to insult me."

"Just go away," Sarah snapped, wrapping up in her cloak and lying down, her face turned away from the pardoner.

It seemed but a moment later when she awoke, but as the fire was down to a few glowing coals, it must have been hours later. She lay still, wondering what had disturbed her. Then a hand touched her shoulder and shook her gently. Sarah scrambled to her feet, her sword in her hand, though she did not remember reaching for it, and a voice said, "Quietly, my princess! Tsk, tsk. You'd wake an army, with all your crashing about. Come with me into the trees." It was the crone, the one who had taken her to Belrepeire.

Sarah didn't hesitate, but followed the old woman into the shadows beyond their camp. "That's a good girl," the crone said. "Still, it's lucky I made sure the others stayed asleep."

"What? What did you do?"

"Nothing harmful, I assure you. I just sprinkled a bit of sleep dust over them before I woke you."

Sarah felt a chill in her breast. "I thought you said it was your *sister* who was an enchantress."

"Dear me, you sound so accusing," the crone replied placidly. "I did say that, and it's true. Still, I picked up a trick or two, growing up in the same household."

"Enchantresses are abominations," Sarah said sternly.

"Ah, yes, I believe I hear the voice of your cloth merchant behind that," the old woman said. "A very good man, your Mordecai, in his own way, but limited. Limited. I suppose it must be comfortable to see the world as being all good or bad, but it does require a bit of effort, don't you think? Is an enchantress who saves a girl's life an abomination?"

"What? Who do you mean?"

"Who do you think it was who dragged you away from the mob that night last February?"

Sarah stared at the crone. "You? But the woman who pulled me into the bushes was a younger woman I'd never seen before."

"It was dark and you were upset, I suppose," the crone said. "Why didn't you stay where I told you?"

"I couldn't! I wanted to rescue them," Sarah snapped. "And if you hadn't dragged me away—"

"You would have joined them on the pillory. Do you think a crowd of screaming fools willing to burn an innocent old man and woman would stop at burning a girl?"

The images of that awful night came rushing back to Sarah, and the pain of her loss filled her breast and paralysed her as it had not in weeks. She saw the crowd of townspeople, a black mass of arms that grabbed at Mordecai and her mother, held them in the air, and bore them to the village square. She heard her mother's frantic voice and saw the flames begin, and most of all she saw the face of the knight who stood beside the growing fires, exhorting the crowds to destroy the evil ones and purify the land. When she was able to speak, Sarah said, "If it was you who saved me, why didn't you save them?"

The crone's voice grew flat and menacing and did not sound at all like the voice of an old woman. "I tried. I tried to cast a spell of blindness over the crowd, then sleep, and nothing happened. Someone in that crowd had magic stronger than mine and kept me from saving Dioneta."

"How do you know my mother's name?" Sarah asked breathlessly. She had been forbidden to say her mother's real name for so long that she had almost forgotten it.

"I knew your mother long before you did, my child. She was much like you at your age. I will find the one who killed her."

"We'll find him together," Sarah said, gripping her sword more tightly.

The old woman shook her head. "No, princess. Not together. You cannot go where I must go. But you may certainly play your part. That's why I'm here. I have instructions for you. Stay with Gawain and Terence on their quest. When you come back to the meadow where Sir Meliagant took the queen and Sir Kai—"

"Who?"

"Sir Meliagant. That much I've learned – that's the knight who took the queen. Find that place, then go east. I don't know how it is, but the signs say that your mother's murder and this abduction are connected somehow."

"Is the knight who hurt Sir Kai the same knight who killed—?"

"I don't know yet, but do what I say. We will find our enemies, and they will be paid. Now, go back to camp and be quiet. If anyone wakes and sees you, say nothing about me."

Sarah nodded, then frowned. "I thought you said you had put some sleeping powder on them?"

"I did, and you could stroll into the camp banging a drum and not wake Gawain or that worm in the black robe, but Terence is a different matter. One doesn't simply put one like that under a spell. Now, go."

Then the crone just disappeared. It wasn't that she moved away so quickly that she seemed to disappear. She simply vanished, and Sarah instinctively began murmuring to herself one of Mordecai's psalms: "Preserve me, O Lord, for in Thee I take refuge." The crone was a witch herself, and every fibre of Sarah's being told her not to trust her. Every teaching she had ever received from either her mother or Mordecai concerning magic told her to stay far away. But this witch had saved Sarah's life – more than once, actually, since she was the one who had left food and a cloak out for her. More important, this witch was as determined as Sarah to take revenge on the ones who had killed Sarah's mother and Mordecai. Sarah crept back into the camp, wrapped herself up in her cloak, and stared into the coals until almost dawn, dreaming of justice.

IV

THE DUNG-CART KNIGHT

Nobody stirred all night while Sarah kept vigil by the fire, so it appeared that the crone's magic sleeping powder had worked. This was good, but it gave Sarah much to consider. Mordecai had always been deeply scornful of the magicians and fortunetellers they encountered at markets and fairs, had always been so certain that their magic was false, intended to snare the gullible, but was it possible that magic could be real? Could Mordecai have been wrong?

Well, he'd been partly right, anyway. Sarah glanced across their dying fire to where Adrian the Pardoner slept in his own camp. That one was a fraud, at least, who claimed to be religious but who cared for nothing but money. When he had seen Sarah's crystal bottle, he had not noticed its beauty or showed the slightest curiosity about the contents of such a vessel, but had seen only how much money he might make from it. Sarah didn't know what was in the bottle, either, but she loved the vial for the unearthly beauty of the crystal almost as much as for the memories of her mother that it evoked.

The next morning, after a light breakfast of day-old bread, Sarah was back in the saddle for a fourth day. Still pondering the question of magic, she guided her horse beside Terence's. "Sir—" she began.

"Just Terence, my lady. I'm not really so grand."

"Neither am I," Sarah replied at once, "so you can call me Sarah."

"As you wish," Terence said, meeting her glance. His eyes were pleasant but, as always, disturbingly acute, and Sarah looked away.

"I've been thinking about what we discussed yesterday," Sarah said. "About magic and faeries and witches and all that."

"Yes?"

"I don't know what to believe," Sarah admitted.

"Yesterday you seemed to know exactly what to believe," Terence commented. "Why this sudden doubt?"

"I've just been thinking some more," Sarah said.

"Is that all? I thought it might have something to do with your visitor last night," Terence said. His voice was low enough that no one else could hear.

Sarah's eyes widened. "What visitor?" she said immediately. Terence looked amused, and Sarah guessed it *had* been silly to act dumb. "So you saw her?"

"Yes, Sarah."

Sarah thought for a moment. "But she said she had sprinkled some sleeping powder over everyone, so no one would awake." Terence said nothing. Still thinking aloud, Sarah added, "But she also said that she wasn't sure it would work on you."

63

"Your visitor knows me, then?"

"I suppose so. She said, 'One doesn't put sleeping powder on someone like that.' What did she mean? What's different about you?"

Terence ignored her question, but he leaned close and lowered his voice even more. "Am I right in thinking that your visitor last night was the crone who led you to Belrepeire?"

Sarah nodded. "Do you know her?"

"Perhaps. I'd have to meet her face to face to be sure."

"Why didn't you get up and talk to her last night, then?"

"She looked as if she had a message for you, and I didn't want to keep her from giving it." He smiled. "On a quest like this, any help we get is welcome. Was I right?"

"About what?"

"Did she have any instructions for us?"

Sarah hesitated. The crone's instructions had been for Sarah, concerning her own search for the knight of the fires. She had said little about the quest for Sir Kai and the queen. "Not much," Sarah said at last. "All she said was that once we get to the place where they were captured, we're to go east. And she said I'm to go with you."

Terence frowned and looked displeased. "I was planning to return you to your family," he said. "I expect this journey will be dangerous."

Sarah let the "family" comment pass; she didn't want to explain anything she didn't have to. "But if the crone said I was to stay with you, you have to let me stay, don't you?"

"Not necessarily," Terence replied. "If this woman is who I think she is, she's as likely to mean mischief as good."

"You mean because she's a witch?" Sarah asked.

64

"No, because she's the sort of witch that she is," Terence replied. "Besides, I imagine she would prefer 'enchantress'."

This brought Sarah back to the question she had started with. "So are there really enchantresses? Who really do magic?"

Terence's eyes showed nothing. "There certainly are in the stories," he said. And that was all Sarah could get from him.

Twenty minutes later they met a knight, on foot. He was soaking wet, and three brightly dyed feathers that once must have waved jauntily above his head were stuck to the side of his helm like drying plaster. One of the feathers, crimson in colour, had bled dye in a pinkish line down onto the knight's shoulders. As their little cavalcade approached, the walking knight removed his helm and stared at them. "Gawain?"

"Good morning, Griflet. You've ... um ... been bathing?"

The knight took a deep, indignant breath. "That cursed Millpond Knight!" Then, catching a glimpse of Adrian the Pardoner riding along behind the others, the knight exclaimed, "You! You said that I should never be unhorsed!"

Sir Gawain raised his eyebrows. "You've been unhorsed, Griflet?"

"Yes! And this Millpond churl makes you joust on a bridge without railings, so if you fall you go right into the millpond, drat it! And me in silk undergarments, too! It's the outside of enough, I can tell you!"

"But how could you be unhorsed?" Sir Gawain asked. "Didn't you give your horse away?"

"The demmed fellow keeps a stable full of spares!" the

knight said. "If I'd known that, I never would have . . . I thought without a horse I should be able to make the fellow fight with swords. You may have noticed, Sir Gawain, that my swordplay is somewhat superior to my jousting."

"I suppose it would have to be," Sir Gawain murmured, his face a picture of polite concern.

The knight cast a suspicious glance at him, then continued. "As I said, though, the chap has his own stable, and he lent me a horse. He even said he'd give me the horse afterwards if I defeated him, sort of a wager, because he was a gambler at heart."

"Doesn't seem that much of a gamble," Sir Gawain said meditatively. The knight squinted at him again, and Sir Gawain added, "On account of his having several horses, I mean."

"So, of course, I accepted, because that man – that man there! – said that I could never be unhorsed!" He pointed at Adrian.

The pardoner lifted his chin and looked down his nose at the wet knight. "When I said that, I thought that you were a man of faith. As the Holy Word says, if you have faith like mustard, you shall move mountains! You must not have had enough faith. It is your own fault."

"Faith like mustard?" Terence murmured.

"That means," Adrian explained knowledgeably, "that your faith is to be sharp enough that you snort with courage."

"A . . . a spicy mustard, then," Terence said.

"Snort!" the damp knight said indignantly. "I would never do so crude a thing!"

"That's hardly my problem, is it?" the pardoner replied.

The knight that Sir Gawain had called Griflet turned away

from Adrian. "Gawain, that man is riding my horse! Make him give it back to me so I can return to court!"

Sir Gawain raised his eyebrows. "But you sold that horse for your magic bone."

"Yes, but it didn't work!"

"I'm sorry, Griflet. A deal is a deal."

"Then how am I to get home?"

Sir Gawain said, "Do you have any money? Perhaps this fellow at the pond might sell you one of his spare horses."

The knight didn't seem to like this suggestion. "Couldn't *you* fight him? You could knock him in his own pond, and then I could take *his* horse."

"No," Sir Gawain said. "I'm on a real quest. I don't have time to go bashing knights into ponds."

"You couldn't unhorse the Millpond Knight, anyway," Adrian said suddenly.

Sir Gawain looked at him curiously. "Why couldn't I? . . . Wait, don't tell me. You sold him a bone, too."

Adrian nodded, and Sir Griflet turned bright red. "You sold that fellow one of Saint Christopher's toe bones? *That* fellow?"

Sir Gawain looked intrigued. "If they both had one of your magic bones, how could either of them unhorse the other?"

Adrian lifted his nose slightly. "As I said, clearly the Millpond Knight has more faith. Also, I think his bone was bigger."

"His bone was bigger?" Sir Griflet gasped, outraged. "That's not fair! I want a bigger bone!"

The pardoner considered this. "As it happens, I do have one more bone, the largest of all—"

"Milord?" Terence said, interrupting the pardoner's

speech with his quiet voice. "We're wasting time."

Sir Gawain nodded, but said, "Yes, but I do feel bad leaving poor Griflet afoot like this. It's a long walk to Camelot."

"Here's a plan!" Sir Griflet said suddenly. "Why don't you joust with this Millpond Knight, and if you unhorse him, then this pardoner fellow has to give me back my own horse."

"What?" Adrian asked. "Don't be silly!"

"Don't you believe in your own toe bones?" Sir Griflet asked slyly.

Sir Gawain almost smiled. "It's a good thought, Griflet, but I really can't take the time to go all the way to some—"

"You won't have to!" the knight shouted triumphantly. "Because here he comes now." All of them looked where the knight was pointing and saw a knight in brightly festooned armour riding towards them. Sir Griflet turned cunning eyes towards Adrian. "Do you believe in your bones or not?"

"Yes, of course, I—"

"Then you think that they'll protect him now?"

"Of course they will!"

"So if he's knocked off, you'll give me my horse back?"

Adrian swallowed, but at last nodded reluctantly.

"Who goes there?" the approaching knight boomed at them as he rode his horse right into their midst and stopped. "More food for my fishes, I'll be bound!"

"We're just passing through," Sir Gawain said.

"No one passes through unless they joust with me," the new knight declared.

"Why not?" Sir Gawain asked. "We're not bothering you."

"Afraid, are you?" the new knight boomed. He wore the visor down on his helm, and his voice echoed metallically inside it.

"Not likely," Sir Griflet said smugly. "This is Sir Gawain."

The Millpond Knight took a sharp breath and seemed to cringe backwards slightly. Sir Gawain turned towards Sir Griflet. "I told you, Griflet, I'm not fighting this fellow for you."

Evidently the Millpond Knight felt he should have an edge in a fight with someone like Sir Gawain. As soon as Sir Gawain looked away, the Millpond Knight went for his sword. Sarah saw him grab his sword hilt and, without really thinking what she was doing, drew her own sword from its place on her saddle. Her blade seemed to spring into her hand, and it came free at the same moment as the knight's. The Millpond Knight swung his sword towards Sir Gawain's bare head, and Sarah's sword came up just in time to meet his stroke. The swords clanged together, and Sarah quickly drew her sword back and swung again. From the corner of her eye, Sarah saw Sir Gawain's sword appear, but he didn't need it. Her second stroke was given off-balance and seemed really quite feeble to Sarah, but when it hit the Millpond Knight in the breastplate he reeled back and tumbled from his horse. He landed with a clank, still holding his sword, though it was bent at a sharp angle where Sarah's sword had hit it.

"Good Gog, Sarah," Sir Gawain said, staring. "You bent his sword."

"And unhorsed him!" Sir Griflet crowed. "I'll take my horse back now!"

The Millpond Knight rose shakily to his feet, threw down his ruined sword, and rushed forwards, but not towards Sarah or Sir Gawain. His eyes were on the pardoner. "You said I could never be unhorsed!" he shouted, grabbing Adrian and dragging him from the saddle. "You said that toe bone would make me invincible!"

Sir Griflet's shrill voice chimed in. "Give me my horse!"

A hand touched Sarah's elbow. It was Terence. "Shall we leave them to sort this out? We've spent too much time here already." Without waiting for a reply, Terence rode ahead, with Sarah and Sir Gawain behind him. Terence set a brisk pace, but even so it was several minutes before the sound of the Millpond Knight's angry shouts, Sir Griflet's crows of triumph, and Adrian's bleating protests died away completely.

"I must thank you, Sarah," Sir Gawain said, guiding his horse close to her. "Your quick parry of that knight's attack may have saved my life."

"You're welcome, Sir Gawain."

"You may as well just call me Gawain," the knight said. "Courtly titles seem sort of silly and pointless once you're away from court. It's one of the best reasons to leave the court, in fact."

"If you like," Sarah replied doubtfully. She wasn't sure she could call a grown man, and a knight at that, by his familiar name.

"But I'm not only grateful," Gawain continued. "I'm curious. I have seen swords bent before, but only by extraordinarily mighty blows. Either you are rather stronger than you look, or else something very odd is going on. How did you do that?"

"I don't know," Sarah admitted.

"Did Kai say anything about your sword when he gave it to you?"

"He said I should use two hands when I swung, because it would give me more control."

"Oh," Gawain said. "Good advice, no doubt, but hardly an explanation. Did, ah, did you spar with your sword when he was teaching you to use it?"

"Oh, no," she said. "After he taught me to draw the sword and how to hold it, we practised with sticks."

"So was this the first time you've ever used your sword?"

Sarah hesitated. "No, there was one other time. At Belrepeire, the guard at the gate was being rude, and so I drew the sword to show him I was serious."

Gawain's lips twitched. "And did he grasp your meaning?"

Sarah shook her head. "Not at first. He laughed at me, then picked up a big spear with an axe at the end."

"A halberd," Gawain said. "So what did you do?"

"He made me angry," Sarah explained. "I could see he wasn't going to give me any help, so I swung the sword and hit the . . . the halberd thing on the wooden part, just below his hands. To show him I was in earnest, you see."

"I hope he caught on this time," Gawain said.

Sarah nodded. "Yes, this time he did."

"A gentleman of discernment. What did he do?"

"He fell down."

"Fell down?"

"You see," Sarah explained, "he was leaning on his spear, and when I hit it, I cut it in two."

Gawain was silent for a few seconds. "May I see your sword?" he asked.

Sarah drew the weapon and allowed him to examine it. After a minute, Gawain returned it, his expression reverent. "Trebuchet," he said to Terence. The squire nodded and glanced curiously at Sarah. Gawain's face grew sombre. "I do not know what magic Trebuchet forged into this steel, but it is stronger than any of us know. Use it wisely, Sarah, and carefully. Remember that the sword that can cut through the shaft of a halberd can as easily cut through a man's arm."

Sarah had not considered that, and the thought that she might have cut off the castle guard's hands was sobering. He had been a surly fellow, in need of a lesson, but losing a hand for rudeness might have been a bit extreme. She replaced the sword in its sheath, eyeing it with awe – and with satisfaction. When she found the knight of the fires, she would be ready.

During the morning of their third day of riding, Sarah began recognizing landmarks in the forest, and before long she found the little meadow where Sir Kai and the queen had been captured. Terence slipped off his horse and began to examine the clearing, and Gawain turned to Sarah. "Which direction did they take?"

Sarah pointed. "That way. East."

Gawain nodded and muttered to himself, "That would have been almost six full days ago now, but perhaps we can catch up. Kai's wounds would have slowed them down."

Sarah made a sour face. "I don't think that Sir Meliagant would have slowed down for Sir Kai's benefit."

Gawain's face grew still, and Terence stopped looking at the field and turned back to stare at Sarah. "What did you say?" Gawain asked.

"Remember that he was going to kill Sir Kai anyway," Sarah said. "So why would he be careful about—?"

"Sir Meliagant?" Terence said. "You've never mentioned the knight's name before."

"Oh," Sarah said. "I . . . well, I didn't know it when I told the king."

Gawain looked confused, but Terence nodded. "Your visitor the other night told you," he said slowly. He looked at Gawain. "You think it's Bagdemagus's son?"

"It would be too much of a coincidence not to be," Gawain said. "What visitor the other night?"

"The crone who helped Sarah at the start of the journey," Terence said. "She came back and talked with Sarah again a couple of nights ago."

"Did she, then? And what else did she say?" Gawain asked Sarah.

"Only that we were to go east, and I was supposed to stay with you."

Gawain frowned. "Stay with us? Why?"

Sarah shrugged vaguely and said, "Who is Sir Meliagant?"

Gawain pursed his lips. "Do you remember when Bedivere was telling Piers about all that was going on, he said that some of Arthur's knights had disappeared?"

"Yes."

"Well, it's actually a bit odder than that. Not only knights but their castles and lands have gone, too."

"How does a castle disappear?" Sarah demanded sceptically.

"I said it was odd, didn't I? The most puzzling disappearance is that of King Bagdemagus. He is one of Arthur's sworn bondsmen and has been a knight of the

Round Table from the very beginning, but he's also the ruler of the Kingdom of Logres, in the heart of England. A few months ago, Bagdemagus was absent from a . . . a court event that he never misses."

"Fancy dress ball," Terence added, mild disdain in his voice.

"Bagdemagus was one of those who began the tradition of the annual ball," Gawain explained. "It's the high point of his year. So, Arthur sent messengers to Logres to see if he was all right. They'd all been there before, knew exactly where it was and how to get there, but they couldn't find it. The whole land was just gone. That was just before the rumours about the fortune-teller's prophecy began to appear."

"And Bagdemagus," Terence added, "has a son named Meliagant."

"Is he one of King Arthur's knights, too?"

Gawain shook his head decisively. "No. Never comes to court at all. I've only seen him once, in fact – at a tournament in Yorkshire." Gawain's face grew serious. "He was very skilled with his weapons." He glanced at Terence. "Are you ready?"

Terence shook his head and returned to his unhurried scrutiny of the scene.

Gawain turned back to Sarah. "You say your old woman told you to stay with us? For how long?"

"She didn't say," Sarah admitted. "She just said after we got here."

"I have to tell you, I'm not keen on it," Gawain said frankly. "Especially now that I hear Meliagant is behind this. I'm sworn to protect maidens, not to put them in harm's way."

74

"I'm not afraid."

"All the more reason you shouldn't go," Gawain replied promptly. "More people die of foolish courage than of cowardice. Besides, what about your family? Shouldn't you be back with them?"

The time had come. "I have no family," Sarah said. "My mother and my guardian died three months ago. I have no one to go back to."

"I'm sorry," Gawain said, after a brief pause. "But . . . do you really want to go with us? Riding all day, sleeping on the ground, eating rarely and poorly?"

"Except for the riding part, that's how I've lived since February," Sarah said. "Besides, the crone told me I was to go with you, and she's hasn't lied to me yet."

"So far as you know," Gawain muttered, but after a moment he sighed and said, "All right. I suppose you're as safe on a quest with us as you would be left alone in the forest. You may come, but on one condition: when I say it is too dangerous or find a safer place for you, you must leave us."

Sarah lifted her chin and said nothing.

Terence returned to his horse and mounted. He glanced once at Sarah, then at Gawain. Then he shrugged.

"You learn anything?" Gawain asked.

"We're not the only ones on their trail," Terence said. "Another knight is ahead of us."

Gawain raised one eyebrow. "Parsifal, you think? No one else should know what has happened."

Terence shook his head. "I don't think it's Parsifal, but we'll see soon. He's not far ahead."

Two hours later they found the unknown knight's horse, stripped of his saddle and gear and left free to graze in a field. Gawain examined it. "Exhausted," he said. "Maybe limping slightly, too."

"It looks like one of Arthur's horses," Terence commented.

Gawain glanced sharply at him, alarmed. "You don't think Arthur came on ahead of us after all, do you?"

"I wouldn't have thought so, but he's been known to slip off incognito before," Terence said. "We should know soon, now that he's on foot, though."

They heard the knight before they saw him. An hour after finding the horse, as they rode through a cluster of buildings that was something more than countryside but something less than a village, they heard the sound of jeering laughter ahead. Topping a small rise, they came upon a group of children shouting and tossing clods at a knight who was riding in the back of a heavy farm wagon.

"Whew!" Gawain said suddenly, wrinkling his nose.

"Dung cart," Terence said.

The knight wore his visor down over his face, which was a good idea considering that he was being pelted with stones and roadside trash, but by no motion or word did he indicate that he even noticed the taunting cluster of children.

"Why are those children throwing things at that knight?" Sarah asked. "Aren't they afraid of his sword?"

"I don't imagine that they've ever even seen a knight without a horse," Terence replied pensively, "let alone a knight riding in a cart that most peasants wouldn't use. It's easy to mock something new. Still think that might be Arthur, milord?"

"Well, it doesn't look like his armour," Gawain conceded.

"Armour? Call that armour?" Terence said with a sniff. "If I put something like that on you, milord, I could never hold my head up in the Squire's Court again. Looks as if the only thing holding it together is rust."

The knight's armour did look sadly stained, and of course sitting in a cart full of manure didn't improve his appearance. Gawain led the others down the hill towards the dung cart. Sarah wrinkled her nose. She had never really minded the smell of manure – it spoke to her of strong animals and farms and growing things – but there could be too much of anything, and this foul cart piled high with steaming dung was certainly that.

"Good borrow, sir . . . ah, sir dight," Gawain said. He sounded as if he had a cold, and Sarah realized he was trying to breathe only through his mouth.

"Good day, Sir Gawain," the knight replied.

A rotten turnip bounced off the dung-cart knight's closed visor, and Gawain turned sharply. "Here dow, you children. Stop that at once!" At his stern voice, the children dropped their projectiles and lapsed into a sullen silence. Gawain turned back to the knight. "You dow me, thed?"

"Yes."

"And, if I bay ask, who are you?"

"No one of importance," the knight replied. He spoke softly, almost in a whisper.

Gawain bowed his head slightly, as if acknowledging the other's wish to remain anonymous. Then he said, "Was that your horse that we passed an hour or so back?"

"No," the knight replied hoarsely. "But it was the horse I rode to this land until it could go no farther."

"Then you are in a hurry?" Gawain asked. "In this cart?"

"The cart moves almost as fast as I can walk in armour, but is not so tiring," the knight replied indifferently. "It is not as fast as I would wish to travel, but it is as fast as I am able."

"But where do you go in such haste?"

"I go where you go, Sir Gawain, seeking the same two people you seek, to rescue them from the knight who stole them away six days ago." Gawain stared at the knight, but before he could reply, the knight added, "Do not let me delay you. Go ahead, and God be with you. Save them if you are able, and if you are not, I will come behind."

"How do you know whom I seek?" Gawain asked. His eyes were bright and clear, and he spoke normally again.

"It doesn't matter. Be sure, my friend, that I've told no one." Gawain hesitated, and the knight said, "Go!"

"Very well, friend," Gawain said, inclining his head again. "I'll leave you. Best of luck to you on the quest as well."

At that, the thick, dirty peasant who drove the cart burst into laughter. "A quest, he says!" the driver said with a chortle. "Best of luck! I'll give you luck, O noble knight!" With that, the driver leaned behind him, plunged his hand deep into the dung, and, pulling out a handful, flung it against the knight's back, where it hit with a wet smack.

Gawain rode his horse up beside the peasant and drew back his gauntleted hand, but the dung-cart knight said, "You waste time, Gawain! I am much in this gentleman's debt. He has given me what I need, and as for his words, what care I? His abuse is to me nothing! Go, I say!"

Gawain lowered his hand and started to reply, but Terence interrupted. "The good knight is right. Let's go."

And so they went, but as they went over the top of the next hill, as if by prior agreement, they all stopped and looked back at the knight in the cart. The children had returned with new stones and clods to throw, but the knight still did not move.

V

THE DIVIDING OF THE WAYS

"Maybe we're on the right road after all," Terence said suddenly, breaking the silence. "This looks promising."

For several hours, Terence and Gawain had been wondering aloud if they were going the right way. The eastwards road that they had taken after leaving the knight in the dung cart had entered the forest and had become the narrowest of trails, winding tortuously through wooded areas that were already as dark as night and now that night was really approaching were almost pitch black. Terence had taken the lead as they entered the trees, and there he had stayed, since there wasn't even room for two horses to ride abreast.

"What is it?" Gawain called from behind Sarah.

"You'll see," Terence replied. "There's some open space ahead, where a little light still comes through."

A moment later they were all in a tiny clearing – barely more than a hole in the tree cover – where there was a little more light and where they could sit on their horses side by side. From the clearing, the path split into two trails, both going on into the forest gloom, but Sarah barely glanced at the roads. Her attention was focussed on the woman who sat at ease on a fallen log, just at the point where the road divided.

The woman was slightly built and austere-looking, dressed in flowing blue-green robes that fell about her legs like silk but that somehow seemed finer, and here at dusk in this black, mossy, and mushroomy forest, Sarah could not imagine a more incongruous sight. The woman clearly was waiting for something or someone, but she did not move as the three of them ranged themselves in front of her. Only when Terence said, "We bid you good day, my lady," did the woman move her head to look at them.

At once dimples appeared on the woman's cheeks, and her eyes lit up. Sarah realized that the woman was hardly more than a girl, perhaps only two or three years older than Sarah herself. The girl smiled happily and said, "But you're Terence! And Sir Gawain! No one said it was going to be you!"

"Ariel," Sir Gawain said, bowing his head. "I should hardly have recognized you."

"Everyone says that I've grown amazingly in the past year, so much so that I'm dreadfully tired of hearing it, in fact. But don't you think I look more grown up, too? Especially in this dress. It's supposed to make me look solemn and dignified. Does it?"

"It did until you began to talk," Gawain said, smiling.

"Oh dear, I'm doing it, aren't I?" the girl said, chagrined. "I was so determined that I was going to be serious and all that, and *not* going to talk too much, and

81

I'm sure I would have done well, but then I saw that it was you, and I forgot myself. How is Piers? And Sir Parsifal? It seems like ages since I've seen them. Are you well? But you look well, so I'm sure I needn't have asked."

"We are quite well, thank you," Gawain said, "except that we are anxious for missing friends."

"Yes," the girl replied. "Queen Guinevere and Sir Kai. You know, I should have expected you to be the ones who came looking for them, now that I think about it, because of course you're Arthur's cousin and greatest knight, and it only stands to reason that you would want to go off to help him if you could. But" – the girl frowned suddenly – "Mother did say that I might not recognize the knight who came. Now why would she say that, I wonder, if she knew it was you? She *must* remember how we spent all that time together in the Castle of Women, when you were wounded."

"Your mother sent you here?" Terence asked when the girl stopped for a breath.

"Oh yes, she said that I was old enough to begin bringing messages to this world now, if I could remember to keep my dignity, which of course I haven't, but since it's only you, it doesn't matter, does it? Among old friends like this, you don't have to act all aloof and, you know, Other-Worldly, do you?" The girl's eyes rested on Sarah, and suddenly her cheeks flushed. "Except that … oh dear, I should have …"

She trailed off, and Gawain came to her rescue. "Ariel, this is Lady Sarah of Milrick, who has been accompanying us on our quest to this point. Sarah, allow me to introduce Ariel."

Ariel smiled brightly and said, "I'm so pleased to meet you. I had expected only men to come along, so this is much better."

82

Sarah nodded soberly. "How do you do?"

Ariel's smile faded slightly. "Have I offended you, Sarah?"

Sarah blinked. "Why no. Why would you think—?"

"It's just that you looked so formal and dignified and you didn't smile when you greeted me," Ariel said. "I was afraid I had said something wrong. I do that sometimes, you know, without realizing it."

"Sarah doesn't smile," Terence explained. Sarah glanced sharply at Terence but could think of nothing to say in response.

"Never?" asked Ariel, wide-eyed.

"I . . . I smile sometimes," Sarah said, but even as she spoke she knew it sounded lame. When *was* the last time she had smiled?

Ariel continued staring, as if seeing a strange beast for the first time. Terence took advantage of her momentary silence to say, "Do you have a message for us, Ariel? Something for our quest?"

"Oh, yes, of course," Ariel said. She schooled her features back into the austere solemnity they had shown at first. "Welcome, Sir Knight," she said in an artificial and formal voice. "You have come to the Dividing of the Ways."

"Actually, we had already noticed that, my dear," Gawain said.

Ariel's formality melted in an instant, and her cheeks dimpled again. "It's what I was told to say, but it does seem silly. I mean, if you can't tell that the road divides here, you're rather an ass, aren't you? And what's the good of an ass on a quest?"

"Why don't you just give us the gist of the message?" Gawain said patiently.

"I had to memorize it so I could give it just right," Ariel said. "Now, pay attention and stop interrupting."

"I beg your pardon, my lady," Gawain said meekly.

"Welcome, Sir Knight," Ariel began again. "You have come to the Dividing of the Ways. You seek the Lost Kingdom of Logres, where the Queen of All England is now held in arduous durance, along with her escort, Sir Kai the Seneschal. Either of the roads you see before you will take you there, but both are fraught with peril."

"Fraught," Gawain murmured.

"Durance," added Terence.

Ariel shot them a stern look, but continued. "The road to your left leads to the Great River of Logres, which may be crossed only by the Underwater Bridge. That to your right leads to the Great Gorge of Listinoise, which may be crossed only by the Sword Bridge. Dangers face you to the right and to the left, but know this, Sir Knight: once you have chosen a road, you may never return from the Lost Kingdom until you have achieved your quest."

"I hadn't planned to," Gawain said calmly. "So, Ariel. Which road do you recommend?"

"Me?" Ariel asked.

"For instance, what is this 'Sword Bridge'?"

"I haven't a notion," Ariel replied frankly. "I don't know anything beyond what I had to memorize. No one would tell me a thing!" She scowled briefly at this, but scowls did not suit her face, and a moment later her expression cleared and she added, "I don't even know what an Underwater Bridge is."

"We've crossed through the water before, milord," Terence said suddenly. "I suggest we try that route."

Gawain nodded, then said, "Very well, but it grows dark

84

now, and there's room in this clearing to pitch the horses. Shall we stop here for the night?" He glanced at Ariel. "Would you stay with us this evening, my dear? I'm sure Sarah could use the company."

Ariel shook her head. "No, I'm supposed to leave at dark. I was just about to take off when you arrived, in fact."

"Then may I speak with you briefly before you leave? I would like to send greetings to your mother."

Gawain went aside with Ariel and began speaking to her in a low voice. Sarah went to help Terence care for the horses and make camp. They were almost finished when Gawain returned and began whispering to Terence. Terence frowned, but said nothing. Sarah didn't care; Gawain could have as many secrets as he wanted, so long as she could get a bite to eat and a place to sleep. She looked about for a likely place for her bed.

"Gawain?" she said suddenly. "Where did your friend Ariel go?"

"She didn't say," Gawain replied.

"But surely it isn't safe for her in this dark forest all by herself."

"Ariel will be all right," Gawain said reassuringly. "She's at home in the forest. Would you like to start gathering some wood for a fire? I'm hungry."

So Sarah put Ariel out of her mind and set about gathering sticks. They ate silently, then rolled up in their blankets in a triangle around the coals and all went to sleep at once.

When Sarah awoke, Gawain and Terence were gone. There were no blankets near the fire, no supplies stacked against the trees, and only Sarah's horse was still tethered to the ground at the edge of the clearing. A neat bundle of food lay beside Sarah's own saddle and saddlebags, but nothing else remained. They had left her behind. Furious, Sarah let out a scream of frustration.

"I was afraid you wouldn't be pleased," said a timid voice behind her. Whirling around, Sarah saw Ariel seated again on the log where she had been when they first arrived.

"Did you know about this?"

Ariel nodded soberly. "Gawain asked me to keep an eye on you and see that you were safe. He said it was going to be too dangerous for you to go with him."

"He might have asked me if I cared for the danger!" Sarah snapped.

"He knew you would want to go, which is why he decided to go in secret, no matter what Terence said."

"What did Terence say?" Sarah asked.

"Terence didn't like it," Ariel explained. "Sneaking out like this. But he didn't want you along, either. He said they couldn't put you in danger when it wasn't really your quest, anyway."

"Not my quest!" Sarah stamped her foot. "What do they know about my quest?"

Ariel looked surprised. "They said you just chanced to see what happened to Sir Kai and the queen, but that you didn't really know them. He said you had just met them for the first time that morning, so the quest really had nothing to do with you." Ariel faltered again as she looked at Sarah's face. "Oh dear," she said. "Were they wrong?"

"Yes, of course they were wrong! Both of them!"

"You mean you really *do* know Sir Kai and the queen?"

"Yes . . . no, not that, exactly . . . I mean, I *liked* Sir Kai, but that's not . . ." Sarah trailed off in confusion, not sure what she could tell this girl and what she shouldn't. All those weeks living alone with her secret hatred had seemed hard, but it was harder still to keep a secret from people whom, at heart, she liked.

"Is there another reason you wanted to go with Gawain and Terence?" Ariel asked.

Sarah nodded.

"Do Gawain and Terence know?" Ariel asked.

Sarah shook her head. "No," she said softly. "I wasn't sure I could trust them."

Ariel's eyes grew round. "You weren't sure you could trust *Terence*?" she said with an expression of incredulity.

"Why should I? He didn't trust me, either," Sarah said defensively. "When I asked him simple questions, he told me all sorts of wild stories in order to keep from answering me."

"What sort of wild stories?"

"About a World of Faeries and magical places that you can't get to from this world and things like that."

Ariel nodded seriously. "Yes?" she said. "And then what?"

"Don't you think that's enough?"

Ariel looked confused. "What's wild about that?"

Sarah let out an exasperated sigh. "Don't tell me you believe in faeries."

Ariel giggled suddenly. "Believe in faeries!" she said. "You silly! What do you think I am?"

"What?"

"I'm a faery, you goose."

"You're a . . . a what?" Sarah stared at her.

"I'm what the people in your world used to call a water nymph. So is my mother."

"My world?" Sarah said faintly.

"Well, of course. Where do you think I went last night after I left you?" Sarah shook her head, and Ariel continued. "Back to my own world, of course. There's a spring just past that oak that's a door between the worlds."

This was going too far. Sarah snorted in disbelief. "You almost had me believing you for a moment," she said.

Ariel only smiled. "Look, Sarah, why do you suppose Gawain was willing to leave you in my care? You don't think he'd trust you to a human girl my age, do you? He knew that if you were in trouble, I could help you."

"What would you do?" Sarah demanded. "You don't even have a sword!"

"I don't know if I should show you. I'm not really supposed to do anything out of the ordinary in this world unless I have to," Ariel said, hesitating for a moment. Sarah raised her eyebrows mockingly, as if to say, "Of course you aren't," and Ariel said, "But maybe this is necessary, after all. I could hide you where no one could see you, like this."

And then Ariel disappeared. One moment she was there, and another moment she was gone, just as the crone had disappeared the other night. That disappearance Sarah had been able to convince herself was a trick of the darkness, but here in the morning sun there was no mistake. Ariel reappeared. "Like that," she said.

Sarah stared, her mouth open but unable to speak. Ariel hurried forwards and laid her hand on Sarah's shoulder. "I didn't mean to frighten you," she said anxiously. "I wanted to reassure you, but I haven't at all, have I? I shouldn't have done that."

Ariel's hand was comfortingly solid, and after a moment Sarah lifted her own hand and rested it on top of Ariel's. "Then there really is a different world. And Terence knows about it, doesn't he?"

Ariel's cheeks dimpled, but she didn't smile outright. "Yes. Terence is a faery, too. Part, anyway. In our world, he's the Duke of Avalon, a very great man."

That explained the crone's respect for him. Sarah said faintly, "And in this other world, you have magic and enchantments and all the things that Mordecai said were wicked. But you aren't wicked, and neither is Terence." Sarah felt as if she needed to sit down, or perhaps to wake up.

"I think our world is more like yours than it seems," Ariel said pensively. "I mean, yes, we have what you call magic, but in that world it isn't magic, if you know what I mean. It's just the way things are. And we have good people and wicked people, just like here. We have mothers and fathers, just like you have . . ."

Ariel trailed off suddenly, looking at Sarah. Sarah met her eyes and saw in them a glimmer of the same acuteness that made Terence's gaze so disquieting. But Ariel's eyes didn't disturb her.

"But you don't, do you?" Ariel said softly. "Have a mother and father, I mean."

"Not any more."

"I'm sorry, Sarah. Was it . . . has it been long?"

Sarah shook her head. "That's why I wanted to stay with Gawain and Terence," she said.

"Can you tell me what happened?"

Sarah hesitated for only a second. "Yes," she said. "I'll tell you."

The early morning was already growing warm, promising an unseasonably hot day, but they made a fire anyway and prepared a breakfast to eat around the flames, and Sarah told Ariel her story.

"I don't know my father; he was gone before I was born. Mother never said where. She was left penniless, but I think she must have been a maid to a great lady once, because she taught me to speak like the nobility and to have good manners and things like that. I still don't know what use good manners are, but I have them anyway."

Ariel nodded sympathetically. "I know just what you mean. My mother would never let me lick my fingers between bites, and now that I'm older, I find that I still don't do it, even when I'm not with Mother and could get away with it."

"Exactly," Sarah said, insensibly comforted at finding an ordinary experience that she shared with this Other-Worldly girl beside her.

"If you and your mother were left with nothing, how did you survive?"

"We were found by a travelling merchant, a man who went from village to village buying and selling cloth. I lived with him all my life – except for one bit – until last February, and he was the only father I ever had."

"What do you mean, 'except for one bit'?"

"Not long after Mordecai took us in, there was a time – maybe six months or so – when he disappeared. We stayed with his horse and wagon and lived off the money in his strongbox. I never knew where he went. You know how when

90

you're really small you don't understand anything that grownups do anyway, so you don't ask too many questions?"

"My mother says that I *always* asked too many questions."

Sarah nodded. She could see that. "Anyway, Mordecai came back, and was so pleased to find that we had only taken what we needed and hadn't touched his wares that he made us sort of his family."

"His name was Mordecai?"

"Yes," Sarah said. "He was a Jew."

She uttered this last sentence almost defiantly, but Ariel only nodded quickly. "Oh, that's why I didn't recognize the name. So you lived with Mordecai the Merchant. Was it a good life?"

"I guess it was," Sarah said. "It was the only life I had, anyway. There were some hard times, of course. Sometimes people wouldn't let him in a village because he was a Jew, but we would just go somewhere else. He always had good cloth to sell, and he always gave a fair price, so we were never hungry. He used to read to me at night and teach me all the rules he lived by, and he called me . . ." For the first time, Sarah's voice broke.

Ariel waited without speaking. It was several minutes before Sarah could speak again. "He called me his princess. That's what my name means in his own language, 'princess'. He chose the name for me."

"So Sarah isn't really your name?"

Sarah shook her head. "It's my real name; it just isn't my first one. Mother didn't want to use our old names, so I became Sarah, and she became Esther."

"So what happened to your mother and this Mordecai?"

"We were in camp near a small village we had never

91

visited before. Mordecai had been given some bad directions and we were lost, you see. At camp that night, Mordecai gave me a present." Sarah gestured at her gown. "This. He had come upon the cloth months before, in Kent, and had bought it. I'm sure it was very dear. Mother sewed it into a dress for me, working a bit at a time after I was asleep, so it would be a surprise. They gave it to me, and Mordecai said that at last his princess had a dress to befit her station. He loved giving it to me so much.

"I was prancing around, showing it off for them both, when we heard voices. The people of the village were coming out to our camp in the woods, bringing torches and axes and scythes and pitchforks. They came to our fire, and Mordecai stood between them and my mother and me and asked what they wanted."

Sarah felt her eyes grow hot, and she took strength from her hatred and continued with her voice steady. "I won't tell you everything that was said, back and forth, but the heart of it was that there had been a plague in the village. Some of their children had died, and they were blaming Mordecai. They said that the Jews had poisoned their well, because Jews always wanted to kill Christians like they killed Christ, and that Mordecai had come to add more poison and maybe to capture and eat some of their children in secret ceremonies."

Ariel's face was a mask of horror, and Sarah could see in her eyes a premonition of what had happened next.

"They had come to kill us. Mordecai tried to talk them out of it. He denied that he had ever harmed a Christian, but they would not listen, so he began shouting that the woman and her child were not Jews, and that they should be spared, whatever they did to him. They didn't listen, and when they dragged Mordecai away, they took Mother, too."

"But how did you get away?"

Sarah shook her head. "I don't know really. When they grabbed Mordecai and Mother, I took up a branch from the ground to attack them, and then I was in the bushes, away from camp. I don't know how I got there, but standing beside me was a woman in grander clothes than I had ever seen. She was so beautiful, except that her eyes were . . . her eyes frightened me. They were so angry that . . . I can't describe it."

"I know exactly what you mean," Ariel said.

"How could you?" Sarah snapped.

"Because that's how your eyes are frightening me right now, Sarah."

Sarah forced herself to breathe calmly for a moment, and felt some of the redness go from her eyes. "Sorry," she said at last.

"Go on. Did you ever find out who the woman with the eyes was?"

"Maybe. Later, I met an old woman who said that she'd been the one who saved me from the crowd, but the woman I saw was definitely not old. Could an enchantress make herself look young?"

"Most of them do, I think," Ariel replied. "Except for hags – that's a nasty sort of witch in our world – but I don't think this would have been a hag, since she saved your life. Hags don't do that sort of thing much."

Sarah shrugged. "Anyway, this enchantress or old woman or young woman told me to stay where I was until everything was over. Then she disappeared."

"You didn't stay, of course." It wasn't even a question.

"No. I could still hear the yelling of the crowd, and I took my stick and followed the sound. I went all the way to the village square, where I hid in a shadow beside a house and saw the knight."

"The knight?"

"There was a man in the middle of the crowd, a man wearing chain mail but nothing on his head, so I could see his face. He stood on a stump in the middle of the square and waved a sword in the air and congratulated the crowd, as if they were soldiers who had won a battle instead of murderers who had captured an old man and a woman. Mordecai and my mother were tied to stakes on each side of him, with piles of wood at their feet. The knight shouted out that these two Christ-killers had been found guilty of murdering the children of the village and were condemned to death. My mother cried, and Mordecai held up his head and looked at the sky and moved his lips – praying, I guess. Then the people of the village set the wood on fire with their torches and burned them."

"You saw this?" Ariel asked, her voice almost too soft to hear.

"Most of it," Sarah replied. "I watched until they stopped struggling, then ran back into the woods to hide. That was where I lived for the next three months and ten days, watching the trails in and out of the village, looking for that knight, so I could find where he lives."

"But how did you survive?" Ariel demanded. "A human girl your age left without food or clothing in the woods in the winter!"

Sarah explained about the old woman who had left her the food and the cloak. "I suppose now that she knew all the time that I was in the woods and was trying to keep me alive. After a few weeks, though, I began to get my food a different way."

"How?"

Sarah lifted her chin. "I stole it from the villagers. I learned how to creep softly through the trees, and I used to raid every storeroom in Milrick." Seeing a small crease in Ariel's forehead, Sarah added, "I wasn't going to, at first. Mordecai had always taught me not to steal, and after he was gone, I vowed that I would keep him alive in my memory by keeping his rules, but then, as I kept watch on the village, looking for that knight, I saw something that changed my mind."

"What was it?"

"Mordecai's cloth. You see, when I had gone back to our wagon the day after the fires, I found only burnt wood and charred metal. I thought that they had burned everything, like they had burned Mordecai and my mother. But they hadn't, of course. They had first stolen everything of value. Within two weeks, every person in the village was wearing new clothes, made up from Mordecai's stock." Sarah's eyes grew hot again. "So you see, they were thieves, too, and no one was left to punish them but me. The only thing left to me of all that we had had was this bottle of my mother's, which I found in the ashes of the wagon."

Sarah drew the crystal bottle from her pocket, and Ariel's eyes grew round. "That was your mother's?" she asked softly. "But . . . that's a faery vial! What's in it?"

Sarah blinked. "I . . . don't know. My mother just kept it

on a shelf and looked at it sometimes. She said it had been her mother's before her. What do the faeries use these for?"

"Like your mother, we mostly like their beauty. But I know that in this world they are often used by sorcerers and enchantresses for their magic cordials." Sarah stared at the bottle, then hastily replaced it in her pocket. How had her mother come by such a thing? Ariel said softly, "And so you lived by taking the villagers' food."

Sarah nodded defiantly and added, "They were the reason I was hungry, after all. Then Sir Kai and the queen came along."

Sarah told Ariel about the events of the past week. She told about the swordplay lessons, the abduction, and her journey to Camelot, as she had told King Arthur, but then she continued, telling about her journey with Gawain and Terence and her second meeting with the crone. It took quite a long time, and all the while Ariel sat silently on the grass by the fire, hugging her knees and staring at the coals.

"So I wonder what we do now," Ariel said at last.

"I have to go after Gawain and Terence," Sarah said. "That's what the crone said for me to do. That's where I'll find the knight."

Ariel nodded. "I know. And when you find the knight, you'll kill him."

Sarah nodded, then said, almost as an afterthought, "I'd like to help Sir Kai, too."

Ariel nodded. "Of course. But your main quest is for revenge, and that's what worries me. You see, I'm supposed to help with the rescue as much as I can – I would have gone with Gawain and Terence if he hadn't asked me to stay with you – but I don't think I'm supposed to help someone get revenge."

Sarah's heart had warmed at the thought of travelling on with Ariel, but now she shook off her momentary weakness and said, "Then I'll have to go on alone."

"But I promised Gawain I'd take care of you," Ariel pointed out. "And if I leave you alone, I've broken that promise." She frowned thoughtfully for a moment, then set her lips firmly and said, "I'll just have to go with you anyway."

"Before you leave, my lady," said a polite male voice behind them, "is it possible for you to assist me?"

Both girls jumped and whirled around. Standing on the path not twenty feet away was a tall man with broad shoulders and long brown hair. He also had a thick brown beard. The man wore a discoloured breastplate, armour on his thighs, and a sword on his left hip, but no other armour. Even without it, though, Sarah recognized the knight they had passed the day before on the dung cart.

"Oh, sir!" Ariel exclaimed. "You startled me!"

"I am desolated, my lady," the knight said, bowing graciously. Despite his coarse appearance, he spoke in a cultured voice with just a hint of a foreign accent. He slung a bundle from his shoulders and set it at his feet. It was the rest of his armour, tied together in a neat pack. "I did not mean to surprise you," he said, his voice still apologetic, "but you were intent on your conversation."

"Did you hear what we were saying?" Sarah demanded.

The stained knight shook his head. "Only your friend's final words, that she would go with you. Please, my lady," he continued, looking at Sarah, "how is it that you have

97

been separated from Sir Gawain and Squire Terence?"

"Do you know this knight?" Ariel asked Sarah.

"We passed him on the road yesterday. He is also looking for Sir Kai and the queen." She turned back to the knight to answer his question. "They left me. They said that the journey was too dangerous."

"No doubt they are correct," the knight said. "But it seems an odd time to make this decision. Had that not occurred to them earlier?"

Sarah shrugged. "They tried to make me stay behind earlier," she admitted. "I wouldn't stay."

"It was your wish to go on this quest?"

"Yes."

"Then you are the girl who saw the queen captured and took word to the king, no?"

Sarah blinked. "Yes. How do you know about that?"

"It is of no importance," the knight said. "But since we are both determined to seek the queen and Sir Kai, may I offer myself as companion?"

Sarah glanced once at Ariel, who was examining the knight speculatively. Ariel nodded slowly. "We shall go together," she said. "I am Ariel, sir, and this is Lady Sarah of – what was it Gawain said yesterday? Of Mil-something?"

"Milrick," Sarah said. "But it isn't really my home. That's the name of the village, where – you know, where I've been."

"I am enchanted," the knight said. His bow was a masterpiece of grace and courtesy. "You may call me Jean."

So it was decided: the three of them would go on together. Ariel explained the two roads to Jean, and they determined that since Gawain and Terence had taken the left-hand fork, they should take the right. They gathered Sarah's gear and Jean's bundled armour (he said that it was faster walking without all of his gear fastened on) onto Sarah's horse, and there was still room for Sarah and Ariel to take turns riding. While they packed, Sarah stole several curious glances at Jean. He wore the clothes of a peasant but – like so many people she had met on this journey – was clearly something else. From his voice and his armour – ill kept though it was – he could only be a knight, but that did not fit the circumstances in which she had first encountered him. She had never heard of a knight who would do something so humiliating as to ride in a cart filled with dung or who could be so indifferent to insults, especially from the lower ranks of society. Even if he was a second-rate knight, though, he carried a sword. Perhaps he might be of some use, after all.

VI

THE HERMIT OF THE TOMB

An hour after the three set off from the Dividing of the Ways, the dense forest thinned, and they began travelling over a moor. There was more light away from the woods, but the trail was hard to see through the heather, and shortly before noon it ended altogether, at a river. The river was just too wide and deep to cross, so they went upstream along the banks, looking for a ford.

Soon they found what they were looking for: a wide, shallow, rocky spot in the river where the water never ran deeper than a person's waist. Sarah was on the mare, and Jean said to Ariel, "If you will sit beside Lady Sarah, my lady, I shall lead the mare across."

"I don't mind the water," Ariel said.

"The current may be swifter than it looks. Please, my lady," Jean replied.

Ariel's dimples appeared, and she ventured a look brimming with laughter at Sarah, and Sarah suddenly remembered that Ariel was a water nymph. Ariel merely said, "Very well," though, and meekly climbed into the saddle beside Sarah. Sarah was suddenly struck with the absurdity of protecting a water nymph from a river – like guarding an eagle from falling off a cliff. It was thoughtful of Jean, though, even if it was unnecessary.

Jean took the mare's reins and started into the water, but Ariel said suddenly, "Jean, should you not speak to this knight first?"

For the first time, Sarah became aware of a knight on horseback, sitting still in the shadow of a tree on the opposite bank. The knight's visor was closed, and he held a long spear, like the one that had injured Sir Kai. "I see no reason to exchange pleasantries," Jean replied, still coaxing the mare into the water.

"Knight!" the man across the river called. "I guard this ford, and I forbid you to cross it."

Jean didn't respond with so much as a glance. He kept leading the reluctant mare forwards.

"You would be wise not to take this ford!" shouted the knight. Again, Jean gave no sign that he had heard. Sarah began to feel concerned. Jean was on foot and wore only half of his armour. If the other knight chose to enforce his command, there didn't seem much that Jean would be able to do.

"Knight! Do not enter the ford against my order, or I shall be forced to strike you!"

"Shouldn't you do something?" Ariel asked Jean hesitantly.

"I am sure he will not hurt you," Jean replied, somewhat absently, leading the mare around a large rock.

"I was afraid that he would hurt you, actually," Ariel replied. Jean only shook his head.

The guardian knight pointed his lance at Jean and

spurred his horse forwards. Sarah caught her breath, but soon saw there was no danger. The other horse was as reluctant to enter the cold, swirling river as Sarah's mare had been, and the knight's grand charge ended weakly just a few feet from the bank, as his snorting and splashing and clearly disgusted mount stopped abruptly.

"Go on, Bucephalus!" the knight called to his horse. "Charge!"

Bucephalus tossed his head and gave his master a look that Sarah had no difficulty interpreting. Meanwhile Jean continued guiding the mare forwards. They were two thirds of the way across now, almost within reach of the knight's lance. Jean turned to face forwards and plodded on through the current.

The knight stopped trying to urge his mount forwards, sat up in his saddle, and said loudly, "Stay, Bucephalus!" Since the horse was already staying and clearly had no intention of doing anything else, this command might not have been strictly necessary, but the knight said, "Good boy," anyway. Ariel giggled, and Sarah rolled her eyes.

Jean kept stepping forwards. Now only about eight feet separated him from the guardian of the ford, and the knight lowered his spear again, pointing it directly at Jean's breastplate. Still Jean ignored it. Another step forwards, and his armoured chest actually touched the point of the spear.

"Stop!" the knight said. Jean stepped forwards, pushing against the lance with his breastplate, and the knight suddenly lunged forwards. The thrusting spear made Jean stagger backwards and almost fall. He caught himself, though, and resumed his forwards march. The mounted knight had more trouble recovering. He almost lost his balance when he thrust and, struggling to keep his seat, nearly dropped his lance. By the time he had recovered, Jean was beside him, and the long lance was useless. Still holding the spear in one hand, the knight dropped his horse's reins and drew his sword. "Now shall you stop?" he demanded angrily.

Jean only reached out with his left hand and slapped the other knight's horse sharply on the flank. Bucephalus twitched and jumped, then turned briskly and headed back to dry land, taking advantage of his slack reins to go where he wished. The knight, unable to balance himself with both hands holding weapons, fell off the horse with a splash.

Jean pressed on, leading the mare up the bank to the other side. Beside them, Bucephalus rose dripping from the water. There was no sign of the knight.

"Merde!" Jean muttered under his breath. He gave Ariel his hand to help her down from the saddle. "Hold the horse, if you please, Lady Ariel." Then he turned and strode back into the river, fished around in the eddies for a moment, then straightened up, clutching the struggling and gasping knight's breastplate with one hand and dragging him from the water. The knight had lost his lance – Sarah saw it floating away downstream – but he still held his sword. Jean dropped him in a heap on the riverbank, then reached down, roughly unfastened the knight's helm, and removed it.

The knight was a young man, with hair that was so fair as to seem almost white and a faint mustache that grew only at the edge of the man's mouth and not under his nose. He probably would have been fairly good-looking, but his face was a faint shade of blue, and he was gagging. Rolling over on his stomach, the knight vomited up several pints of river. Jean watched until the knight had finished and was breathing again, then nodded and walked back to the mare. "Shall we go? The trail had been pointing eastwards for the last hour, so we can continue in that direction."

Sarah and Ariel nodded, careful not to stare at the limp form on the ground behind them. But then the knight began to make a strange sound, and Sarah realized that he was crying. Ariel touched Jean on the arm. "Can you not help him?"

"I already saved his life, did I not?" Jean replied.

"Yes, but can't you help him now?"

Jean looked dourly at her, then said, "Me, I do not think so. But for your sake, I will try." He walked over to the sobbing knight and said, "Brother, what ails you?"

"I have lost my honour."

"If your honour was so slight as to be lost by falling in a river, then it was not worth having."

"No," the knight said. "Not the fall! But you! You wouldn't even fight me! Am I so far beneath you?"

"I am pressed for time," Jean explained. "I have not leisure to fight people I meet along the way."

"You wouldn't even look at me!"

"I did not want to encourage you. As I said, I have not the time. Besides, what if we had fought and I had defeated you? You would have lost your honour anyway, no?"

"But no! To be defeated by another great knight is a feat worthy of note! Only to be ignored and then pushed into the river, like a lackey—"

"I didn't push you," Jean pointed out. "You fell."

This didn't seem to be helpful. The knight burst into racking sobs again, and Ariel said gently, "Jean."

Jean looked back at her. "But he is so stupid, my lady!"

At that, the knight stopped crying. "You dare to insult me!" he cried. Rising to his feet with difficulty, the knight lifted his sword and drove it into the ground between him and Jean. "I take such words from no man!" he said proudly. "Draw thy weapon, and I shall take mine as well!" It would have been a fine, dramatic gesture, Sarah thought, had he not driven his sword into the spot where a moment before he had emptied his stomach.

Jean looked distastefully at the sword in the puddle, then shrugged, closed his right hand into a fist, and hit the knight in the face. The knight rocked backwards, then sat down hard. "If it will give you pleasure and save your honour to be defeated, then let us make haste and defeat you," Jean said.

With a roar of indignation, the knight crawled to his feet and gripped his sword. Jean slapped the man's hand away and knocked him down again. For the next two minutes – no more – Sarah watched the guardian of the ford bob up and down like a twig in a river. Jean never drew his sword and never seemed hurried. He parried the two or three feeble sword strokes that the knight managed to make by slapping the flat of the sword away with his bare hand. Jean's hands were even quicker than Sir Kai's, Sarah realized, and as she watched she noticed that Jean's feet were always in exactly the right position to give him perfect balance. At last, one of Jean's slaps actually knocked the sword from the knight's hand. Jean punched the knight once more, then picked up his sword and pointed it at the man's bare neck. "Do you yield?" he said wearily.

The knight nodded, and Jean drove the sword back into

the ground, in a clean spot, and turned away. "Let us go now. The day does not grow longer."

They had gone only a few steps, though, when the guardian of the ford called out, "Sir Knight?" Jean stopped and looked back at the knight, who said, "Thank you."

Jean closed his eyes briefly and replied, "It was nothing."

"It was an honour to fight such a knight as you," the knight said.

Jean nodded curtly, then turned back to the trail. As he walked, though, he said, "And to think that once I *was* a knight such as you. *Incroyable!*"

He spoke these words softly, under his breath, but Sarah heard. She examined their companion with a new curiosity. She had had difficulty thinking of Jean as a real knight – her first picture of him, sitting amid the manure in an old farm cart, had probably been responsible for this – but his handling of the knight at the ford had altered her opinion. It wasn't that he had overcome the knight so easily, but that he had been so confident that he could.

"You didn't seem afraid back there, when you fought that knight," she ventured.

"Afraid? Of him?" Jean replied. His voice held no scorn, only mild surprise, as if it had never occurred to him that one might be afraid. "No, Lady Sarah."

"You didn't even draw your sword."

Jean shrugged. "A sword is a terrible thing. With a sword, one kills. I did not wish to kill."

"Have you ever wished to kill?" Sarah asked. Jean did not answer, so after a moment, she said, "But you know how to fight with a sword, don't you?"

106

"Some have said so," Jean replied.

"Would you teach me?" Jean looked up at her, his blue eyes bright under his heavy eyebrows. "Sir Kai started to teach me, when he gave me this sword," Sarah added, "but then he was hurt."

"No, I will not teach you. A sword is a terrible thing," Jean repeated.

That evening, as their shadows began to stretch long before them on the heath, they came to a compact house built into the side of a small hill that rose incongruously out of the flatlands. The house was constructed of unhewn stones, closely fitted together and chinked with mud. Jean stopped and stared at the house, his eyes alight. "But how marvellous! See how beautifully it is built! Each stone in exactly the right place, as if designed for that spot and no other!"

Sarah agreed that the house looked very snug and secure, but she didn't see what had drawn such admiration from Jean. There was not the slightest decoration anywhere, not even flowers in the bare yard. Whoever lived here was male, she decided, and immediately she was proven correct. A balding man in long black religious robes appeared at the doorway.

"Good afternoon, travellers," the man said. His voice was gentle.

"Good afternoon, Father," Jean said, bowing reverently.

"Oh, no," the man said. "I am not a priest, only a humble dweller of the moors."

"But your robe, is it not Benedictine?" Jean asked.

"Yes," the man said. "I am a monk, although I live away from the brotherhood now, but I have not been ordained. In these parts, they call me Brother Constans."

"Did you build this house?" Jean asked.

The old man smiled. "I am still building it. It has been ten years already, and I think in another three years, I shall have my bedroom finished. But the guest room is ready. I hope you will stay with me this evening. The moors are cold after dark, when the wind rises, but there is always a fire at my hearth."

With a bow Jean accepted, then turned to the girls. "I am Jean Le Forestier, and this is Lady Ariel and Lady Sarah."

"My home is honoured," Brother Constans said, sweeping the ladies a courtly bow that seemed out of place in his monkish garb.

Ariel laughed delightedly. "But how graceful! Is that how they teach novitiates to bow at the Abbey now?"

Brother Constans's eyes wrinkled at the edges. "I have not always been a monk, my child." He turned his eyes to Sarah and smiled with evident pleasure. "Sarah," he said. "You are welcome, princess."

Sarah stared. "Why did you call me that?"

"It is what your name means, of course. Did you not know? But yes, I see you do." He led them into the house and showed Ariel and Sarah to what he called the guest room, where two pallet beds lay on the floor. Then he turned to Jean. "Come – how did you give your name again? Jean? – come outside, and I will show you my work."

The two men went out a rear door, and Sarah, watching them through the door, saw the hermit showing Jean around a field littered with stones. He gestured about, evidently describing where the new room would be, and Jean began nodding and talking. It was the most Sarah had seen their escort speak since they had met him. A stir at her side caught her eye, and she looked over to see Ariel beside her.

"What an odd man," Sarah said.

"I like him," Ariel replied.

Sarah agreed that the monk seemed nice enough. "But how strange," she said. "To build the guest room before building his own room. Surely he doesn't have that many guests out here."

"You wouldn't think so," Ariel conceded. "I thought at first that it was just his polite way of giving up his own room to guests, but the guest room beds haven't been slept in for some time. The blankets had dust on them."

"Dust?"

Ariel nodded. "He probably never noticed. I suppose a holy man is still a man, after all. I shook your covers out already."

"Thank you. So where do you think the hermit sleeps?"

"Maybe on the floor," Ariel replied. "Or maybe there's another room behind that door."

Sarah noticed for the first time a heavy oaken door built into the side wall, just where the house joined the little hill. "Do you think that the hill is hollow?" she asked.

"But of course, Sarah," responded the monk, who had drifted near enough to hear Sarah's question. "The hill is not a real hill, you know. It is a house just like this one that I build, only much older. Would you like to see the inner room?" Sarah didn't reply, but the old monk seemed to take her silence as an affirmative, and he turned to Jean. "Come and see, my friend."

Walking back into the house, Brother Constans took up a candle and lit it at the fire in the hearth. "Follow me," he said, "and see why I live alone out here on the heath." His eyes glinted, and he added, "Don't tell me that you haven't wondered." He opened the oaken door and led them into a spacious room with stone walls. In the flicker of candlelight, Sarah could see figures and words carved in the stones, but the words seemed to be in a different language. At the far end of the room was a large stone box, exactly the size of a bed.

"This is a crypt," Jean said.

"Yes," the old monk replied.

"Who is buried in that tomb?"

"No one yet."

"Yet?" Jean's right hand rested casually on the hilt of his sword.

"Don't be concerned," Brother Constans said with a chuckle. "I am not a madman who waits to kill travellers, like Procrustes in the story of the ancients. The tomb waits here as a hallowed resting place for one of the great heroes of the land, and I am its guardian until that time."

"What hero?" Jean asked.

"Sir Lancelot du Lac," Brother Constans said calmly. He rested one hand on the stone coffin and patted it fondly. "A great man indeed."

Jean said nothing. To fill the silence, Sarah commented, "Someone told me that Sir Lancelot had gone away from the court. How do you know he isn't already dead?"

"I know only what I am told. Sir Lancelot has more to do for England, deeds that will lift his name higher than it has ever been raised, and when he dies, he will be laid to rest here."

"And when will that be?" Jean asked. His voice was very quiet.

"That I was not told." The old man looked at Jean and smiled. "But if it is not soon, then it is to come someday. You did not think that Sir Lancelot would live forever, did you?"

Ariel spoke for the first time. "Why were you chosen to keep this place, Brother Constans?"

The monk turned back towards the door. "I'll tell you, but first, shall we have some soup?" He led them back into the new part of the house, where he pulled several wooden bowls from a cupboard and ladled soup into them from a pot that hung over the fire. Standing at his place at the small table, the monk bowed over his bowl, briefly and silently, then sat and looked at Ariel. "You see, my dear, Sir Lancelot is the reason I am a monk at all. It happened nearly twelve years ago, just after Sir Lancelot had taken Joyous Garde."

"What's that?" Sarah asked.

"A castle," the monk replied. "Do you mean you haven't heard of it?" Sarah shook her head. "Well, let me begin there, then. At that time, there was a mighty knight by the name of Sir Turquin, who held a great hatred for King Arthur and all his knights."

"Why?" Sarah asked.

Brother Constans shook his head. "I do not know what reason Sir Turquin would have given, but it doesn't matter. He hated because he was a man who hates, and that was his own choice. It is the same with every hatred. So, because of his hatred, Sir Turquin would ride about England looking for knights from the Round Table, and when he found one he would defeat that knight and drag him off in chains to his castle, which was called Dolorous Garde. Many of Arthur's knights found themselves in those dungeons, including even Sir Kai the Seneschal. If you haven't heard of Joyous Garde, I suppose you haven't heard of Sir Kai, but—"

"But I have," Sarah said.

"Ah, then you know that any knight who could defeat

111

Sir Kai was indeed a mighty warrior. Sir Kai spent nearly six months in prison, where he was Sir Turquin's prize captive. Sir Turquin fed him with slop left from the hogs, gave him no blankets, even in winter, and heaped upon him all the abominations he could imagine. I am told that he forced Sir Kai to share his cell with every sort of outcast he could dredge up."

"What do you mean?" Ariel asked.

"He searched the land for all the most despised sorts of people, then put one of each in Sir Kai's cell with him: a leper, an old Egyptian woman, a Jew, and a raving madman.

"King Arthur sent out his greatest knights to find Sir Kai, but since no knight had ever met Sir Turquin and returned to tell of it, no one knew where to look. At last, though, Sir Lancelot found him. Sir Turquin was on his way back to Dolorous Garde, nearly at the gates, bringing a captured knight – I forget which one—"

"Gaheris," Jean said.

Brother Constans nodded. "Yes, that's right. Anyway, Sir Lancelot killed Sir Turquin, set the prisoners free, then renamed it Joyous Garde and made it his own home in England."

"He didn't have one already?" Sarah asked.

"Sir Lancelot was originally from Benouic, in France, you see. And so the king's enemy was defeated, and Sir Lancelot became the most honoured knight in England."

Sarah nodded slowly. "More than Sir Gawain?"

"Sir Gawain was away at that time, thought to be dead, but even if Gawain had been at court, Sir Lancelot would have eclipsed him," Brother Constans said. "Do you not agree, Jean?"

"Sir Lancelot was not worthy to buckle Sir Gawain's armour for him," Jean said quietly. "But come, how does all this lead to you? How did Sir Lancelot inspire you to enter the monastic life?"

"That came, as I said, just after Joyous Garde. I was a knight then, though not of the Round Table, and a man of bitter gall and choler. Then I was called Sir Pedwyr."

"You?" Jean exclaimed. "Sir Pedwyr?"

Brother Constans nodded serenely. "I," he said. "I was a different man, then, I hope. I was quick to see offence, and eager to avenge it, and no one felt my wrath more than those I most loved. It is often that way, I believe. Most of all, I loved my wife, the Lady Serena; therefore, I suspected all men of wanting to take her from me, and I suspected her of unfaithfulness with every man who bowed to her."

Sarah remembered Adrian the Pardoner's holy bones for people who wanted to betray their spouses. "You didn't love her at all," Sarah said, "if you didn't trust her."

Brother Constans's eye rested on Sarah approvingly. "You are right. I loved her as far as I understood love," he replied. "But, as you say, it was not a love that is worthy of the name, and it ended as such a love can only end. One day, for a reason that I no longer remember, I came to believe that Serena had betrayed me, and I set out to kill her. She saw me coming with my sword drawn and, knowing me, ran. I had just caught up with her when Sir Lancelot came upon us.

"He drew his sword and stopped me, then made me promise not to kill her. I promised, and Sir Lancelot sheathed his sword. He should not have done so: he didn't realize that people who cannot trust others cannot themselves be trusted. I cut off my Serena's head before his eyes." The monk's voice was sober but calm. Sarah gasped, and Ariel's eyes filled with tears. Jean's face was utterly still. Brother Constans glanced at him, then continued.

"Sir Lancelot beat me, angrily and severely. He never drew his sword, but when he was done, I was covered with bruises and hardly able to move. When he was done, he broke my sword and said that if I did not do what he said, he would beat me again, more severely."

"What did he say to do?" Ariel asked.

"He bid me take my wife's head to Rome and present it to the Pope, begging forgiveness."

"And did you?" Jean asked.

"I did. On the long journey, I learned to be horrified of what I had become, and kneeling in Rome I found forgiveness. It was the beginning of my life. I have often suspected that Sir Lancelot meant only to give me a punishment horrible enough to fit my crime, but he gave me new life instead. All that I used to be died that day at the holy city. The marks of Sir Lancelot's fists were but the scars of new birth." Brother Constans looked at Ariel. "And that is why I was chosen to guard this place. It is a way that I may show gratitude to the one who was midwife to my salvation."

Jean shook his head slowly. "He little deserves such gratitude, Sir Pedwyr. He was – *Bah! Quel hypocrite!* – that he should presume to judge you for your wrath, when he himself was betraying his own king! Have you not heard that of your Sir Lancelot?"

"I have heard that he loved the king's wife, Queen Guinevere," Brother Constans said gently, "but I no longer listen to reports of others' sins."

Sarah frowned at a sudden memory. "But it might be true. When Sir Meliagant abducted the queen, he said that she would learn to love him, and when she said she was already married, he laughed at her and said that she had not cared about that when Sir Lancelot was at court. I didn't know what that meant, but now I see. The queen was unfaithful to the king, with Sir Lancelot, wasn't she?"

"I cannot say, princess," the monk replied.

"It was true," Jean replied, "but do not blame the queen. The fault is Sir Lancelot's."

"Is that why Sir Lancelot went away from the court?" Ariel asked Jean.

"Yes."

"How do you know that?" Sarah demanded.

Jean glanced at Brother Constans, who smiled and said nothing. Jean looked back at Sarah and shrugged. "I was once called by the name Sir Lancelot," he said.

"I came to the court of King Arthur – it was almost fifteen years ago – filled with the lust for fame, desirous of being called the greatest of all his knights," Jean said.

They had moved from the table and were now sitting together around the hermit's large fireplace. Jean and the hermit sat in plain but well-made wooden chairs, and Sarah and Ariel sat together on a rug before the fire. It wasn't really cold, but the muted sound of the wind outside made it pleasant to sit there in the stillness and warmth.

"But that was my problem, you see. I did not wish to *be* the greatest knight, only to be *called* so by others, and so I did whatever other people thought the greatest knight should do. The world decreed that the greatest knight should be the greatest fighter – that was easy for me – but also that he should be a graceful dancer, should wear the finest clothes, should have a private priest, should walk with a dainty step, and above all, should languish for love." He glanced at the monk. "That was my scripture, *bon frère*, to do . . . to do whatever was *la mode des chevaliers* – the fashion of knights. I did not seek to be, only to seem.

"And so I had to languish for love, but my love could not be for an ordinary woman. She had to be one whose beauty and grandeur would adorn my knighthood. No woman was so beautiful or grand as the queen, so I languished for the queen. For seven years, I mooned over her so that I could be in every way *comme il faut*."

"Then you didn't love Queen Guinevere at all," Ariel said softly. Her dark eyes glittered with the depth of her concentration, reminding Sarah again of Squire Terence's eyes.

Jean hesitated, then looked at Brother Constans. "It is as Sir Pedwyr said. I loved her as I understood love to be, but it was not enough. It was nothing like the king's love for her."

"The queen didn't tell you to leave her alone, though, did she?" Sarah asked abruptly. "She has to take some of the blame, don't you think?"

Jean said nothing, and after a moment Brother Constans said gently, "He can tell only his own story, my child. Please, Jean, continue."

"I cannot describe the fear I lived with," Jean said ruminatively.

"Fear?" Sarah asked. She thought of the calm, unhurried manner with which he had dispatched the knight at the ford, without even drawing his own sword. "But what could you be afraid of?"

"Everything, don't you see? I had become what I sought to be: the knight called perfect in every way. But to maintain such a reputation! Impossible! Had any man ever seen me in shabby clothes, had I ever stumbled on the dance floor or trod on my lady's toe, my name for perfection would have collapsed altogether. Especially, I had to win every tournament. I could not be put to shame.

"One day," Jean said, his eyes darkening and his expression growing severe, "as I rode in the forest, I came upon a woman sitting beneath a tree, crying. Her falcon, she said, had flown away and was caught in that tree. Her husband had given her the bird, and now it was lost, its leather jesses tangled in the branches. Could I not climb up the tree and rescue it for her? So, of course, I did. It was always my duty to help maidens. One cannot climb trees in armour, so I removed my armour and went up, only to hear a knight beneath me shout in triumph. It had all been a trap, a way to catch me in the tree without my armour or weapons. The knight wished to become famous as the one who slew Sir Lancelot."

"What did you do?" Ariel asked.

"I broke a branch from the tree to use as a cudgel, then leaped upon him. I beat him, took his own sword away, and killed him with it." His eyes were bleak. "I did not have to kill him, you understand. But I could not have it told how I had been put in such an embarrassing position." His jaw tightened convulsively, and he whispered, *"Salaud."*

Then his eyes cleared, and he looked at the others. "Your pardon, my friends. I have lived alone so long that I have grown much in the habit of speaking to myself."

117

"But how did that come about?" asked Ariel. "Living alone, away from the court, I mean."

"It had to happen one day, of course. I fell from my lofty heights. It was shortly after the falcon episode. Sir Gawain returned from a great quest, having earned so much glory that I grew jealous, and the king called a tournament. At this tournament, I defeated Gawain but then was defeated by an unknown knight. Then, to make my shame greater, the queen rejected me before all the court and turned her eyes back to her husband. Like a house of sticks when one stick is removed, my honour collapsed."

Ariel said, "What was it you said to that knight back at the ford? Something about honour?"

Jean nodded. "If your honour is so frail that you can lose it in one defeat, then it is not worth keeping. I left the court, vowing to live the rest of my life alone in some hermitage." He glanced at Brother Constans, and his severe expression lightened. "That was the worst fate I could imagine, you see."

"A dreadful prospect," Brother Constans replied placidly. "Did you find a hermitage?"

"Nearly. I found an empty woodcutter's cottage in Cornwall, and I've lived there ever since, hunting for my food and cutting wood for the nearby villagers. It was there I took the name Jean. I have cut wood for seven years now. It has not been an easy life, but it has been my own life, and I have been content."

"And no one from the court knew where you were," Ariel said wonderingly.

"That would be too much to ask," Jean said, "but I was fortunate, and the only people from Camelot who discovered me were men and women of honour who told no one. Sir

Gaheris and Lady Lynet, his wife, know me. Squire Terence, of course. What secrets are hid from that one? Also, Sir Parsifal and his page boy, Pierre – or Piers, I should say."

"Piers?" Sarah and Ariel repeated, in unison.

"Yes. Piers is the one who came to me two – or is it three? – days ago and asked me for the love of King Arthur – and also of Queen Guinevere – to dig up my armour and help Sir Gawain search for the captives. Piers said he was supposed to find Sir Parsifal, but he did not know where to look for him. He knew where to find me. He told me to keep the quest secret, then gave me directions and his horse. The horse was weary already, but I rode it until it could go no farther, and then I set it free and began to walk."

"Except when you rode in a dung cart," Sarah said.

"Yes, except for then," Jean replied.

"And so you are a knight again," Brother Constans said.

Jean shook his head. "No. I am a woodcutter with a sword. I am Jean Le Forestier. Sir Lancelot . . . he did not ride in dung carts. I do."

VII

THE CUSTOM OF THE LAND

Sarah walked beside Jean, casting him occasional sideways glances but too bashful to ask any of the thousand questions that the story he had told the night before had evoked. How could a man who had been so famous as a knight be "content" cutting wood? Had he never had regrets? Did he still love the queen? Is that why he took up his armour again? And, more immediately, what had gone through his head when Brother Constans showed them the tomb that awaited Sir Lancelot? But, shy before the famous knight, Sarah held her tongue. Instead, she rested her hand on the hilt of her sword, stretched her legs into a longer stride, and watched the horizon for the towers of a castle.

Before they had left the hermitage that morning, Brother Constans had told them how to get to the home of a nobleman, whom he simply called the "Vavasour", who might be able to help them. The Vavasour was a sworn vassal of King Bagdemagus and of his son Sir Meliagant and should be able to direct them to Bagdemagus's home, the Castle Logres. And, so long as they didn't tell the Vavasour their purpose, he might even help them on their journey. "Beware, though," the monk had said. "Beware of this land. It has changed in the past year. I don't know how, but it has become a place of threat and omen. In this land, darkness is the natural condition; even the sunlight has to force its way in."

Ariel had looked very serious at this, but Sarah thought it made no sense and had barely repressed a shrug. Then Brother Constans had looked at her and said softly, *"Yevarekh adonai veyishmarekh."*

Sarah stared. The monk's pronunciation was strange, but the words were familiar. Mordecai used to say them to her at night as a blessing. "How do you know those words?"

"A hermit has time to study," Brother Constans had replied. "I cannot play with rocks all day, you know."

Sarah's reverie was interrupted suddenly. "Castle ahead," Jean said. "This must be the home of that Vavasour fellow. Let us hope he can guide us to Sir Meliagant."

Half an hour later they came to the castle gate, where they sent a message by the guard and shortly afterwards were being welcomed by the Vavasour himself. He was a portly fellow in a velvet blouse that was trimmed with the finest ermine but showed the outlines of old grease stains on the front. He rushed out of the castle keep, his face beaming. "Visitors! Good gracious, how delightful! You've no idea how rare it is to have noble guests these days!" Then he stopped as he looked at their little retinue. "But, you *are* nobles, aren't you? My guard said a knight and two ladies were at the gate."

"I am a knight," Jean said calmly. "And these are indeed

ladies. We have come to you for help on our quest."

"You're on a quest?" the Vavasour asked dubiously.

"We are."

"Without a warhorse? And with no lance?"

"I left my horse behind three days ago," Jean explained. "It could carry me no farther."

"Three days? You've been on foot for three days? A knight?" the Vavasour was clearly shocked.

"Not all the way," Jean replied evenly. "Some of the way I rode in a dung cart. Could you give us directions to the Castle Logres, please? We must see King Bagdemagus and his son."

"A dung cart," the Vavasour said, almost in a whisper. Then he shook himself and his troubled expression disappeared, replaced with a beaming smile. "Forgive me. I've quite forgot my manners. You must dine with me and my sons. We shall be serving a midday meal soon, and any questing knight is welcome to join us, even one who . . . well, never mind that."

Jean bowed politely. "We thank you, sir, for your offer, and we certainly would not refuse any assistance you gave us, but our quest is of an urgent nature. We should be on our way at once."

The Vavasour's smile turned at once into a scowl. Sarah had never seen anyone change moods so quickly or so often, much more often than he changed shirts. "It is the custom of this land," the Vavasour said indignantly, "that an invitation to dinner is sacred. You refuse my hospitality at your own peril."

"This is the custom of the land?" Jean asked. "We must fight for the right not to dine with you?"

"It is our custom. Now, accept you my invitation or no?"

Jean sighed very softly. "But of course we accept, sir."

The Vavasour's face cleared at once and again assumed a jovial expression. "Capital!" he cried. "I shall inform the household that we have three more for luncheon. Make yourselves at home!" Then he disappeared into the castle, leaving them alone in the courtyard.

"Curious notion of hospitality," Jean murmured. He helped Ariel from the mare's saddle, then said sharply, "What is it, my lady?"

"I don't know," Ariel said softly. Her face was pale, and her fingers trembled. "Something is not right." She tried to smile. "Perhaps it is something I ate."

Jean took her arm. "Let us walk about for a moment," he said. "Sarah, could you bring the mare? We will find some feed and water for her."

They walked along the castle wall until they found the stables. Ariel had more colour after her walk, but when Jean turned from her to help Sarah with the horses, she grew pale again. The faery's ashen cheeks looked ghastly, and Sarah swallowed hard, experiencing the unfamiliar feeling of being anxious about another person.

A moment later, a maidservant stepped out of the keep, carrying a bucket of food scraps, and Jean stopped her. "Please, *mademoiselle,* could you help us?" The maid curled her lips as if to retort, but then Jean smiled at her, and she stopped and blushed. "This lady is ill and needs to lie down," Jean said. "Could you show us to a bedchamber?" The girl blushed again and led them at once into the castle. Sarah glanced curiously at Jean, understanding for the first time how he might have been able to win the heart of the queen. He was so rough and scruffy that she had wondered about that, but when he smiled, his face had been enchantingly transformed. With a haircut and a shave, he might be quite good-looking, she realized.

The maid took them to a dim room in which was a large bed. Jean carried Ariel, who could barely walk, to the bed and laid her on it. Spying a pitcher and some goblets on a sideboard, Jean poured a cup of wine for her, but Ariel shook her head. "No, no wine. I shall be well, I'm sure, if I can just close my eyes for a moment."

Jean nodded. "Stay with her, Sarah. I shall find our host."

Sarah felt a sudden panic. "Alone? But what if she needs something?"

"Then help her," Jean said. "Have you never cared for someone who was ill?" Then he left.

When Jean had gone, Sarah stood uncertainly over Ariel for a moment. No, she *hadn't* ever cared for someone who was ill. She had lived almost her entire life with her mother and Mordecai, and it had always been her mother who took care of others. And of course, since she had been alone, she had had her hands full just caring for herself. When would she have had time to care for another? Ariel closed her eyes and began to moan. She was definitely *not* getting better.

Sarah sat on the bed beside Ariel, who began to thrash about with her hands. Sarah caught them and held them still. At Sarah's touch Ariel seemed to grow calmer. "If only my mother …" Ariel whispered. "She would have a cordial …"

Sarah's eyes widened. *She* had a cordial, didn't she? Ariel had said that her mother's crystal bottle probably had a magic cordial in it. Stepping away from the bed, Sarah dug the bottle out of her cloak and quickly removed the top.

While Ariel moaned and started to roll restlessly around the bed, Sarah poured one drop into the cup of wine that Jean had left on the sideboard.

Then she stopped. What was she thinking? She couldn't give Ariel a cordial that she didn't know anything about. What if it was poison? What if it turned her into a frog or did some other horrid magical thing? Sarah pushed the wine away and went back to hold Ariel's hands. That helped, at least. It seemed that when Sarah was touching her Ariel breathed more easily. Experimenting, Sarah let go with one hand, and at once Ariel's restlessness increased; Sarah took her hand again, and she grew calmer.

"I can do that much, at least," Sarah said, and she climbed into the bed beside Ariel, took her in her arms, and held her close. Almost at once, Ariel's eyes opened.

"Sarah?" she said, her eyes focussing.

"You seem calmer when I'm touching you," Sarah explained.

Ariel nodded. "And you feel nothing? No oppression or heaviness in your heart?"

Sarah hesitated. She always felt a heaviness in her heart. "I feel as I always do," she said at last.

"It's a spell," Ariel said. "Something against the Seelie Court. You must take me out of this castle. Where's Jean?"

"He went to find this Vavasour person," Sarah said.

Then the door burst open and Jean entered the room, followed by the Vavasour and an old man in dirty grey robes who held a white basin filled with knives and other sharp tools. "Which one is the patient?" the old man demanded.

"Lady Sarah?" Jean said, looking with surprise at the two girls lying side by side.

"I was cold," Ariel said. "Sarah was warming me. It has done me much good. I feel better."

"You still look very pale," Jean said.

"I'd better bleed her," the man in the grey robes announced.

"This is my own leech," the Vavasour announced. "Doctor Hermaphras. He'll have you right as a trivet in no time."

"I don't need to be bled," Ariel said. She leaned forwards to sit up, and Sarah sat up beside her, keeping her body close.

"All my patients say that," Doctor Hermaphras said, setting down the bowl and choosing a knife.

"I'm sure they do," Ariel replied steadily. "But as you see, I'm quite well." Her voice trembled, and Sarah put an arm around her back. Ariel nodded and sat straighter.

"Well, what's all this botheration, then?" demanded the Vavasour of Jean. "You made it sound as if she were on her deathbed, which I never believed, and here I find her all well."

"Indeed, sir, I am as pleased at her recovery as you are," Jean said, his voice calm.

"I should bleed her anyway," the doctor said. "Just to be safe, don't you think?"

"No," Ariel said to him. "I don't want you to bleed me."

"All my patients say that," the doctor replied.

"If you're well, then let us go eat," announced the Vavasour.

"No," said Sarah.

"Eh?" the Vavasour asked.

Ariel had said she needed to get out of the castle. Sarah thought furiously. "We cannot. Jean . . . I mean Sir Jean here . . . didn't want to tell you, but we're . . . we're fasting.

126

It's a vow we've taken: no rich food or wine, only dry bread and water. That's why we have to leave at once, you see. We have to finish our quest quickly."

Jean and the Vavasour both stared at her, for which she didn't blame them at all. It did sound pretty stupid. Jean's eyes narrowed, but he said nothing. The Vavasour, however, burst into raucous laughter. "But you can't go questing without real food!" he said. "No wonder your lady is burnt to a socket! Come, break your vow and have something to eat, or you'll all be ill!"

"Shall I bleed them all, then?" asked the doctor.

Jean looked at Sarah, who put an entreaty in her eyes. Jean said, "I'm sorry, sir, but we cannot. A vow is a vow."

"But how can you fight without food to give you strength? Where will you find courage without wine?" the Vavasour demanded. He nodded at the sideboard, where the cup of wine with Sarah's cordial in it still sat, and laughed. "Don't you wish you could do this?" And then he took up the cup and drained it in a gulp.

Sarah held her breath, watching the Vavasour, wide-eyed. He made a face and put the cup down, but he didn't turn into anything unpleasant, and he didn't die, and after a second, she let her breath out slowly.

"Nasty stuff, that wine," the Vavasour said in a quiet voice. "Must be spoiled. I'm sure it will give me indigestion again." Then he turned back to Jean and spoke, again in his normal, hearty tones. "Come, then. What do you say?"

Jean started to answer, but before he could speak, the Vavasour said in his quiet voice, "They can't really expect me to believe this silly tale about fasting. Laying it on much too thick! Surely they don't know that I'm supposed to

127

delay everyone who comes looking for Logres. But if they do know, then they might suspect poison."

"I assure you, sir," Jean said sternly. "It is no such thing."

"Eh?" the Vavasour said in his hearty voice. "What such thing?"

"We do not suspect poison, sir."

"Who said anything about poison?" the Vavasour bellowed. Then, in the quiet voice, he added, "How did he guess what I was thinking? Is he a wizard? No, no, he couldn't be. Meliagant said no wizard could enter these walls. Wizard or not, poison's not such a bad idea, though, now that I think on it."

Sarah stared in astonishment at the Vavasour, who saw her gaze. "Now what's she looking at?" he wondered in his quiet voice. "Demmed rude girl, I'd say. Some washerwoman's whelp in a fancy gown, she looks like. Deuce it, there comes the indigestion. I shouldn't have had that wine."

He turned back to Jean, who was also staring. "I told you," he said loudly, "it is the custom of this land to take hospitality seriously, and we don't poison our guests, whatever may be the custom where you are from." Without a pause, he continued in his quiet voice, "Wish I knew where that was, too. Fellow looks like a peasant. Dung cart, indeed! What sort of a base-born creature would ride in a dung cart? He's no more a knight than that silly ass Hermaphras."

"I beg your pardon?" quavered the doctor.

"Eh? I wasn't speaking to you, good doctor. I was talking to this knight."

There was an awkward silence. "We . . . really should go, now," Jean said at last. "Our quest—"

"Quest, indeed!" the Vavasour said in his quiet voice.

"Making trouble for Meliagant, more like. How can I keep them here? Poison it shall have to be. Or I could have that dashed fool Hermaphras bleed them. Either way, they die." The doctor clucked faintly, but the Vavasour ignored him and bowed to Jean. "Very well," he said in his normal voice. "I suppose you have to keep a vow. But let me at least give you fresh water bags before you go. I'll bring them to you in the courtyard." Then he added quietly, "That should give me time to add poison. Now where did I put the poison? Deuce take this indigestion! I shall tell the cook to leave off vegetables from now on; they make me gassy. Now is the poison in the chest under my bed?"

It was the cordial, Sarah suddenly realized. Somehow the potion in the wine had broken down the barrier between what the Vavasour thought and what he said aloud. Now he spoke every private thought aloud, yet didn't know he was doing so. "Oops, there went one," the Vavasour announced calmly. "Deuced vegetables. I'd best go stand by the doctor. If anyone notices, they'll think he did it."

Jean gave Sarah and Ariel a piercing look and casually put his finger over his lips, then turned to the Vavasour. "I thank you for your generous offer, my lord, but we have more than enough water for our journey. There is one way that you could help me, though. The dry bread that we've been eating has been giving me indigestion."

The Vavasour's face was instantly filled with sympathy, but his lips softly said, "Bah! You don't know the first thing about indigestion, I'll wager. The pains I suffer every night!"

Jean ignored him and continued. "Do you think that it would help my indigestion to be bled by this good doctor?"

"Eh? Why, yes, of course!" the Vavasour declared

heartily. "Nothing better for indigestion than a good bleeding!" He started to add something in his quiet voice, but he had no chance. Jean bashed him on the back of the head with the pitcher of wine. Wine spattered all over the room, and the Vavasour fell on his face on the floor.

"Forgive me, friend," Jean said to the astonished doctor. "I mean your master no harm, but I could see no other way to help him."

"Help him?" the doctor asked weakly.

"But of course, good doctor. You heard how he suffers with his digestion. He needs to be bled – why he as much as said so himself! – but he is one of those people who does not like to give himself over to a physician. Is that not so?"

"Yes. Yes, that's very true," the doctor said, a trace of whiny indignation creeping into his voice. "He never lets me bleed him."

"That's just what I thought," Jean said smoothly. "Your master is far too sanguinary and must be bled at once. It is why I felt that the best thing I could do for him would be to give him into your learned care. Surely it is worth a knock on the head to be healed from a life of pain."

"Yes," the doctor said dubiously. "But when he awakes—"

"When he awakes, he will see how much good your art has done him, and he will never resist you again," Jean said. "You will be so honoured in the court, then!"

The doctor's face grew dreamy for a moment. Then he nodded with sudden decision. "It is for his own good, after all," he said. "Help me get him onto the bed."

A minute later Ariel, held tightly by Sarah, stood by the bed, and the Vavasour was stretched out in her place. "We must go on our quest now, good doctor," Jean said. "But you no longer need our help. Farewell, and do not spare your tender mercies to your master. Remember that he has not been cupped in years."

The doctor nodded pensively. "Yes," he murmured to himself. "I'd better get a second basin." He was choosing a stained blade from his collection when the three travellers left, with Jean carrying Ariel and Sarah leading the way. A few minutes later they had retrieved the mare and were all outside the castle walls.

Jean put Ariel in the saddle, and Sarah walked beside her, one hand resting on the faery's leg, but Ariel no longer needed a human touch. Away from the castle, her colour began to return at once. "It was an enchantment," Ariel said after a few minutes. "A spell against the Seelie Court. I've heard of such charms, but few can do them."

"What is this 'Seelie Court'?" Jean asked.

Ariel hesitated, glancing between Sarah and Jean, but then said, "I am not supposed to speak of it openly, but you have saved my life, the two of you, and I have to trust you. The World of the Faeries is divided into two parts, the Seelie and the Unseelie Courts. The Seelie Court is made up of those who live honourable lives and bear no ill will to their neighbours, especially to those in this world, the World of Men. The Unseelie Court – they are the others."

Jean looked stunned, then he looked at Ariel. "And you? You are from this Seelie Court?" Ariel nodded. "You are a faery, then, like in a tale for children?"

Ariel smiled apologetically. "I don't really know the children's stories of this world. I haven't been here very often."

Jean looked at Ariel doubtfully. Sarah knew what he was feeling – she had felt the same mixture of resistance and

131

confusion when Terence had first told her of the World of Faeries – but they had no time now for him to grow used to the idea gradually as she had. She said, "So you think that there's some enchantment on the Vavasour's castle that works against faeries?"

"It's the only explanation," Ariel said. "I grew ill the moment I stepped inside the gates and began to get well as soon as I was out, but neither of you was affected at all."

Sarah added thoughtfully, "And you felt stronger when a human touched you, as if we were some protection against the spell."

"That's right," Ariel said, nodding slowly.

"And," Sarah concluded, "the Vavasour himself said something about the spell. Remember? He said that Meliagant had promised that no wizard could enter the castle. He must have been talking about the enchantment."

Jean shook his head, as if he had walked into a spider's web and was trying to shake it off, then said, "That means that Meliagant, or someone with him, is a sorcerer."

"Or sorceress," Ariel said. "When my mother told me about this enchantment, she said only the great enchantress Igraine had ever grown strong enough for such a thing. But that was not dangerous, because Igraine was a friend of the Seelie Court."

"Igraine?" Jean asked. "The old Duchess of Cornwall?"

Ariel nodded. "Yes, she who's been dead for more than forty years of this world's time. Someone else must have grown strong enough for that spell ... I should tell my mother."

"Is your mother also an enchantress?" Sarah asked.

"No," Ariel said. "She is the Lady of the Lake."

Even Sarah had heard stories of the Lady of the Lake, though of course she had never believed them, and she blinked at Ariel in amazement. As for Jean, he looked as if he had been hit with a cudgel. "The Lady of the ... she really exists," he whispered in an awed voice.

Ariel, growing stronger with every second, pressed on. "But that wasn't the only enchantment in that castle. My wits were not at their best, but what was wrong with the Vavasour? Did I dream all that?"

Sarah said nothing, but Jean said, "No, you did not. Something happened to him. He was speaking his thoughts aloud, and never knew it. Good thing, though. If he hadn't told us he was planning to poison us, I would have accepted his water bags."

"And if he hadn't told us about his digestion, you couldn't have handed him over to the doctor," Sarah said. "That was very clever of you, by the way. Do you think the Vavasour will survive the doctor's care?"

"Me, I would not wager a groat on it," Jean replied with a shrug. "But what do you suppose happened to the Vavasour? He was not speaking his thoughts at first." Jean glanced warily at Sarah. "Are you, *par chance*, an enchantress, too?"

Sarah felt sorry for him. "Not that I know of," she said reassuringly.

"Maybe it's part of the larger spell that is on that castle," Ariel said. "In any case, I suppose we should just be grateful, even if we don't know."

Sarah dropped her hand into her cloak pocket and closed it over the crystal bottle. A part of her wanted to tell her companions about the bottle and the cordial, but she

133

couldn't. Now that she knew what effect the cordial had, it gave her a sense of power, and she had lived too long a powerless orphan, nursing vain dreams of revenge, to give that up. Now, with a faery sword and a magic potion, she might be able to serve her enemies as they deserved after all.

But, even as she decided to keep her potion secret, an uneasy twinge of conscience disturbed her. Why should she feel guilty about keeping a secret from Ariel and Jean, though? Sarah glanced at them again, allowing her gaze to rest on Ariel's face for a long moment. Ariel must have felt eyes on her, because she looked down from the mare and smiled back.

Sarah blushed and looked away, her heart swelling with unaccustomed feelings. When Ariel had begun to thrash about back in the bedchamber, something had changed in Sarah. At that moment, and through all the time that she had lain beside Ariel, holding her close, Sarah had thought of nothing but of Ariel and how to help the faery. For those long minutes, frightened on someone else's account, Sarah had not thought of her mother, of Mordecai, of the night of the fires, or of her thirst for vengeance. Everything had been subsumed by her frantic desire to help Ariel.

Sarah wasn't sure how she felt about this change. It seemed disloyal to the memory of her mother, to have thought first of another person, even for a few minutes. But as she peeked again up at the faery girl, she realized that she was still doing it – solicitously watching Ariel's movements and complexion to make sure she was truly well. It was odd – warming and yet frightening – to discover that her own peace of mind depended partly on someone else's well-being.

They travelled east. They had received no directions

from the Vavasour, of course, but the trail that they had followed from the Dividing of the Ways had never veered from an eastwards direction, and so they went that way. Before going a mile, they were rewarded by coming upon a clear eastwards trail.

Towards the middle of the afternoon, Jean said, "Knight coming towards us," and Sarah glanced up. She was having her turn on the horse and had been drowsing in the saddle, but this break in the monotony of travel was enough to stir her. Approaching them rapidly was a knight in grey armour, holding his helm in one hand and staring fixedly at them. Sarah's throat suddenly tightened.

It was the knight of the fires.

The old coldness encased her heart, with all its bite and bitterness – that still, deadening sense of numb hatred that had been her daily companion through all those months alone in the forest. She looked at the knight's face and saw it as it had appeared that frozen night, gloating victoriously in the orange light of his murders. Sarah's eyes grew hot and dry; her hand gripped the hilt of her sword.

The knight was now near enough to speak, and he called out, "Are you a knight?"

"I am," Jean replied.

The knight smiled widely. "Good!" he declared, pointing at Ariel, who walked beside Sarah. "I'll take her!"

Jean stopped walking at once, halting Sarah's mount with a hand on the bridle. "I beg your pardon?" he asked mildly.

"You can keep the little one," the knight said. "I want that one."

"These ladies are travelling under my protection," Jean said, his voice calm.

The knight glanced at Jean and laughed. "Then you don't know the custom of the land?"

"The custom of the land?" Jean repeated.

"It is the custom of this land," the knight said, "that a lady who rides alone is to be regarded as sacred and may not be touched by any knight, but if she rides under a knight's protection, then anyone who can overcome that knight may take her for himself." He leered at Ariel and added, "I've been waiting a long time to find a lady worth—"

"This is the custom of the land?" Jean asked contemptuously. "It is a vile custom."

"By decree of King Bagdemagus himself."

Jean frowned. "I am somewhat acquainted with Bagdemagus myself, and I do not believe that he would issue any such decree. Leave us alone."

The knight drew his sword, and his eyes lit with something like the glee they had shown when he had killed Sarah's mother and Mordecai. "Not without my prize," he said. Then he charged.

The knight carried no lance, but his charge on horseback against an unmounted knight put Sarah vividly in mind of Sir Meliagant's charge against Sir Kai. This charge turned out quite differently, though. Jean's sword appeared in his hand, as if by magic, and he parried the other knight's blade with one hand while reaching up and catching hold of the knight's armour with the other. A moment later, the knight was in a heap in the dust, having been pulled abruptly from the saddle.

"Ariel, Sarah! Get back out of the way!" Jean shouted.

Ariel hesitated, but Sarah did not. Slipping lightly from the saddle, she grabbed the bridle with one hand and Ariel's arm with the other and pulled Ariel and the horse roughly away from the scene of battle. "He can't fight well unless he knows we're out of reach," she explained as she tugged. Only when they were more than ten yards away did she stop and turn back to look.

The knight of the fires had risen to his feet and was facing Jean warily. Jean stood straight, holding his sword almost nonchalantly at his side. He did not look to be on his guard, but his swift move to unhorse his opponent must have given the knight reason enough to be cautious. The knight struck – tentatively, Sarah thought, as if testing Jean's reflexes – and Jean parried the blow easily and resumed his casual, watching stance. The knight lunged, and Jean stepped aside and watched him stumble by him. Jean didn't even move his sword. Sarah scowled. Even she, with as little training in swordplay as she had, knew that Jean could have ended the battle there, with one sword stroke, as the knight had run past him.

"Don't be noble! Kill him!" she muttered through clenched teeth.

"What did you say?" Ariel asked, her eyes wide.

"It's him," Sarah replied. "That's the knight who killed my mother."

The knight whirled around and lashed out wildly. Jean parried that blow, then a second one. The knight slashed again, low this time, trying to cut Jean's unprotected legs from beneath him. Jean blocked the stroke, then struck his first blow of the fight, and the knight's sword flew from his hand, landing nearly ten feet from them.

"Stop this at once," Jean commanded sternly. "I could have killed you four times already. Do you wish to die?"

137

The knight did not reply, merely gripping his sword hand and grimacing in pain.

"Do you yield now?" Jean asked. "And do you vow never more to pursue this foul custom?"

The knight growled something unintelligible, then ran across the field to his sword, taking it up again. He charged, swinging wildly, and Jean, his face grim, neatly cut off the knight's hand at the wrist. Sarah watched as the severed member, still holding a sword, floated away from the knight's arm in a gentle arc, then bounced into the grass. Ariel gasped and looked away, as Jean called over his shoulder, "Bring a leather thong to me at once."

Ariel didn't move, so Sarah pulled a length of leather from the mare's pack, then slung her own sword over her shoulder and walked to where Jean stood over the moaning knight.

"You will not need your sword, Sarah," Jean said. He looked down at the knight and said, "Hold still. We will bind up your arm so you won't bleed to death. Sarah, I'll hold the knight down. You tie the thong around his wrist and tighten it until the blood stops. I'll show you how."

Sarah stared, furious, and didn't move. Did he expect her to save this knight's life? Jean misunderstood her hesitation and said, "Try not to look at the blood."

"Let him die," Sarah said and threw down the leather thong.

Jean looked sharply at her face, then back at the knight. Driving his own sword into the ground beside him, he knelt over the fallen knight and began to twist the thong around the knight's stump. The gushing blood slowed, then stopped. Jean rose to his feet and stepped back behind the knight's feet. "I do not kill unless I must," Jean said. Sarah didn't know if he was talking to her or to the fallen knight; her eyes were fixed on the man's face. His eyes were glazed in pain, and his face was grey, but he was conscious.

Sarah knelt beside his head and said softly, so that Jean would not hear, "Do you remember the night you murdered a woman and an old Jew?"

The man stared at her, uncomprehending.

"You burned them alive in a village called Milrick," she said. A red mist began to cloud Sarah's vision, and she fought to keep her voice steady. "It was in February."

"Saint Valentine's Day," the knight whispered. "They were sorcerers."

"They were not sorcerers." Sarah's voice barely made any noise at all.

"The Templar said they had poisoned the well. He told me to kill them."

"The Templar?" Sarah repeated.

"They were Jews, anyway."

Sarah leaned closer. "The woman was my mother," she said.

The knight's eyes widened, and Sarah saw fear in them. Then the knight shoved Sarah backwards, using his left hand. She fell against Jean, who stumbled momentarily, and by the time Sarah had recovered her balance, the knight had seized Jean's sword. He drew back his arm for a blow, and Sarah snatched her own sword from its scabbard, drawing it faster than she ever had before, and struck with all her might.

Then it was over, and everything was still, but for the distant sound of a woodpecker tapping a cheerful rhythm on a dead tree.

"*Sacre . . .*" came Jean's whisper from beside her. He said no more but only stared at the scene at his feet.

Sarah's stroke had cut cleanly through Jean's sword blade and then, without slowing, had cut off the knight's head. Sarah knelt and cleaned her blade on the grass, then sheathed it again. Her stomach was tight and she was slightly nauseated, but she felt no emotion: not sorrow, not horror, not triumph, not joy, not remorse.

"Sarah?" came Ariel's voice from a few steps behind her. It was faint with shock and horror.

Sarah did not reply. "I'm sorry about your sword, Jean," she said. "Perhaps you can use the knight's sword instead."

"Sorry about my sword," Jean repeated slowly. "What about him? Are you sorry for him?"

Sarah shook her head. "I think of it as the custom of the land," she said. Then she turned away from them both and started back towards the mare.

VIII

THE SWORD BRIDGE

They returned to the road, but a grim silence had fallen over the companions. Ariel, whose bubbling laugh and merry chatter had lightened the journey to this point, was solemn and silent, and twice Sarah caught the faery watching her, wide-eyed. Both times Sarah met her gaze unflinchingly, and Ariel looked away. Even Jean was more silent than usual and gave Sarah occasional long, measured looks.

Jean's disapproval was only to be expected, Sarah admitted to herself. Jean didn't know about the night of the fires and what the knight had done then. But Ariel's silence rankled. What had Ariel thought Sarah was going to do when she found the knight anyway? Scold him? Sarah shrugged and resolutely stopped looking at Ariel, concentrating instead on her own thoughts and feelings.

These were muddled enough without worrying about Ariel's reaction, anyway. For months now Sarah had thought of little but vengeance, dreamed of the day when the knight of the fires should be punished. Now he was dead, by her own hand, and she felt no triumph, only a cold numbness. She should be rejoicing and gloating, as the knight had done over her mother and Mordecai, but she could not. She felt empty and incomplete, just as she had felt before killing the knight. Maybe, she thought, it was because her vengeance was incomplete.

"What is a Templar?" she asked, speaking to no one in particular. Jean gave Sarah one of those unhurried looks but did not reply at once. "Well? What is it?" she demanded.

"Some of the knights who went on crusades to the Holy Land call themselves Templars," Jean said at last. "They wear a white tunic over their armour, marked with a red cross, and they swear allegiance to no king but only, they say, to the Church."

"Do you know where any Templars are?" she asked.

"No. King Arthur does not welcome them in England – sometimes they feel that they are a law unto themselves – and he encourages them to go back to the Holy Land. Some sorts of holiness are most admirable from a great distance. But matters may be different now. As you know, I have been away from court many years." Jean looked away from Sarah, but he added, "May one ask why you wish to know?"

"I heard the knight back in the field say the word," Sarah replied.

"Yes, so did I," Jean said. "I did not hear what you said to him, however."

Sarah did not reply, and after a moment Jean turned away and continued to walk in silence.

By the time they made camp, Sarah was thoroughly sick of the journey, the silence, and above all the invisible barrier that had come between her and the others. They ate a silent dinner, and then Ariel curled up in her blankets and went to sleep. Sarah looked at her still form for a few minutes.

"You mustn't blame her, you know," Jean said quietly.

Sarah started slightly, then schooled her face into a non-committal expression. "Blame her for what?" she asked.

"She has never seen bloodlust in one so young as you," Jean said. "When she's older, she will no longer be surprised to find cruelty in anyone."

"Cruelty!" Sarah exclaimed bitterly. "Ariel knows how much that knight deserved to be killed! She knows! That wasn't cruelty – it was justice!"

Jean nodded soberly. "It usually is," he said. "Sleep well, Sarah." Then he rolled up in his own blankets, leaving Sarah staring alone into the coals.

It was probably only a few minutes later when she heard a whisper of sound behind her, and she rose quickly but silently, sword in hand.

"You are very quick with that sword, my dear," came a creaky voice. It was the old woman of the woods. "A good thing you are, too."

Sarah let out her breath slowly, then gestured behind her. "They don't think so," she said.

"They are fools, then," the crone said, dismissing Ariel and Jean with a careless wave. "You did well back there in the field. That knight who's with you was going to leave him alive, wasn't he?" Sarah nodded. "Fools," the crone repeated.

"Were you watching?" Sarah asked, stepping closer to the old woman.

"I am often watching you," she replied. "Tell me, dear, was the knight you killed awake when you got down beside him? Did you talk to him?"

143

Sarah nodded. "I wanted him to know who I was."

"Splendid!" the crone beamed, but her smile was not pleasant. There was no happiness in it, only a sort of angry satisfaction. Sarah wondered suddenly if that was how her own face had looked after she had killed the knight. "Did he say anything to you?" the old woman asked.

"He said that he was only doing what the Templar told him to do," Sarah said.

The crone's smile disappeared. "What Templar?" she asked.

"He didn't say."

The old woman scowled, then asked, "Did he say anything about a woman?"

"A woman?"

"A woman, perhaps a sorceress, who might have planned the villagers' attack."

"No."

"Then we shall have to ask this Templar when we find him," she said softly, and her voice – no longer the voice of an old woman – made Sarah's scalp prickle. The crone reached out and rested one hand on Sarah's shoulder. "Stay with the other two for now. You aren't far from the bridge to Logres. Wait for me there, and I shall make inquiries about a Templar."

Then the old woman was gone, leaving only emptiness where she had been. After a moment, Sarah curled up in her blankets, taking in that emptiness with every cold breath.

Ariel was silent the next day, too, but she no longer seemed horrified, only sad, and the time or two that Sarah saw Ariel watching her, the faery's eyes did not seem shocked, as they had the day before, but wistful. Once or twice, Sarah thought Ariel was going to speak, but she didn't. About mid-morning they came to the Sword Bridge.

There was no mistaking it: it was a long, bright, wicked-looking metal blade that stretched across a chasm so deep that the bottom was hidden by fog, or a low cloud. The sword faced up, so that anyone trying to walk across would have to step right on the sharpened edge.

"The Sword Bridge," Jean said. He examined it for a moment. "It seems to be impossible. Perhaps there is another way across."

Ariel shook her head. "I was told that there were only two ways into Logres: by the Underwater Bridge that Sir Gawain and Terence took, and this way."

Jean nodded. "Let us see how sharp the edge is." He picked up a thick stick and, kneeling at the edge of the sheer cliff, ran it lightly along the blade. The blade cut the stick easily. Jean backed up. "Sharp enough," he said.

Ariel, who had stepped up beside Jean, moaned suddenly, crumpled, and fell towards the abyss. Jean grabbed her quickly and pulled her away, but by the time he had caught her in his arms, she had gone completely limp. Jean laid her down in the grass, and after a moment her eyes flickered open. "What happened?" she asked.

"You swooned," Jean said. "At the edge of the cliff. Did you feel faint before you stepped to the edge?"

"I don't know," Ariel said haltingly.

"Are you often made giddy by heights?" Jean asked. Ariel shook her head. "Have you ever had . . . fits like this before?"

Sarah could be silent no longer. "Don't be stupid, Jean." Ariel and Jean both looked at Sarah with surprise. "Look at her face, how pale it's gone. Haven't you seen that before?"

"Ah," Jean said, understanding at once. "It's the enchantment, isn't it? The one that was at the Vavasour's castle."

"But stronger," Sarah added. "Logres is protected by more than just a sharp bridge. Ariel can't go any farther."

Ariel protested, arguing that her momentary weakness had just been a lingering ill effect of her sickness at the Vavasour's castle. Jean and Sarah didn't reply. They waited until her strength returned, as it did shortly, then walked with her to the cliff again. Again Ariel grew pale and for a second time she nearly fainted. "Sarah's right. I can't go with you any longer," she said miserably.

"Sarah will stay with you," Jean said.

Sarah might have resisted Jean's assumption of authority, but since the crone had said to wait for her at the bridge anyway, she just nodded and glanced over her shoulder at the wide chasm. "Unless we figure out how to get across the bridge, none of us are going anywhere," she said practically.

Jean's eyes followed Sarah's, then focussed thoughtfully on the Sword Bridge. As soon as Ariel had recovered again, he went to the mare and began unloading the parts of his armour that he had tied there. "I shall have to cross the bridge from underneath," he said, "swinging hand over hand."

"And how will you do that without cutting off your fingers?" Sarah asked, but she was already seeing his plan.

"Like this," Jean said, putting two pieces of armour together to make a double layer of iron. They looked like leg plates – Sarah didn't know what they were called. "I'll put armour on my hands."

"The sword won't cut armour, I suppose?" Ariel asked.

146

"Eventually, it will. A strong blow with a sharp blade will cut through even a breastplate. That's why we wear chain mail beneath. This blade is certainly sharp enough, but it won't be striking at me. Here, let me test it, to see how many layers of armour I shall need."

Jean rested the double layer of iron in the palm of his right hand and walked back to the edge of the cliff. There he knelt, placed the armour on the edge of the Sword Bridge, and pushed down. The sword cut cleanly through both layers of iron, as if they had been made of rotten cork wood, and Jean leaped back, blood welling from his hand. Sarah stared at the wound and, before the blood hid it, saw a flash of white bone. "*Sacre*—!" Jean exclaimed, his face registering more shock than pain.

Ariel dressed Jean's cut palm, binding a cloth over the wound with two leather straps from the mare's tack. "What can be done?" the faery asked tremulously.

"That is no normal sword," Jean said. "It must be part of the spell that protects Logres. Any blade that could cut that cleanly through iron can cut through anything."

"Maybe not," Sarah said.

Jean and Ariel looked at her, and Sarah swallowed. She hadn't meant to say anything about her idea, but for a moment, amid concern for Jean's hand and a desire to help him on his quest, the words had slipped out unbidden. Now that she had spoken, though, she wouldn't go back. Taking a deep breath, Sarah said, "Let me try something. May I use another piece of your armour?"

Jean nodded, and Sarah chose at random a piece that looked as if it had been designed for a forearm. "Don't rest your hand on it," Jean said.

Sarah turned her head slowly and met Jean's gaze, then rolled her eyes expressively. "Thank you for that valuable advice, Jean. Just how much of a knock-in-the-cradle do you think I am?"

"I suppose it was a bit obvious, wasn't it?" Jean admitted, grinning ruefully. His face was transformed briefly by this flicker of self-deprecating amusement. "But what do you mean to do?"

"Watch," Sarah said. Stepping close to the Sword Bridge, she swung the armour down on the edge of the blade. As she had expected, the blade cut the armour easily, and the top half tumbled slowly down the abyss. "Now," Sarah said, "watch this." With a swift movement, she drew her own sword and swung down on the Sword Bridge. The two swords rang at the collision, but when Sarah lifted her sword, it was still in one piece. There was not even a dent or a mark on Sarah's sword to show where it had hit the bridge.

Jean's eyes widened. "Please, Sarah, may I see that sword?" Sarah let him take it from her hand, and he examined it reverently. *"Quel sabre! Merveilleux,"* he murmured.

"It is a magical sword," Sarah said. "It was made by a faery armourer named Trebuchet" – Ariel's eyes sparkled at the name, and she nodded quickly – "and was given to Sir Kai." Sarah's face lightened at a memory that suddenly struck her as absurd. "I think perhaps even Sir Kai didn't know of this sword's strength. He was planning to give it to his son. But instead he gave it to me."

"Kai has a son now?" Jean asked. "But this son cannot be very old. Kai had no children when I went away."

"I think Sir Kai said his son was two years old," Sarah said.

Jean's face remained grave, but the edges of his eyes wrinkled with amusement. "Yes," he said. "It is perhaps not a toy for the nursery. Nor, I would have said, for a young girl." Sarah met his searching gaze, and Jean continued, "But Kai is no fool, and if he gave it to you, he must have seen something remarkable in you."

Sarah shrugged off the compliment. "The important thing is that the magic of the Sword Bridge cannot cut through the magic of this sword. There must be some way we can use that to get you across."

"It will mean giving up your sword," Jean pointed out. "And it may end up at the bottom of that gorge – if it has a bottom. Even if I get across, I won't be able to return your sword."

Sarah nodded. She had already recognized that drawback, and in fact that was why she had hesitated to mention her idea, but she realized with faint surprise that she was willing to give up her sword if doing so could help Jean.

And so the three of them sat by the cliff – back a few yards from the edge, for Ariel's sake – and discussed a dozen different plans for Jean to get across the bridge using Sarah's sword. They rejected all of them. They could think of ways to use the blade to protect Jean from being cut in half, but not to get across such a thin bridge without falling off.

At last Jean came up with a plan that satisfied him and, over the protests of Ariel and Sarah – who thought the plan was madness – began to make preparations. Jean's idea was to fasten Sarah's sword in place down the centre of his torso, from his chin to his groin, then lie down face first on the bridge, allowing Sarah's sword to protect him from the blade. Then Jean intended to pull himself forwards with his hands, pressing them only against the flat side of the Sword Bridge.

"You'll split yourself right down the middle!" Sarah said bluntly. "We'll have Left-side Jean and Right-side Jean."

"No no," Jean assured her. "If aught goes awry, you won't have either of me. I'll be at the foot of the cliff."

"What about your wound?" Ariel asked. "We've just now stopped the bleeding. You'll start it up again and bleed to death right on the sword." Jean ignored her, and after a moment she said, "Oh, if you're set on it, wait here."

Ariel took a hatchet from their gear and walked over to a stand of stubby trees a furlong away from the cliff. A minute later she returned carrying some branches she had cut. "Rub the sap of these boughs on your hands. It will make them sticky and help you pull yourself forwards."

Jean smiled. "Thank you."

A few minutes later, Jean was ready. To make himself as light as possible, he had removed all of his armour except his breastplate, and with some of the cut-up bits of armour he had fashioned some clasps to hold Sarah's sword in place on his chest. "Take care of each other," Jean said calmly. Then he lowered himself face first onto the edge of the cruel blade.

It worked. The Sword Bridge didn't cut through Sarah's sword or, for that matter, through the knight that rested on it, and Jean reached forwards, laid his sticky palms on the flat of the blade, one on each side, and began to inch his way forwards. He held himself steady by bending his legs and pressing his ankles against the flat of the sword behind him. "Will it work after all?" Ariel whispered.

Then Jean stopped. Sarah stepped to the edge of the cliff. "Jean, what's wrong?"

"Your sword is loose," Jean replied calmly. "The blade of

the bridge has cut away the stays that were holding it in place. If I move, it will fall out from under me."

"Can you move back? You're only about two feet from this edge."

"No," Jean said. "Your sword is completely unattached. I'm very sorry about losing your sword like this. It is a priceless treasure. If you see Gawain and Terence, and Guinevere and Kai, tell them I tried."

"Oh, shut up," Sarah said. She turned to Ariel and said, "He needs someone to hold the sword in place while he pulls himself forwards."

Ariel's face grew still, but she nodded. "I will wait for you here," she said. "And Sarah? I'm sorry."

"Sorry?"

"For being so shocked when you killed that knight. I knew it was what you meant to do . . . but I . . ."

"It doesn't matter," Sarah said.

"But I want to be your friend still," Ariel said. She reached out and took Sarah's hand in her own. "Friends?" she said.

Sarah nodded and whispered, "Friends." Then, turning away from Ariel, she walked to the edge of the cliff and said, "Jean? Hold on tight. I'm going to jump onto your back now."

"What?"

"Then I can reach around your neck and hold the sword steady when you move forwards."

"You're mad!"

"Yes, I think so."

"I forbid it, Sarah!"

"How do you plan to stop me? Are you ready? When I say three. One, two, three." Then Sarah jumped from the edge of the cliff.

She landed on Jean's back and felt herself sliding forwards, but she caught herself by hooking her hands under his arms. The Sword Bridge quivered and sang at the impact, but Jean clamped himself onto the sides of the sword with such ferocity that they didn't slip to either side. Sarah let out her breath, then moved her hands carefully around Jean's neck, groping blindly but carefully until she found the hilt of her sword. "I've got it," she said.

"You foolish child!" Jean said between gritted teeth.

"Yes," Sarah replied. "But there's nothing to do about it now."

"I'll take you back at once," Jean said. "Hold the sword steady." He began to push, to slide them back to the edge, but they didn't move. "We're caught on something. We can't move backwards."

"Then let's move forwards," Sarah said. Jean began to speak, but Sarah cut him off before he could say a word. "Don't be a fool, Jean. We can't move backwards, and we can't hang here forever. Forwards is our best hope, and if you don't mind terribly, I'd rather you didn't waste any more strength arguing with me. We may need that strength before we're across."

For the next eternity – all Sarah could say for sure when it was over was that it had taken more than an hour and less than a day – they crept forwards, with Jean sliding forwards an inch at a time while Sarah held the blade steady beneath him. More times than she could count her sword slipped slightly and Jean winced as he received a cut, but these nicks were all superficial, and each time Jean was able to lift himself up again enough for Sarah to correct the position of her sword. Sarah's fingers ached from holding the sword, and the hilt of Jean's sword, which he had tied to his back, dug into her chest. As Ariel had predicted, the wound in Jean's right palm began to bleed again, and Sarah watched in morbid fascination as drop after drop floated down the cliff into the cloud below them.

Then she couldn't watch any more. When they were about halfway across, the cloud rose and surrounded them. She could no longer tell how far they had gone or how far they had yet to go. She could barely see the outline of Jean's dark hair in front of her. Twice they almost fell, but they continued inching forwards. Sarah could hardly feel her numb fingers, but still she held firm. Jean's huge shoulder muscles trembled spasmodically at each pull forwards. At last, as Sarah reached ahead to reposition the sword for the thousandth or ten-thousandth time, her hand brushed something. "Jean, stop!" she whispered.

Jean did not speak, but he obeyed. Cautiously, Sarah extended her arm and her fingers felt a tuft of grass, then solid ground, just over a foot in front of them. "We're at the other side," Sarah said. "The other side, Jean. Hold tight. I'll climb off, then reach back and hold the sword in place for you."

"Go," Jean gasped.

One hand on the edge of the cliff to steady her, Sarah carefully raised herself to her knees on Jean's back, and from there it was easy. A moment later, she collapsed in thick grass on solid ground. She didn't rest, though, but immediately scrambled around and reached back over the precipice.

Her fingers found Jean's hair, soaked with sweat and with the moisture of the cloud. She allowed her fingers to follow the line of his beard down to his shoulders and chest. At last they touched the hilt of her sword. "I've got it," she said.

153

Jean pulled himself an inch, then another. It should have been easier to move without Sarah on his back, but it seemed as if every movement was the very last one that his muscles could possibly make. "Here," Sarah said. Holding her sword with only one hand, she put her other hand over Jean's hand. "Reach out," Sarah said. "You're inches from the edge."

Jean let go and allowed Sarah to guide his hand to the cliff edge. It seemed to give him strength, and he buried his fingers in the thick grass and pulled himself forwards. Then his forearms and elbows were on solid ground. Sarah still held her sword in position so that Jean would not lose a leg at the very end, and then Jean gave himself a great heave from his elbows, came over the edge, and crumpled in a limp heap on top of Sarah.

How long she lay there, trembling and gasping and crushed beneath the joyful weight of inconceivable relief, Sarah was not sure, but Jean's laboured breathing had still not returned completely to normal before Sarah pushed the knight off her and rose to her feet. "We have to tell Ariel we made it," she said. "She can't see us through this fog. Ariel! Ariel!"

There was no answer. "She cannot hear you, either," Jean said. Sarah called as loudly as she could, but no answering shout came back.

"We shall have to wait until the fog lifts – or drops," Jean said. "It will be hours before I will be able to move, anyway."

Sarah hesitated. She hated leaving her friend in suspense. "Let me try this," she said. Stooping, she picked up her sword from the grass at her feet and felt her way through the cloud back to the edge of the cliff.

"Be careful," Jean said.

Sarah felt a strange and unfamiliar sensation rising in her breast, an irrepressible, wild hilarity, and then the wall broke and a quiet but earth-shakingly unexpected sound came from her lips: a giggle. "Be careful?" she said. "You tell me to be careful? You mean, I shouldn't take any risks?" She giggled again, and then began to laugh in earnest.

Jean, his voice shaking, said, "*Mordieu!* Did I really say that?" And then he, too, began to laugh, and for another few minutes they lay helpless, convulsed at the absurdity of being careful now.

At last, their laughter subsided, and Sarah said wonderingly, "Do you know? I haven't laughed in four months."

"Bah! You are an amateur," Jean replied. "Me, I have not laughed so in seven years. Now, what were you doing at the edge of the cliff?"

"Remember when I hit the Sword Bridge with my sword, back on the other side? Remember that loud ringing sound?"

"Of course! Hit it again. Ariel will know what it is."

Sarah felt her way to the edge, then reached out with the sword tentatively until she found the end of the bridge. She raised the sword, then swung it down. A loud clang rang out over the gorge, but Sarah's sword didn't rebound off the Sword Bridge as it had before but instead cut right through it. Sarah stumbled forwards, almost falling over the edge.

"What happened?" Jean demanded.

"I cut through the bridge," Sarah replied. A fresh wind, rising from nowhere, struck her face and swept her hair behind her. At once the cloud began to dissipate. First she could see her feet, uncomfortably close to the precipice. She stepped back. Then she saw Jean, lying nearby in the grass, covered with blood, his clothes in tatters. She sheathed her sword, pushing it back under the edge of her cloak, and knelt beside him, but he shook his head.

"They are all shallow cuts, save the one on my hand. Look! Across the gorge!" Then she looked up and saw, across the now bridgeless chasm, Ariel standing by their horse, watching. Sarah waved to her friend, but Ariel shook her head. The faery pointed at a spot behind Jean and Sarah, then disappeared in the fading mist. Sarah turned to look behind her.

Ten men with longbows stood not ten yards away, each with an arrow notched and ready. In the middle of the archers stood a knight in chain mail and a velvet robe. "Welcome to Logres, travellers," the knight said, smiling without a trace of humour, or even of humanity. "We love to entertain guests here. I shall be your host for your stay. I am the prince of this land."

Jean climbed weakly to his feet. "Sir Meliagant," he said.

"The same. I must trouble you to give me that sword that is hung over your back," Sir Meliagant said to Jean. Without comment, Jean removed his sword and dropped it on the ground at his feet. Sarah held her cloak tight, to conceal her own sword.

Sir Meliagant's smile faded, and he demanded sternly, "Now, how did you get here?"

"Across the Sword Bridge," Jean replied.

"Impossible! The Lady said that no one could cross it!"

"Then the lady was wrong," Jean replied. "What she

should have said was that no one could cross it alone."

Sir Meliagant led them up a slight rise, then down a long hill towards a brightly festooned castle. At any other time, Sarah would have stared at all the decorations that covered nearly every stone on the outer wall, but it was hard to concentrate on all the heraldry while trudging heavily in front of ten archers and listening to Sir Meliagant give the guards instructions on which rooms she and Jean were to be locked in.

Just outside the castle gate, though, these depressing arrangements were interrupted. As Sir Meliagant walked through the open trellis, a grey-haired man in a lemon yellow doublet and a lime green cloak stepped out and smiled benignly. Sarah saw frustration flicker across Sir Meliagant's face, but it was swiftly replaced with a smile. "Father!" he said. "What are you doing out of your chambers at this time of day?"

"Visitors!" the brightly dressed man exclaimed with delight. "Are they . . . noble visitors?"

"No. They are peasants," Sir Meliagant said at once.

"If it please you, sire," Jean said clearly, "I am a knight, and this is the Lady Sarah. I perceive that you are King Bagdemagus, ruler of Logres and Knight of the Round Table. I bring you greetings from your friends at that court." Jean delivered this speech in a grand, courtly manner, and accompanied his words with an elegant bow that left no doubt as to the truth of his words. Not even his ragged, bloodstained leather clothing and wild hair and beard could hide the fact that this was a cavalier of a great court.

Jean's speech had quite different effects on the two

principal listeners. Sir Meliagant's eyes widened with surprise, then hardened into a baleful glare. His father, King Bagdemagus, however, clapped his hands and beamed with delight. "You've been to court?" he demanded.

"Not in some time, sire, but I know how you are esteemed there by Sir Griflet and others of your closest friends."

The king's eyes brightened. "Dear Griflet! You must indeed be from Camelot if you know of our friendship. Why did Meliagant say you were a peasant?"

"Your son was deceiving you, sire," Jean said promptly.

King Bagdemagus burst into delighted laughter. "That's my son, you know. He never can keep names and faces straight. Silly of him! How I shall laugh at him about it later! But you must come in at once! I have so missed having visitors since . . ." the king trailed off hesitantly and sneaked a furtive look at his son. But the look was gone in a second, and the king continued, "It's been so long."

Sir Meliagant bowed briskly. "Yes, Father. I was just about to conduct them to their rooms. As you can see, they are not fitly dressed to be received. It is no wonder that I took them for peasants in such garb. I ask you, Father, have you ever seen a knight dressed so meanly?"

Bagdemagus looked troubled. "It is true, sir, that your raimant ill suits your station. I wonder at it! 'Pon my soul, I wonder at it!"

Jean bowed again, perhaps to remind the king of his courtly grace and distract him from his clothing, and said, "You are very right, sire, and normally I should shrink from presenting myself in such attire at this most brilliantly decorated castle." Bagdemagus beamed with pride at the compliment, and Jean said, "But we are on a most dangerous quest and have undergone many trials."

"It is still unseemly," Sir Meliagant said abruptly. "Allow me to escort them to their rooms to change their clothes, and quickly – before anyone sees such gaucherie at your most elegant castle."

"Yes, that's true," Bagdemagus said, nodding feebly. "Don't want to give anyone a bad impression. Take them away, I suppose."

"We will gladly enter your castle," Jean said, "but I ask, on your honour as a knight of King Arthur's Round Table, to receive us at once. Perhaps we could go to a private room."

The king glanced hesitantly from Jean to Sir Meliagant and back, then said, "He did say on my honour, Meliagant. Must keep up the honour of the court. Guards, bring them to the blue receiving hall . . . No, no, not the blue room! Heavens, what was I thinking? In this robe! Take them to the green hall."

Jean and Sarah were led down a long corridor to a heavy oaken door, where they stood and waited outside. King Bagdemagus and Sir Meliagant had left them, going to the hall by a different route, Sarah supposed. She looked over at Jean, who was leaning against the door frame, his face grey with weariness and, no doubt, loss of blood. Sarah stepped up beside him. "Are you faint?" she asked softly.

Jean nodded. "But I must keep my wits for this interview."

"Shouldn't we have gone to our rooms and rested first instead of demanding to see the king right away?"

Jean smiled bitterly. "Rooms? What sort of rooms do you suppose we will be given?"

"I know that Sir Meliagant was talking about locking us up," Sarah said, "but now that his father has seen us, surely he won't do that. I mean, this king doesn't seem especially clever, but he doesn't look like someone who would put guests in a dungeon."

Jean shook his head. "Could you not see? It is Meliagant who rules here, not the king. He did not defy his father to his face, but once we are out of Bagdemagus's sight, Meliagant will do to us just what he wants." Jean leaned closer and lowered his voice. "You still have your weapon, no?" Sarah nodded, and Jean smiled approvingly. "Never have I quested with a more valorous lady. Now listen to me. If Meliagant tries to kill us out of hand, draw your sword and get it to me. If he puts us in a dungeon, hide it."

Sarah nodded again, and then the great door opened and a servant in a pale yellow suit with green trim ushered them into the hall. It was a spacious room with a high ceiling, every inch of which was hung with diaphanous green silk, giving Sarah the feeling of being in a green tent. In the centre of the hall, seated on a large throne covered with green velvet, was King Bagdemagus, his long green robe arranged artfully around his feet. ("So that's why we had to wait so long in the corridor," Sarah thought. "He was striking a pose.") At the king's right, on a smaller throne, sat Sir Meliagant, his purple velvet blouse strikingly out of place in this sea of green, and at the king's left, on the smallest throne of all, sat a girl in a white gown, calmly stitching at a sewing frame. The girl looked to be about Sarah's age, and was quite pretty, or would have been had she shown any expression at all, but her face was as empty as a corpse's. Sarah stared at her, but when the girl turned her eyes towards her, Sarah looked away.

"Welcome to my court, Sir Knight!" King Bagdemagus announced formally, waving one hand in greeting, but carefully, so as not to disturb the arrangement of his robes. "I am King Bagdemagus, sovereign of this realm of Logres, and I greet you. What is your name?"

"I am called Jean, and this is Lady Sarah."

King Bagdemagus frowned. "I don't know anyone of that name from Camelot."

"Probably a false name," Sir Meliagant said at once. "You must be careful of knights who refuse to give their true name. Perhaps he is an assassin."

"I am no assassin," Jean said.

"He's dressed like an assassin," Sir Meliagant said. Bagdemagus nodded slowly. "After all, murder is an act of such horrible taste that you could hardly expect an assassin to know how to dress."

This casual suggestion that murderers could be identified by their clothes made Sarah blink, but the king seemed to accept it as logical. He frowned at Jean.

"Sire, we have not come to harm anyone but only to seek Sir Kai and Queen Guinevere, who were taken prisoner not long since."

"Prisoner?" King Bagdemagus said, startled.

"You see how rumours start," Sir Meliagant said smoothly. "Really, Sir Jean, you must be careful before you repeat such silly stories. Sir Kai and the queen are honoured guests at this castle. They came at my invitation for a prolonged visit."

Sarah stared. She had expected Sir Meliagant to deny all knowledge of Sir Kai and Queen Guinevere, and this open

161

avowal of their presence surprised her. Jean, too, seemed taken aback, but after a moment he said, "And they may leave when they wish?"

"But of course," replied Sir Meliagant. "They have only to ask. But naturally, their manners are far too delicate to dream of offending their host, my father."

"Sir Kai? Delicate manners?" Jean asked blankly.

"How could it be otherwise?" Sir Meliagant said.

"And they are well?" Jean asked.

"Alas, no," replied King Bagdemagus mournfully. "They have been quite ill and are keeping to their rooms at present. Indeed," he added, "they have not even felt up to receiving a visit from me."

A flicker of annoyance crossed Sir Meliagant's face, and Jean followed up on this revelation at once. "Then you haven't even seen them?" he demanded of the king.

"But of course not. It would not be … would not be courtly to impose my presence on them when they are ill … is that not right, son?"

"Quite right," Sir Meliagant said. "It is the most basic of polite behaviour. Indeed, I am surprised that this knight should even ask such a question. I must tell you, Father, that I have my doubts about this man's claim to be a knight. Dressed like that! And, though I have been far too delicate to mention it before, I must draw your attention to this supposed knight's hair and beard. No courtly valet ever gave that hair a trim, I'll vow."

The king pursed his lips primly and looked with disapproval at Jean's hair.

"Sire," Jean said, "your son is trying to change the subject. If you have not seen Sir Kai and Queen Guinevere,

162

how do you know that they are not prisoners?"

"How could they be prisoners if they came at my invitation?" Sir Meliagant said, laughing unconvincingly. "Do you think that I brought them here by force?"

"Yes," Jean said.

"He's mad!" Sir Meliagant said to his father. "That's why his hair and clothes are in such a state!"

"He's not mad!" Sarah said, speaking as loudly and as clearly as possible. "He's telling the truth. You did take Sir Kai and the queen by force. I saw you do it."

In the silence that greeted this speech, Sarah saw the first hint of life in the young girl's eyes. Until that moment she had sat on her throne, imperturbably setting stitches in her embroidery and looking as blank as the sky on a clear summer morning, but when Sarah spoke up the girl's eyes darted quickly to Sarah's face, then immediately back to her stitching.

"The girl is mad, too," Sir Meliagant said.

"I am not mad," Sarah said. "Sir Kai and the queen were on their way to Camelot when you came upon them in the forest near the village of Milrick. Although Sir Kai was on foot, you charged him on horseback with your lance and wounded him in the hip. Then you took his sword and brought them away. You were wearing grey armour and riding a huge white horse."

The girl with the embroidery suddenly clapped her hands together and said in a sing-song voice, "Why, that sounds like your stallion Snowstorm! Can we go riding later? You never let me ride Snowstorm, but I'm sure I'm quite old enough now."

Sir Meliagant's eyes flashed with irritation, and King

163

Bagdemagus's brow furrowed slightly. "I assure you, Father," Sir Meliagant said, "the girl is dreaming or mad. There are other white horses in the land than mine."

"If you wish to know the truth, King Bagdemagus," Jean said quickly, "there is nothing simpler. Go see Sir Kai and Queen Guinevere at once. If all is as your son has told you, then you will know that we are mad. But if you find them imprisoned and find Sir Kai with a wound on his hip, then you will know that your son has been lying to you."

Sir Meliagant's face reddened with suffused rage, but he spoke calmly. "I cannot recommend such a breach in good manners. What will the queen think of you?"

The king's face trembled in indecision, but when he spoke he said, "I think I must go and look. Surely I can explain to the queen my concern for her."

Sir Meliagant rose from his seat and took a deep breath, his eyes darting fire at Jean, but then he bowed to his father and said, "As you wish, Father."

King Bagdemagus stood and stepped carefully over the train of his robe. "I shall go at once, my son, where I am sure I shall prove your honesty."

"Of course, Father, but, forgive me, were you planning to wear those clothes?"

At that, the king stopped. "Why? Why do you ask?"

Sir Meliagant shrugged apologetically. "It is nothing. It's only that when I saw the queen this morning she was sitting up and was wearing an orange dressing gown. I wonder, will that not clash with your green and yellow robes?"

"Good heavens!" King Bagdemagus exclaimed, horrified. "How fortunate that you said something! I shall go change my robes at once."

Hurriedly, Jean said, "But the queen could not care for such foppery, surely!"

King Bagdemagus took a deep breath, obviously mightily affronted. "Foppery?" he repeated coldly.

Sir Meliagant looked at Jean, his eyes glowing with triumph, but he only said, "Don't listen to this boorish lout, Father. You go to your chambers, and I shall be along in a moment to help you choose just the right outfit."

King Bagdemagus hurried from the hall, and as soon as the door was closed behind him, Sir Meliagant turned back to the archers who had stood behind them through the entire interview. "Take them to the new dungeon rooms, on the old guest wing. Lock them in separate rooms. I shall be along soon."

"Bagdemagus will never go and see Guinevere and Kai, will he?" Jean asked quietly.

"Of course not," Sir Meliagant said with a sneer. "I'll tell him that she wants to have her hair done before he visits and he'll forget all about it soon enough. He's nearly as much a fool as his half-wit daughter." He jerked his head contemptuously at the girl in white, who was still calmly sewing on her throne. "Now I must go and rid my dear papa of all the nasty ideas you've been putting in his head. Enjoy your quarters!" And with one more laugh, he strolled from the room.

The guards circled Jean and Sarah and pointed them back out the main entrance, but before they left, Sarah glanced over her shoulder at the girl. She was staring at the side door through which Sir Meliagant had just gone, her face no longer expressionless at all.

IX

NIGHT IN LOGRES CASTLE

The room where the guards put Sarah was not, strictly speaking, a dungeon. There were sconces all along each wall for candles, just like the ones in Lady Marie's room at Belrepeire, and there was a large (albeit cold) fireplace on one wall. Clearly this room had been built as a bedchamber. With no heat or furnishings, however, and with no light save what filtered in through two narrow slits in the wall, it was quite as unhospitable as any dungeon.

The first thing Sarah did after she heard the key turn in the lock behind her was hide her sword as Jean had told her to do. Hiding a sword in a bare room was not so easily done, but at last she found a way to wedge it up the cold chimney, propped up on an uneven brick. That done, Sarah wrapped herself in her cloak and huddled in a corner. In seconds, she was asleep.

She was awakened, what seemed only moments later, by the sound of her cell door slamming. In the fading light from the slits in the wall, she could vaguely make out the shapes of three men. The nearest one spoke, and she recognized Sir Meliagant's sneering voice at once. "I've come to check on my guest," he said. "Is your bedchamber quite comfortable, my lady?"

Sarah blinked and tried to shake the heavy sleep from her eyes, but she managed to say, "Quite comfortable, sir. It's a lovely room."

Sir Meliagant laughed coarsely. "Why, thank you. I decorated it myself."

Sarah was almost awake now. "I thought so, sir. Something about the walls reminded me of your heart."

Sir Meliagant's smile disappeared. "Mind your tongue, child, or you'll regret it. So, you were in the woods watching when I took Kai and the queen, were you?"

Sarah decided not to answer. Sir Meliagant's voice sounded ugly. "And who did you tell, may I ask?"

"King Arthur."

Sir Meliagant began to swear, fluently and angrily, pacing back and forth around the room. His low, guttural voice rose slowly until by the time he was done it was almost as shrill as a woman's. In his speech, Sarah figured as a meddler, a strumpet, a poke-nose, and a dozen things that Sarah didn't recognize. She rose to her feet, clutched her cloak around her as if it could provide some protection, and waited for Sir Meliagant to end his tirade. When at last he ran out of breath and rude epithets, he stepped up to Sarah and slapped her across the face, hard enough to knock her back against the stone wall. Sir Meliagant gave her a final glare, then turned to the two guards behind him. "Search her. Take everything that she might use as a weapon. Then beat her." He strode from the room, slamming the door behind him.

Sarah scrambled to her feet, wondering if she could get over to the fireplace to retrieve her sword, but the guards didn't move. At last one said, "Clem?"

"Not I," the other replied. "I've a daughter her age."

The one who had spoken first nodded slowly and turned to Sarah. "Beggin' your pardon, missy, but we has to search you. Don't worry, though, no one won't hurt you."

Sarah blinked in surprise, unaccustomed to kindness from strangers. "Won't you be in trouble if your master learns you didn't do what he said?"

"Ay," said the one called Clem. "But I'd rather face him than face my Meghan after I'd just beaten someone else's daughter."

The guards searched her, awkwardly and apologetically, but the only thing they found, in the pocket of her cloak, was her little crystal bottle. "What's this?" asked Clem.

"It's a ... well, it's a bottle."

"We see that, my lady. What's in it? Poison?"

"No, it isn't. I promise you."

"What then?"

Sarah shook her head. "I won't say. But it isn't poison."

"We'll have to take it with us."

Sarah started to argue, but she couldn't. These guards were already taking a grave risk by not beating her, for she had no doubt how Sir Meliagant dealt with disobedient servants. She said, "I understand." The guards backed away, carrying the bottle. As they reached the door, Sarah said, "If your master asks, I'll tell him you were heartless and cruel and brutal and inhuman to me."

Clem nodded. "That'd be right kind of you, miss."

"Thank you," Sarah said. Then they left, and Sarah went

back to her corner and returned to sleep.

Again, it seemed only minutes before she was awakened by sounds at the door of her room. It must have been hours, though, because there was no longer even a faint sliver of daylight from the archers' loops in the wall.

The lock clicked and then a faint orange glow showed where the door opened a crack. "My lady?" came a frightened voice. "Miss?"

Sarah didn't answer, but she rose to her feet and began carefully stepping over to beside the fireplace, where she could reach her sword.

"Is anyone in this room?" came the trembling, rather high-pitched voice.

Sarah's shoes crunched in the dirt on the stone floor, and there was a gasp outside the door. "Oh, who's there?" the voice said. Sarah was almost sure it was a woman's voice, or even a child's. "Don't hurt me!" the voice said weakly.

"Oh, for heaven's sake," Sarah exclaimed. Her voice sounded loud. "Why are you so afraid? I'm the one who's a prisoner, aren't I?"

The door opened wider, and a small head peeked around the door, lit by a candle. It was the girl from the throne room. "It *is* you," she said, with obvious relief. "I thought you might be the knight."

"It wouldn't matter if it was," Sarah said. "Jean wouldn't hurt you, either. What are you doing here?"

The girl stepped into the room. "I couldn't sleep, thinking of you." She examined Sarah in the candlelight, a puzzled expression growing on her countenance. "You don't *look* hurt. I heard the guards tell Meliagant that they had beaten you."

"Oh ... ah ... well, I'm being brave and trying not to show it."

"They didn't beat you at all, did they?" Sarah tried to think of a reply, but the girl said simply, "I'm glad. I'm glad you're not hurt, and I'm glad to know that there are still a few decent people left in this castle. I must find some way to reward those guards. I don't suppose you know their names, do you?"

"One was called Clem," Sarah said. "Did you come up here to help me?"

The girl nodded. "I couldn't leave you up here hurt. I didn't know what I could do, but I thought I might be able to help. It's bad enough that my brother locks up grown men and women, but a girl! It's a new low, even for him."

"Meliagant is your brother, then."

"Only by blood," the girl replied. They stood awkwardly silent for a moment, and then the girl said, "My name is Charis. I'm King Bagdemagus's daughter."

"I'm Sarah."

Again they were silent. At last, Charis said, "I suppose I'd better be going then, if you're all right."

"What?"

"You said you weren't hurt."

"I wasn't beaten, but I'm still a prisoner."

Charis sighed. "That's true, but I don't see what I can do about that."

Sarah stared. "You can let me out, of course."

Charis's eyes opened wide with fright. "Oh, I couldn't! What if someone found out? Meliagant would figure it out! He'd be so angry with me!"

"So what? Tell your father that your foul brother is abducting people and locking them up."

"You don't understand!" Charis said bitterly. "I tried to help you, back in the green hall, by reminding Father that Meliagant always rides a white horse, but you see how little good that did. He never believes me over his foul son."

"But you could prove you're telling the truth, couldn't you?"

"Father doesn't care about the truth. No, that's wrong. He does care about the truth: he doesn't like it. It makes him worry. He believes only what's comfortable."

Sarah stepped forwards. "Well, I'm sorry if your brother gets angry at you, but I'm not going to let you lock me back up. You can come with me, or you can go back to bed, but I've got to go now."

"Where?"

"To find Jean."

The girl's face was pale with terror and tight with indecision. Sarah gave up on her and walked around her, out the door, and into the corridor. A moment later, though, Charis was at her elbow. "You'll need these," she said, producing a ring of heavy keys. "Come on. He's probably down this way."

Together the two girls walked down the long corridor, tapping on each door and calling for Jean in the loudest whisper they dared.

"When I was small," Charis whispered between doors, "this was our guest wing. Father always had visitors, and this was the liveliest place in the castle."

"And your brother turned it into a jail?"

"He likes to have prisoners more than he likes to have guests."

"Don't you have a real dungeon?"

"Only a small one. And it's full right now."

"Sir Kai and Queen Guinevere?" Sarah asked.

"I suppose," Charis replied. "I've never seen them, though."

As they came to the very last door, Sarah knew they had found it. Three drops of blood marked the stone just outside the latch. "Open this one," she said to Charis.

Trembling but determined, Charis fumbled with the keys and began trying them. The fourth key turned, and Sarah pushed the door open. A huge shadow appeared from nowhere, gripped her roughly over the mouth and dragged her into the room. Charis, left standing in the corridor, uttered a muffled squawk but didn't scream. Then the hand released her. "Sarah?" asked Jean's voice.

"Yes, it's Sarah," she answered indignantly, rubbing her mouth with her hand. Her fingers came away wet and sticky. "Were you trying to kill me?"

"I was, yes," Jean replied calmly. "Next time you rescue me, let me know it is you, please. If you hadn't been so small and light, I might not have realized who you were."

Sarah dried her hand on the sleeve of her cloak and then rubbed the sleeve over her mouth. "Is your hand still bleeding?" she asked.

"Yes, it will not heal. Good evening, my lady." This was evidently addressed to the shaking Charis. "Forgive me for startling you." Charis nodded wordlessly, and Jean added, "I perceive that we owe our deliverance to you. Allow me to offer you my thanks."

"You're welcome," she said faintly.

"Let's get away from this castle," Sarah said. "Charis, if you lock our doors and then go back to bed, maybe no one will know that you were the one who let us out. We can be miles away by morning."

"But of course we are not leaving the castle," Jean said.

"What?" Sarah asked.

"We did not come here only to run away." Jean turned to Charis. "Forgive me for trespassing on your good nature, Lady – Charis, you say? – Lady Charis, could you conduct us to Sir Kai and the queen?"

"They … they're not on this wing," Charis said. "They're in the real dungeon. I can't get you in there. These are the spare keys that the groom of the chambers had when this was a guest wing, but only Meliagant has the keys to the dungeon."

"Perhaps we shall think of something," Jean replied imperturbably. "Would you take us there?"

Sarah could see Charis's fear surge. Evidently her humanitarian impulse to tend Sarah's injuries had not included giving aid to her dreaded brother's enemies. But to Sarah's surprise, the girl replied, almost in a whisper, "All right. Follow me. I'll take you by an old corridor that no one uses now."

It was a long and circuitous route through more dark passageways than Sarah would have thought one castle could have, but Charis never hesitated at any turning. At last she slowed and pointed down a long stairway. "The dungeons are down there."

"Thank you, Lady Charis," Jean said. "Do you know if there are guards?"

"No guards," she replied at once. "My brother doesn't want guards to overhear his interviews with the queen. He believes that she will fall in love with him in time."

"Your brother? Meliagant?"

"Yes."

Jean rested his hand on Charis's shoulder. "Why then,

this is an act of greater courage than I had thought, Lady Charis. I'm glad to see that I was right about you."

"Right about me?" Charis stammered.

"Yes. I felt sure, back in the throne room, that you were not as indifferent to what was going on as you let on, nor so empty-headed."

Even in the faint light of the candle, Sarah could tell that Charis was blushing, but the girl only said, "It isn't hard to fool my brother. He thinks all women are weak and stupid anyway. I mean, honestly, can you imagine a worse way to make a woman love you than to lock her up in a dungeon? But he thinks we're all fools."

"It is, perhaps, what will be his undoing," Jean replied. "Come, Sarah. Let us go find our friends."

"Wait," Charis said. "My brother comes to see the queen often, even at night. You take the candle, and I'll wait here and watch. If I hear him coming, I'll throw something down the stairs as a warning." Sarah noticed that Charis's voice hardly trembled at all now.

Jean gripped her shoulder again, then took the light and led Sarah down the long, dark stairs. Sarah counted forty-eight steps before they reached the bottom and found themselves in a small room, only slightly larger than Sarah's bedchamber cell. Before them was a row of thick iron bars, set into the stone floor and ceiling, and behind the bars was a single cell with two pallet beds in it. Both beds were occupied.

"My lord," said a woman's voice from one of the beds, "it is hard for me to imagine that I might grow to hate you even more than I do, but if you persist in disturbing my sleep, I feel sure that I shall learn to do so."

"You must forgive me, your highness," Jean said. His voice sounded almost amused. "I was not free to visit earlier."

The figures on both beds stirred, and one of them sat upright. "Am I dreaming?" asked the woman's voice.

"No, Guinevere," Jean said.

"Lance?" she whispered. "Is it you?"

Sarah remembered with a shock what Jean had told them back at the hermit's cottage, how he and the queen had had a love affair before he left the court.

"It is I," Jean said. Immediately, the queen leaped from her bed and ran to the bars. "I've come to set you free," Jean said.

The queen's eyes glowed in the candlelight, but at Jean's words her face tightened, and she took a small step back. "And then?"

"And then return you to your husband," Jean said gently.

"Yes," the queen said. "To Arthur. Have you seen him? Is he coming?"

"I have not seen him, no," Jean replied. "I hope to see him soon, though, when I bring you home. You are well?"

"Yes. Hungry and cold, but I'm not hurt. Oh, but Lance, I'm so worried about Kai."

A rumbling voice rose from the other bed in the cell. "Lancelot, is it? I might have known. Every time I get myself in a dungeon you come along and get me out of it."

"Quite like old times, is it not, Sir Kai?" Jean replied.

Sir Kai began to push himself up from the bed, and Queen Guinevere ran over to him. "Be careful, Kai, you'll start the bleeding again."

The knight grunted. "Too late."

Sarah, who had been in Jean's shadow, stepped up to the

bars and asked, "Is it the wound in your hip, Sir Kai? The one from the woods?"

Both the queen and Sir Kai looked quickly around, and then Sarah saw the glint of a smile on Sir Kai's face. "Is that you, Sarah?"

"It's me," Sarah said.

"The girl from the woods!" the queen exclaimed. "Sarah! Kai said that you would bring help, but I didn't believe it."

"I'm not usually wrong about people," Sir Kai said. He glanced at Jean and said, "I was wrong about you once, Frenchman, but I learned my mistake. I was sure I was right about Sarah here, though – as soon as I saw her I thought, 'There's one who will stand fast.' And here you are."

"You were more right than you knew," Jean said. "When I tell you what she has done, you will be amazed. But we shall have time for this later. Now we must get you out of here."

"But, Lance," the queen said, "that's what I started to tell you. I'm not sure that we can move Kai. That wound in his hip, it just won't heal. He's lost so much blood, I'm afraid it will kill him to travel. Have you horses ready?"

Jean shook his head.

"And do you have the keys to open the door here?" Sir Kai added. Sarah looked inquiringly at Jean. She had been wondering about that, too.

"No," Jean said. "But I fancy we won't need them." He smiled at Sarah. "Don't you think that your sword will cut through these bars?"

Sarah's heart sank, and her stomach felt like lead. "Oh, Jean," she said. "I forgot to bring it." Jean stared at her blankly. "I still have it," Sarah added quickly. "It's hidden in my room, like you told me."

"Oh," Jean said.

"Look here," Sir Kai said. "You couldn't cut through these bars with a sword anyway, not even that sword of Trebuchet's."

"Perhaps you don't know all the power of that sword," Jean said. "We should not be here at all if it were not for that blade. As for cutting through bars, I've seen Sarah slice right through a sword and armour and a knight's neck in one blow with that weapon."

The queen gasped, but Sir Kai only said, "You did, eh? Was it the fellow you were looking for, child?"

"Yes," Sarah said softly.

"Did it help?" Sir Kai asked.

"No."

"You shall have to tell me about it another time," Sir Kai said. "Right through sword and armour, you say? Trebuchet did say that it was no ordinary sword. Well, you'll have to go back and get it, won't you? You won't budge these bars by pulling on them."

"Have you tried?" Jean asked suddenly. "I have known of places where bars have seemed strong but were really rotten with rust." He handed the candle to Sarah, then gripped two bars and gave them a mighty pull. Nothing happened, and after straining for a moment, Jean let go and stepped back. Sarah saw blood welling from the gash on his palm.

"Lance!" Guinevere exclaimed. "Your hand!"

"These bars won't budge," Jean said.

"Stay there!" the queen commanded. She hurried across to her bed and grabbed the one thin blanket that lay on it. "Put your hand through the bars," she said imperiously. Jean did, and she wrapped the blanket tightly around his wound. "There. Now keep your hand above your head until it stops bleeding."

Jean removed the blanket and handed it back to her. "It won't help," he said. "My wound, like Kai's, will not heal."

A sudden rattling noise came from the stairs. "Jean!" Sarah said. "It's Charis. Someone's coming."

Jean compressed his lips, then nodded curtly. "Very well," he said. "Goodbye, my queen. We shall come back soon. Come, Sarah. Run!" Then Jean took her hand in his and all but dragged her up the forty-eight stairs, taking three and sometimes four at a time. The candle went out halfway up, but Jean's feet never missed a step. They arrived at the top just in time to grab the trembling Charis, retreat down the hall, and hide. Sarah could hear footsteps approaching just around a corner, and she fought to keep from gasping too loudly for air. The steps rounded the corner, and the hallway before them was washed in bright torchlight, but the three were pressed into a recess in the wall and the person with the torch – Sir Meliagant, she supposed – did not see them. He began down the dungeon stairs, and she and Jean began to gulp air.

"Did you find them?" Charis asked. Her voice was quiet but it didn't shake.

"You waited for us," Jean said.

"I couldn't just leave you. I thought I might stop my brother and delay him or something."

"Here is another one who will stand fast – like you, Sarah," Jean said approvingly. "Yes, we found them, but we were not able to free them this time. We must get back to our rooms to retrieve something. Do you think that you could come and let us out again tomorrow night?"

"Of course," Charis said. "I've been thinking about that. Since you are not wounded like Sir Kai, my father might expect you to join him for breakfast. If he forgets, I can do my brainless-girl act and remind him. Maybe I can get you free before night falls. Now, you'd better follow me."

For the third time, Sarah was awakened by sounds from the door to her cell. She looked up. Daylight streamed through the slits in the wall, revealing three armed guards waiting for her. "Get up," one said gruffly, pointing a spear at her. "The king wants you down for breakfast."

Out in the corridor, more guards waited, along with archers with arrows pointed at Jean. They all looked grim and menacing. "Good morning, Lady Sarah," Jean said. "These courtiers have come to conduct us to breakfast."

"Courtiers?" Sarah repeated.

"But of course! Can you not tell by their fine clothes and manners? Indeed, the hospitality of this château surpasses anything I have ever seen! To send so many fine lords to escort us to breakfast! Why, I barely had time to scramble into my velvet morning clothes! And how about you? Had you time to dress?"

Sarah stared. Jean was wearing the same tattered and bloodstained leather jerkin he had worn the night before. "Yes, of course," she said faintly. "I'm dressed."

Jean smiled at her. "And what about your necklace? You know, the necklace that Sir Kai gave you. Are you wearing it?"

Sarah swallowed. There had been no time to get the sword. "No," she said. "I didn't have time." She whirled around and said to the guard who had awakened her, "Please, could I go back in my room for a moment?"

179

"We've no time for foolishness," the guard said. "Move along."

They walked together down the corridor, both moving stiffly. Evidently crossing the Sword Bridge had used every muscle in Sarah's body, because they all hurt this morning. Before long, they came to a brightly decorated room where King Bagdemagus and Charis sat at one end of a long table covered with cakes and bread and sausages and other food. Sarah realized suddenly how starved she was. Charis smiled at Sarah, and the king rose to his feet. "Welcome, friends!" His brow clouded. "I say, had you no time to change your clothes before coming downstairs?"

Jean bowed in his smoothest courtly manner and replied at once, "But of course I did! Do you like my jerkin? Don't you think 'tis marvellously done? I daresay, since you have not been to court for several months, you have not seen the latest fashion?"

The king's eyes widened. "The latest fashion?" he whispered.

"Yes. Is it not marvellously droll? All the court now is dressing in rustic clothes and playing shepherds and shepherdesses. I had my own seamstress snip each of these cuts in the jerkin and paint them with a crust of rubies – as if I had been defending the sheep from wolves, you see."

"Crust of rubies?" the king repeated.

"To look like blood. It was frightfully expensive, but I said, 'Spare no cost! If a man is out of fashion, he may as well be dead!'"

King Bagdemagus cast a self-conscious look at his own rich silk doublet. "They even wear these clothes to breakfast?" he asked.

"It is permitted," Jean replied promptly, "but the finest of all the courtiers continue to wear silk in the morning – as you do. Indeed, I realize now that I am being absurd, telling the famous King Bagdemagus about the current fashions! Of course you already know all this, do you not?"

"Of course, of course," the king said hastily. He returned to his seat, his mind clearly preoccupied with matters of fashion.

Sarah sat beside Charis, who leaned over and whispered, "That was brilliant! Except now poor Father will spend the rest of his day hunting up shepherd's clothes to wear to dinner. Cutting holes in them, too."

Sarah grinned. It *was* clever of Jean. Yesterday, the king had seemed most struck by Sir Meliagant's comments on the poor condition of the travellers' clothes. Now Jean had taken that ground away and convinced the incredibly convincible Bagdemagus that it was they who were in fashion. She leaned over to Charis. "Where's your brother?" she asked.

"I haven't seen him yet," Charis replied in a low voice. "It's how I was able to convince Father so easily to bring you down. Unfortunately, the guards he sent are loyal to Meliagant, which is why they had all those weapons pointing at you."

Sarah began to eat, forcing herself not to bolt her food. Jean sat beside King Bagdemagus and made bright and utterly vacuous conversation with him about fashion and courtly customs. She heard him explaining in detail how long it took him before the mirror to obtain the modish "wild-and-unwashed-hair-and-beard" look that was so necessary for one who wished to be considered *au courant*, which Sarah guessed meant "in fashion". Twice Charis was seized with muted fits of giggles, and even Sarah smiled several times. She was afraid that Jean was overdoing it, but the king only nodded sagely, committing all of Jean's imaginary lunatic fashions to memory.

Then the door slammed open, and a furious Sir Meliagant burst into the breakfast room. He held a bundle of cloth in one hand and had begun to snarl something when he saw Jean and Sarah and stopped. His colour rose another level, and he demanded, "What are they doing here?"

King Bagdemagus quailed under his son's fiery glare. "But they are our guests, are they not? I ... invited them to breakfast. Should I not have?"

Sir Meliagant turned a baleful glare at his father, and Charis immediately said, in a chirpy, empty-headed voice, "Oh, it was my idea! I thought it would be so delightful to have us all together for breakfast. I don't know how I remembered that we had visitors, for of course we don't in the usual way, but I did, which I think was very clever of me, don't you, dear brother?"

Sir Meliagant turned his eyes from the king to Charis, and Sarah read scornful dislike in them, but Charis had been successful in defusing her brother's initial fury – or at least deflecting it from her father. "Well, we shall have to see to our visitors another time," he said menacingly. "As for now, we have a more pressing matter. Look at this!"

He held out the bundle of cloth, a thin woollen blanket with dark stains all over it. King Bagdemagus peered at it distastefully, then perked up suddenly and glanced at Jean. "I say, do you think that would make a good shepherd's robe?"

"This," Sir Meliagant announced furiously, "is Queen Guinevere's blanket!"

"My goodness," the king said. "You're right! Even the queen has adopted the shepherdess fashion. I shall have to see about a new robe—"

"These are bloodstains!" Sir Meliagant declared.

Sarah stiffened and peeked at Jean. Charis stared at her plate and seemed to shrink. If Sir Meliagant had found the bloodstains from Jean's wound on the queen's blanket, did that mean he had discovered their visit the night before?

"Dear me," King Bagdemagus said. "Shouldn't her maid have dealt with that? No need for you to carry the laundry about, dear boy."

"Do you not understand, Father?" Sarah had seen Sir Meliagant angry before – in fact, she had hardly seen him anything except angry – but she had seen nothing like this uncontrollable rage. "This is Sir Kai's blood!"

Sarah blinked, then stared at Sir Meliagant. "Sir Kai?" the king said weakly.

"Yes! Sir Kai is wounded. Last night, he came to the queen's bed, and they disported themselves with lust! Here is the proof! His wound bled on her sheets, but they did not see it. She has betrayed me with Sir Kai!"

King Bagdemagus's eyes widened, as he finally understood, but a slight frown creased his forehead. "Betrayed King Arthur, you mean, don't you?"

Sir Meliagant clamped his mouth closed and fumed for a second, then said, "Yes, of course. She has betrayed the king. And for that she must die! I shall have a gallows built at once."

Jean spoke for the first time since Sir Meliagant entered. "Is she not to have a trial?"

"What need is there of a trial? Here is the proof!"

"Why, to hear her side of the story, of course."

"A woman's testimony! Bah!"

"Sir Kai might testify as well," Jean pointed out.

"It would be his word against mine, and of course he would lie! There will be no trial . . ." Sir Meliagant trailed off, and a cunning sneer spread on his face. "Unless Kai wished to challenge my word in a trial by combat!"

"Trial by combat?" Jean repeated.

"Yes, of course. The old law says that when a case comes down to the testimony of two opposing witnesses, then the matter may be decided by single combat. Yes, that would be fine."

"That law," Jean said, "also allows for a champion to step in, does it not?"

"Yes, I believe it does," Bagdemagus said, nodding. "I remember that."

Sir Meliagant scowled. "And you would take Sir Kai's place in this combat? No! I would never demean myself so as to fight an unnamed knight for the queen's honour!"

"Oh, I have a name," Jean said, imperturbably. "I am called Sir Lancelot."

X

THE WOUNDED LAND

Sir Meliagant turned pale with anger – and, Sarah thought, with fear – but he had no chance to reply. King Bagdemagus, upon hearing Jean's name, leaped to his feet with delight and rushed to embrace him, chattering like a magpie about how delighted he was to have such a distinguished guest and how sorry he was not to have recognized him at once, what with Lancelot's beard and new style of dress, and did Lancelot remember that time at the annual ball when they had both worn clothes of the same shade of crimson and had made everyone else jealous and so on.

Sir Meliagant watched his father fawn over Jean for a while, then spoke. "Very well, indeed, Sir Lancelot," he said, with only the fire in his eyes betraying his hatred. "We are delighted to have you with us. Shall we set our combat for one week from today?"

"Yes, yes!" exclaimed King Bagdemagus. "It will be just like the tournaments at Camelot! Do you think we should send invitations to other knights as well?"

"No, Father," Sir Meliagant replied. "A trial by combat is between two people only."

"Very well," the king said, sighing regretfully. "It sounds a shabby affair, though. I shall have to decorate the hall! Shall we have it in the Crimson Room, do you think?"

"Wherever you wish, Father. But I see that Sir Lancelot is weary still from his days of travel. He should go back to his room to rest."

"Oh, yes, quite," replied the king. "And I must go put on my shepherd's clothes!"

"Your what?" Sir Meliagant said, momentarily diverted.

"My shepherd's clothes, of course. It's all the crack in Camelot, you know. But I can see you don't. You've never been quite as *au courant* as I, have you?"

Sir Meliagant shrugged. "Put on whatever you want, Father, but by all means go back to your room now. I shall deal with matters here."

"Oh, Father!" Charis said suddenly. "Do you know what I've just discovered? The Lady Sarah here, Sir Lancelot's companion, is a lady-in-waiting! You *know* that I've been wanting to have my own lady-in-waiting! *Do* say I can have her? Please?" Sarah turned to stare at Charis, aghast at the simple-minded tone that Charis adopted whenever she spoke in Sir Meliagant's presence and offended at being spoken of as if she were a puppy Charis had found.

"But of course, my dear," King Bagdemagus said. "You're quite old enough now for a lady attendant. How delightful for you! Meliagant, will you send for the royal seamstress? I must have some new clothes made at once. And Sir Lancelot? I shall look forwards to seeing you at dinner!"

Then they all separated. Jean was taken away by the guards, presumably back to his cell; King Bagdemagus returned to his own chambers; and Sarah and Charis went to Charis's rooms, where Charis immediately barred the door.

"How can you do that?" Sarah asked as soon as they were locked in the room.

"Do what?"

"Act so brainless! Talk in that silly little-girl voice! Aren't you embarrassed?"

Charis reddened. "Sometimes. You have to understand that I don't like it, but it's the only way I can get anything. My father does whatever Meliagant says, and Meliagant has no thought for a mere female. Acting as he expects me to act is my only tool. If I stood up to him, he'd just be angry, and I'd accomplish nothing."

"Have you ever tried?"

Charis scowled. "You've seen my brother! How do *you* think he'd respond to a rebellious female?"

Sarah nodded. "I see what you mean, of course. But I just ... it just seems so ... so *shifty* – to get what you want by pretending to be dumber than you are."

Charis coloured again, but she replied only, "You should be glad I did. If I hadn't, you'd be on your way back to your cell, like Sir Lancelot."

Sarah couldn't argue with that. "I suppose we ought to set about getting him free and then rescuing the queen and Sir Kai. Your brother gave us a whole week to figure something out."

"Yes," Charis said. "I wonder why he did that. It's not like him at all to wait for anything. I wonder what he's up to."

"Whatever it is, let's not wait with him," Sarah said

decisively. "How soon can we go and set Je— Sir Lancelot free?"

Charis thought a moment. "I'll wander around the halls and see what I can learn. You stay here with the door barred. No point in reminding Meliagant that you're not in his prison. When I come back, I'll knock four times, two fast and two slow, all right?"

Sarah nodded, appreciatively comparing the decisive young lady who stood before her, weaving plans against her brother, to the timid, trembling girl who had opened her door the previous night. Maybe, she reflected, it wouldn't be so long before they found out what Sir Meliagant would do to a rebellious female. Jean had been right: here was one who would stand fast.

Sarah had plenty of time to reflect on Charis's transformation, because the princess was gone for hours. Sarah paced and sat, sat and paced, and worried. She worried about Jean – what if Sir Meliagant simply had him killed? – and about Charis, wandering the castle and perhaps being caught listening to what was not intended for her. Then, for good measure, she worried about Sir Kai and Queen Guinevere and about Ariel, who must still be anxiously awaiting them across the gorge. Sarah wondered how it had happened that she suddenly had so many people to worry about. It seemed to her that caring about other people's well-being was very fatiguing and a great nuisance, but she supposed it was too late to go back now.

At last there came a knock at the door – *rap-rap, rap, rap* – and Sarah threw aside the heavy wooden bar for Charis to come in. "About time," she said.

"Sorry," Charis replied, entering. "I brought food."

She put down a sack and they barred the door again.

"What did you find out?" Sarah demanded.

"I couldn't get to Sir Lancelot," she said. "There are guards placed all up and down the corridor where you were last night. I suppose that's a good sign, though. I thought Meliagant might just have him executed, but even Meliagant wouldn't be so afraid of him that he would guard his corpse."

"He *was* afraid of Jean . . . of Sir Lancelot, wasn't he?"

Charis nodded with satisfaction. "When Sir Lancelot revealed his name, I thought my dear brother was going to swoon. I've never seen him turn that colour before." Then her smile faded. "I couldn't get to the dungeons, either. There are now guards at the dungeon stairs. I waited to see when they changed guards, but so far they haven't."

"So what are we going to do?" Sarah asked.

But Charis had no ideas. Sarah wanted to retrieve the sword she had hidden in her cell, but Charis said that at least four of Jean's guards were stationed in view of that door. The two girls stayed in Charis's room all day, discussing the problem, and all they could think to do was to check that night to see if there were fewer guards after dark.

They couldn't avoid dinner, however. Charis joined her father and brother at the banquet table each night, and, since Sarah was now a lady-in-waiting, she had to be there as well. Sarah hesitated, but Charis assured her that Meliagant never paid any attention to mere females. At first, it seemed that Charis was right. They arrived at the banquet hall at the same moment as Sir Meliagant, but he hardly even glanced in their direction, staring past them at the astounding sight of his father in full, "courtly" shepherd's costume.

"What foolishness is this?" Sir Meliagant demanded.

"Is it not the most precious pastoral garb?" his father replied delightedly. "I don't know when I've had so much fun as I had this afternoon with Tuttle and my seamstress." Here the king nodded at an embarrassed-looking gentleman beside him, evidently his personal valet. "It was Tuttle's idea to sew a silk lining inside the sackcloth, which I'm most grateful for. Horribly scratchy, that stuff is. Wonder how real shepherds endure it? At least . . . real shepherds do wear sackcloth, don't they?"

"I haven't any idea," Sir Meliagant said curtly.

The king's brow cleared. "Well, I think it looks fine, don't you?" The king turned around so that everyone could see his new clothes. They were indeed ridiculous, an impossible combination of coarsely woven wool and fine silk, ragged tears and precious gems, cracked leather and luxurious ermine. He even carried a real shepherd's crook, and he could not have looked more foolish if he had been trying.

"Dashed nonsense!" Sir Meliagant snapped, and for once Sarah agreed with him.

The king looked pained, although not so pained as his wretched valet. "No, no," Bagdemagus said. "I assure you, it's what everyone is wearing at court. Lancelot said so! I say, where is Lancelot?"

"He's indisposed, and won't be here," Sir Meliagant said, turning away from the king and taking his place at the table. The rest joined him, and the meal began.

Through most of the meal, Sarah stood correctly behind Charis's chair, helping to serve her "lady" and hating it, but it seemed that acting meek and docile worked: Sir Meliagant hardly looked her way. King

Bagdemagus continued prattling about his new clothes and twice managed to knock his own wine goblet over with his shepherd's staff. "Bless me," he announced jovially after the second time this happened. "I do wonder why shepherds carry these things anyway! They must be forever knocking over their crystal! And what do they do with them when they're on horseback or in carriages, I wonder?"

Sarah could only stare, and even the brittle-tongued Sir Meliagant seemed unable to reply adequately to such an inane statement. It didn't matter. The king was chattering as much to himself as to anyone else and did not require a response.

At last the meal was over, and when the king rose to leave, Charis, who had been waiting, followed at once. "Just a moment, dear sister," Sir Meliagant said.

Charis stopped, her smile frozen on her face. "Yes?"

"I'd like a word with you." Sir Meliagant's eyes were on the king's retreating form.

"Very well," Charis said brightly. "Sarah, you go back to my room and wait for me, all right?"

"But it is not all right," Sir Meliagant said smoothly. At that moment, the door closed behind King Bagdemagus, and Sir Meliagant's smile faded into a sneer. He jerked his head at the guards, who pointed their spears at Sarah. "It is with your new lady-in-waiting that I would like to speak." Reaching into his robe, Meliagant produced Sarah's crystal bottle. "My guards say that they took this from you. What is it?"

"It's … it's nothing," Sarah said lamely.

"I am not, I believe, a fool," Sir Meliagant said. "Nothing but a magic cordial would be kept in such a bottle. But you are not, I'd swear, a sorceress. Come, girl! What is it, and how did you come by it!" He stepped forwards menacingly.

"It's for my complexion," Sarah replied, remembering her talk with Adrian the Pardoner.

Sir Meliagant ignored her. "It is not a poison," he said thoughtfully. "I know because I gave some to my father's detestable little lap dog, and nothing happened. Pity. But I can see that you need to be persuaded." He nodded to one of his guards, who stood nearby. "Raven? Cut off her left hand, please."

Charis laughed brightly. "Oh, what a clever joke, dear brother! But you mustn't frighten my poor lady-in-waiting. She doesn't know your little pleasantries as I do! Why, she might think you were serious! And Sarah! You naughty puss! Do you really have a lotion for clearing the complexion? Why, how clever of you! You must let me try some!" Charis giggled.

Sarah kept her lips tightly closed and watched Sir Meliagant's face. Only by a fleeting expression of irritation did he show that he had even heard his sister's artless prattle. He jerked his head towards Sarah, and the guard he had spoken to drew his sword and approached her.

"Why, Meliagant! I declare! You're taking this joke right to the end, aren't you?" Charis's laughter was brittle and forced now, but she pressed on doggedly. "How I shall tease you about this later! But Sarah, I've just remembered that I left my scarf on the floor of my room. Run off and get it for me, won't you?"

Sarah saw from the corner of her eye that the guard with the sword had stepped quickly to one side, to get between her and the door, but Sarah kept her eyes on Sir Meliagant and didn't move. Sir Meliagant said calmly, "Actually,

192

Raven, why don't you first see my beloved sister out of the room? Then bar the door and return to me."

"Yes, my prince," the guard said. He took a firm step towards Charis.

"If you take another step, Captain Raven," Charis said in a very different voice, "I shall be forced to tell my father about the two loyal guards whom you murdered while they were on guard duty. I shall also tell what you did to their wives afterwards. He will have your head, you know. I will insist on it."

The captain froze, staring at Charis, and even Sir Meliagant seemed taken aback. "Well, well, dear sister. You appear to have been listening more than I was aware. I wonder what else you know." Charis was silent, and Sir Meliagant said, "Have I underestimated you?"

Sarah spoke. "All right, Sir Meliagant. I'll tell you what the vial contains." She paused, waiting until every eye was on her. "It isn't really mine, anyway. It belongs to Sir Lancelot. He thought you wouldn't search a woman."

Sir Meliagant smiled. "I thought as much. And where did he get it?"

Sarah chose a name at random. "From the Lady of the Lake."

Sir Meliagant's smile disappeared, and his eyes widened. "So. The Lady was right. All right, child. What does the cordial do?"

Sarah thought furiously. The name of the Lady of the Lake seemed to have struck a chord in Sir Meliagant. Now she had to think of something else he would believe but that he couldn't confirm by testing it on a lap dog. "The potion . . . doubles your skill with a sword."

Sir Meliagant searched Sarah's eyes, then smiled. "You may even be telling the truth. We shall see. Raven, conduct them to their room."

The light had been gone for at least three hours before Sarah and Charis dared open their door and look out. At various times during the long evening, they had heard voices outside their door, and they halfway expected to find a guard posted there, but the corridor was empty. Charis closed the door behind them, then led the way down the dark passages of Logres Castle.

They had decided not to bring candles with them – with more guards in the corridors there was too much risk of a light or a shadow being seen – but Charis did not hesitate, even in the paralysing fog of absolute blackness. "Here," she said. "This is where I hid the keys last night." Sarah heard a faint clink of iron on iron, then felt the tug of Charis's hand. "We'll check the dungeon first," she said. "It's nearest."

She led Sarah to a winding stairway, and they descended into even blacker darkness. Charis moved on the stairs as lightly as a sure-footed mountain creature. Sarah was not so agile, however, and by the time they reached the bottom of the stairs she had several new scrapes and bruises on her legs and elbows. "All right, you'll need to watch your step now" was Charis's only comment. "This stair comes out in a recess in the wall near the dungeons, and if there's a guard, we don't want him to hear you banging into things."

Sarah started to retort that she hadn't intended to bang into things, but at that moment Charis squeezed her hand tightly, and then Sarah heard it, too: voices. Both girls froze and flattened themselves against the stone wall.

"Is the guard gone yet?" hissed a woman's voice.

Sir Meliagant's unmistakable voice replied, but without its usual arrogance. "I sent him to watch the prisoners at the bottom of the stairs," he said. "He won't hear us."

"Good," replied the woman. "I am very nearly displeased with you, Meliagant. How could you let an outsider into this castle?"

"I'm very sorry, Lady," Sir Meliagant said. "But you did promise that no one would be able to cross the Sword Bridge."

"Silence!" Then, a moment later, "Nevertheless, I should be most curious to know how any man could have done so. But this is not just any man. How did Lancelot find out about the queen's capture?"

"A girl told him."

"A girl! A sorceress?" The woman's voice was tight and sharp.

"No, Lady! I'd swear it! She was some peasant girl who saw me attack Kai and overheard our conversation! Bad luck, but not sorcery!"

"I don't like it, though. Lancelot is the one man who should not be here."

"What should I do with him? Shall we wait for the trial by combat? I set the date for a week from now, because I wanted to talk to you first. I can kill him, you know."

"You?" There was scorn in the woman's voice. "Not in your wildest imaginings!"

Sir Meliagant hesitated, and when he spoke, Sarah could hear the anger throbbing behind his deferential tones. "Perhaps not normally, Lady, but this time I can. His right hand is wounded, and you know that won't heal while he is

195

in the Wounded Land. Besides, I have an extra edge."

"Don't imagine that my magic will save you from his sword, Meliagant."

"Not your magic, Lady – his own magic."

"What are you talking about? Lancelot has no magic."

"Not of his own, perhaps, but he has magical friends. He had with him a magic cordial that is said to double the swordsmanship of anyone who drinks it."

"Nonsense. I've never heard of such a potion, and, even if it existed, where would Lancelot get such a cordial?"

"From the Lady of the Lake," Sir Meliagant replied promptly.

Now the woman was silent, and when she spoke her voice trembled slightly. "So. I warned you Nimue might take a hand, didn't I? She has always had an interest in Lancelot. And a potion that increases swordsmanship sounds like her. The wench has always been obsessed with swords."

"Shall I use the potion then, at the trial?"

"No, little man, you shall not. I know you would love to be the one who kills the great Sir Lancelot, but I prefer to do things my way. Leave him to me."

"Will you just kill him, then?"

"Don't be a fool. You know nothing of the magical world, but we do have rules. If I were to murder someone under your own roof, it would utterly destroy all the spells that I've cast here to protect you from outsiders. That's why we couldn't just execute the queen and Sir Kai. The Law of Hospitality is a horribly ill-conceived rule, which I shall change once I control everything, but for now we must at least appear to honour it. No, as I say, leave Lancelot to me."

"Yes, Lady."

"He will not appear at the trial," the woman said. "And by not appearing will forfeit the test. Guinevere will be proven guilty, by law, which will release us from the Law of Hospitality. Then you will kill them both."

"Yes, Lady."

"My time is coming, Meliagant. With Guinevere, Kai, and Lancelot gone, Arthur will be alone."

"Yes, Lady. Except—"

"Except what?" she snapped.

"What about Sir Gawain, Lady?"

"Ah, yes, my meddlesome son and his revolting squire. A pity that he isn't here for me to deal with as well. I find it so disappointing that my own son is on the side of my enemy. Has he no family loyalty?"

"What would you do with him if he were here?"

"Crush him, of course. Farewell, Meliagant. I shall be back soon. Be ready for me."

Then there was a rush of wind, then stillness, then the sound of Meliagant's footsteps retreating down the corridor.

"An enchantress," Sarah said, sinking slowly and sitting on the steps. "An enchantress is behind it all. Just what the crone said."

"What crone?" Charis demanded.

"An old woman, an enchantress herself, that I met on my journey here. She asked me if I had heard anything about an enchantress involved in the queen's capture."

"Not just any enchantress, either," Charis added. "Didn't that woman say she was Sir Gawain's mother?"

"I wish I could tell Terence," Sarah said softly. "That's Sir Gawain's squire."

"We have to talk to other people first," Charis said, standing. "We must warn Sir Lancelot that that woman is going to do something to him."

Sarah rose hastily to her feet and took Charis's hand. "You're right. Lead the way."

But when they came to the prison wing, they knew at once they were too late. Nearly a dozen guards lay sprawled along the hallway, deep in charmed sleep, and at the end of the corridor, Jean's door stood open. He was gone.

For two days and two nights the girls roamed the castle corridors, but although they were able to retrieve Sarah's sword and hide it in Charis's room, they found no sign of Jean. On the third day, Charis obtained permission from her father (without even using her brainless-girl act) to go riding in the surrounding countryside with Sarah. Sir Meliagant overheard their plans but, to Sarah's surprise, made no objection. Indeed, he seemed almost amused. "Go ahead," he said, looking right at Sarah. "Ride wherever you want, if you think it will do any good."

If Sir Meliagant meant that they would find nothing, he was right. They rode to the gorge where the Sword Bridge had been, but there was nothing there, and Sarah saw no sign of Ariel on the other side. Then they rode into the forests around the castle, but every direction they took they came to a barrier they could not cross. Sometimes it was a deep chasm, but most of the time it was a rushing river. They couldn't have escaped even had they wanted to: Logres Castle was completely surrounded by water.

It was good to get away from the castle and from the fear that someone was listening behind every door, though. The girls talked freely as they rode. Charis told of her life at Logres, an increasingly confined life since her brother effectively usurped her father's power, leaving the king nothing to do but play with his clothes and redecorate the rooms.

"But your father . . . I'm sorry, Charis, but does your father *want* to do anything except play with clothes and decorate rooms?"

Charis was silent for a moment, then sighed. "Perhaps not. Perhaps he's not the cleverest man, let alone the cleverest king, but in the old days everyone loved him, so he can't have been *too* horrible a ruler. Better than Meliagant, anyway."

Sarah couldn't argue with that. For her part, she told Charis about her childhood with her mother and Mordecai, and then about their murders. She realized with a pang that she had not thought about her grief for the past few days, but she wept as she told the tale, and her heart yearned for her mother with a renewed ache. Then she told Charis about meeting Sir Kai and the queen and about the ensuing quest. When she was done, Charis was silent for a long time. At last she said quietly, "Now I am humbled. All I had to complain of was being confined and ignored."

"Our stories aren't that different," Sarah said. "We've both had what we love best taken away by men. I lost my mother. You lost yourself."

"But you set out to make things right."

"No, I set out to get revenge."

"But I did nothing at all. I wish I were brave like—" Charis's hands flew to her mouth, and she stifled a squawk of alarm. "What is that thing?"

They were riding alongside the river, only about two miles from the castle itself, and had just ridden out of a thicket into a small clearing, where the most horrible beast Sarah had ever seen or imagined lay dead in the grass. It was as large as Mordecai's wagon and was covered with black scales from the tip of its tail to the top of its seven long, snaky, headless necks. Lying in the grass before them was one of the severed heads. The girls' horses shied away.

Sarah patted her horse's trembling neck. "I don't know what it is. I'm glad I'm seeing it this way instead of alive, though. Who do you think killed it?"

"Whoever did it was hurt," Charis said. She pointed at the head. Its fierce teeth were clamped together in the rigor of death, but Sarah could see caught in those teeth a twisted and bloody length of chain mail.

"Gawain," Sarah said softly.

The girls dismounted and began to hunt in the bushes near the little clearing. Sarah found one footprint, half hidden under a bush, but other than that they saw nothing. After almost an hour, they walked back towards their horses. Sarah bit her lower lip anxiously. "He must be alive, or we would have found his body, but where could he have crawled and hidden so well?"

Charis said something that sounded like "Urlp."

Sarah glanced anxiously at her friend. Charis was staring at their horses, where a pale man in leather clothes leaned weakly against her mount. It was Terence.

"Lady Sarah," Terence said. His voice was faint and his face wan.

"Squire Terence," Sarah said, instinctively stepping

forwards and holding out her hand.

Terence took her hand in his and almost at once began to look stronger. "Thank you," Terence said. His face grew less ashen, and his lips curved. "I see that we were wrong, after all. We should have brought you with us from the crossroads."

"I don't think so," Sarah replied, "although I'll admit I was angry enough when I woke up that morning. But I came on with Jean, and that was probably better."

"Jean?"

"The knight we passed in the dung cart that day," Sarah explained. "This is Charis. She's King Bagdemagus's daughter, and she's helping us."

"Pleased to meet you, my lady. Then you've found them? Sir Meliagant was behind the abduction?"

"No, that was ... someone else. But Sir Meliagant is involved, and things are in a terrible fix. How is Gawain?"

"Bad," Terence said. "He has a wound in his side from that creature over there, and although it's been three days, it just won't seem to—"

"Heal?" Sarah interjected. Terence nodded. "It won't, you know. Sir Kai and Jean are wounded, too, and they won't heal, either. It's an enchantment."

Terence shook his head briskly, as if shaking off cobwebs. "I thought you didn't believe in enchantments," he commented.

"Please don't be stupid," Sarah said. "We don't have time. Can Gawain fight?"

Charis suddenly clapped her hands. "Of course! Sir Gawain can take Sir Lancelot's place and fight Meliagant at the trial!"

"Sir Lancelot?" Terence demanded. Then something lit his eyes. "Now I see! Jean Le Forestier! Was he the knight in the cart?"

"Yes, yes," Sarah said to Terence. She nodded at Charis. "That *is* what I was thinking. Again, Terence, can Gawain fight?"

"He shouldn't," Terence said. "He's lost a lot of blood. But that's his own decision. Come on, I'll take you to him."

A minute later Terence ushered them into a shelter made of woven branches and leaves. Sarah realized that in her search for Gawain she had walked not ten feet away from it and hadn't seen a thing. Inside the shelter, Gawain leaned against a tree. He looked weak, but his eyes lit up when he saw Sarah. "My lady!" he said, reaching out to her. "Can you forgive me for leaving you in your sleep? It was ill done and officious of me, and I have regretted it almost since I left."

Sarah nodded, smiling, and something lightened in her heart. "It has worked out for the best, I think," she said, sitting beside the wounded knight. "Is your wound bad?"

Gawain smiled. "I've been hurt worse."

"Really, milord?" Terence asked, one eyebrow lifted. "When was that?"

Gawain shrugged. "All right. I've been hurt nearly this bad before." He glanced at Terence, then sighed. "Yes, it's bad."

Sarah slumped dejectedly. "Then we're in trouble."

"Tell us the story, why don't you?" Terence said, sitting beside her. "You don't mind if I hold your hand while you talk, do you? I don't know why, but I feel stronger when I'm touching you."

"Of course you may. Take Charis's hand on your other side, too. That will help as well." She looked consideringly at

Terence. "How much of your blood is faery blood, anyway?"

Terence looked startled, but he said, "Half, my lady. On my father's side."

"That explains it, then," Sarah said. "You're faery enough that the enchantment affects you, but you're human enough that you could at least come here." At Gawain's and Terence's bewildered expressions, Sarah explained, "You see, there's an enchantment on the whole land of Logres, something that keeps out the Seelie Court. Ariel wasn't able to enter it at all. I'm not sure why, but it helps if the faery is touching a human. There's another enchantment, or maybe another part of the same one, that keeps wounds from healing. Meliagant called this 'The Wounded Land'. Sir Kai and Jean – I mean, Sir Lancelot – have unhealed wounds as well."

"Sir Lancelot?" Gawain repeated, dazedly.

"And you say this enchantment is over the whole land of Logres?" Terence asked. Sarah nodded, and Terence shook his head slowly. "What sort of enchanter is strong enough to cast a spell over a whole land?"

"Not enchanter," Sarah said. "Enchantress."

Terence's grip on Sarah's hand tightened. "Do you know the name of this enchantress?"

Sarah shook her head, then took a deep breath. "No, but you do. It's Gawain's mother."

The knight and the squire looked soberly at each other. "You were right," Gawain said at last. "You never really believed she was dead."

"Every generation, a different plot," Terence said. "So this time she's using Sir Meliagant?"

"Yes," Sarah said. "And unless we can find Sir Lancelot, Meliagant will execute Sir Kai and the queen."

Gawain said again, "Sir Lancelot?"

"He was the knight we passed in the dung cart," Sarah explained. "He and I came on together, crossing by the other bridge."

"I hope your bridge was easier than ours," Gawain remarked.

"I was about to say the same to you," Sarah replied.

Then she told their story, as concisely as she could, omitting only the part about her killing of the knight of the fires. As she concluded, she explained about the trial by combat that was to take place in four days and about Jean's disappearance. When she was done, Gawain closed his eyes tiredly. Even the effort of staying awake through Sarah's tale seemed to have been too much for him. Terence caught Sarah's eyes and shook his head slowly.

"He's too weak, isn't he?" Sarah asked.

"Yes," Terence replied.

"Don't be ridiculous," Gawain said, without opening his eyes. "I'll rest here for three days, then trot off and fight Meliagant if you haven't found Lancelot. I'll be fine."

"As you wish, milord," Terence said. "But if you are to fight, you should rest now."

"Yes, Mother," Gawain replied, but he slumped forwards gratefully. Terence jerked his head towards the forest outside, and the three rose, still holding hands, and went out.

"He can't fight like that," Sarah said bluntly. "And he won't be able to in three days, either."

"No," Terence said. "I shall have to fight instead."

"With me holding your hand all the while to help you stay on your feet?" Sarah asked scornfully. "You were about to faint when we saw you by our horses."

"I know," Terence said with a sigh.

"Our only hope is to find Jean," Sarah said. "Have you seen anyone?"

"No," Terence said. "We've seen no once since we killed the beast."

"Then you *did* kill that creature," Charis said, in an awestruck voice.

"Yes, though I still hardly believe it myself," Terence said. "It nearly had us. After we left you, Sarah, we came to the densest forest I've ever seen. Even I couldn't slip through it, and after an hour of trying to cut a way for our horses, we left them behind and went on foot. For three days we hacked and slashed. My own sword is ruined. If we hadn't had Gawain's sword Galatine, we'd never have got through at all."

"Gawain has a special sword?" Sarah asked.

"Yes, given him by the Lady of the Lake."

"Made by Trebuchet?"

Terence nodded, a slow smile lighting his face. "You seem to know a great deal more now than you did when I last rode with you, Sarah. Yes, made by Trebuchet – a faery sword like yours."

"What happened when you got through the forest?" Charis asked.

"We came to the Underwater Bridge that Ariel told us about. It was easy enough to identify, just a bridge built in a great stone arch, with the top a few inches below the surface of the water. The river wasn't even very fast there. It looked simple. Of course it wasn't."

"That monster?"

"Yes. As soon as we started across, it came out of the river and attacked." Terence shook his head. "Gawain sent me back to the shore so I wouldn't get in his way, and he drew his sword and slashed right at the closest of the heads."

Charis shuddered. "And cut it off?"

"No, he missed. The sword didn't touch a thing. He kept on striking out and hitting nothing, and all the time he was being bumped to the side. The creature was trying to knock him off the bridge, you see, but Gawain wedged one of his feet into a crack between stones, and although he was bashed back and forth, he didn't go over. Finally, the creature must have got impatient, and he took a bite. That was how we figured it out. You see, I was watching Gawain all the time, and when the monster bit him I saw the wound appear – but I didn't see the mouth that gave the wound."

"What?" Charis and Sarah said, in unison.

"It was magic, of course. The monster's real heads were invisible and the heads that you could see weren't really there. That was why Gawain kept hitting nothing. So I called out to him to strike where the beast's heads were *not*."

Sarah tried to imagine fighting a battle where you ignored the enemy you could see and struck where you could not. "That must have been rather hard."

"Gawain said it was the hardest battle he ever fought, because he wasn't just fighting a monster, he was fighting his own instincts. But it worked: his first blow cut off a head. Strangest thing I ever saw. He struck into the empty air to his left, and I watched one of the monster's heads, off to the right, fly off into the river." Terence shook his head slowly. "By the end, it was a question of who would last the longest. With every head Gawain cut off, the monster got slower, but Gawain was weakening, too. At last, Gawain closed his eyes and began just swinging wildly and blindly –

I'll never tell him this, but he looked exactly like Sir Griflet in a tournament – and that was how he got the sixth head. After that, the monster tried to get away. It crawled out on the opposite bank. I came out on the bridge and helped Gawain free his foot. Then we finished off the beast."

They sat in silence for a moment, and then Terence said bitterly, "But it was all useless. We killed the monster at the crossing, but neither of us can live in this Wounded Land. We can't even go back: the Underwater Bridge crumbled as soon as we were across. Worst of all, we can't do what we came here for. In three days, if you don't find Lancelot, the queen and Sir Kai will die."

XI

THE TRIAL

For three days Sarah and Charis rode back and forth across the lands of the Castle Logres. They cut through dense forests and climbed into rocky crevices, searching every hidden spot, every narrow corner, but they found nothing. Jean had simply disappeared. And every day they took food to Gawain and Terence, but neither grew stronger.

The night before the trial was scheduled, behind the barred door of Charis's room, Sarah drew her own sword from its hiding place and looked at it speculatively.

"No," Charis said. Sarah didn't reply. "Sarah, listen to me," Charis continued, urgently. "My brother is an absolute rotter, but he's good with a sword. When he used to go to tournaments, he almost always came back the victor. You wouldn't have a chance against him."

"But this is no ordinary sword," Sarah said.

"No sword will work if the person holding it is dead," Charis pointed out.

"I have a better chance against him than Gawain does right now, or Sir Kai."

"We still have tonight to find Sir Lancelot," Charis said.

"Where?" Sarah demanded. "He's been hidden by an enchantress! How can we find someone who's been hidden by magic? What if he's in the one place we can't see? Remember Gawain's bridge monster, whose heads were everywhere but where they appeared to be? No, it's up to me."

Charis shook her head firmly. "Meliagant wouldn't fight you anyway. He'd never lower himself by fighting a female."

"Then I'll need some boy's clothes. And a helm with a visor."

Charis argued for several more minutes, but at last she grudgingly agreed to help. She cut Sarah's hair, found some boys' breeches in a trunk, and even crept down to the arsenal beside the guards' barracks and took the smallest helm and coat of mail that she could find, along with armour plates for Sarah's legs. She never stopped arguing against Sarah's plan, but as the night went on, her main point – that there must be another way – grew increasingly weak, and at last she lay down on her bed, covered her head, and recommended that Sarah get some sleep before morning. "You'll want to be well rested before you die, you know," she said bitterly.

"Just a little while longer," Sarah replied, taking some practice strokes with her sword. "I have to get used to wearing mail and trying to see through this visor."

Sarah tried to keep her tone cheerful, but she knew that Charis was right. Against a real swordsman, she had no hope of victory. In the morning, she would doubtless be killed, but she didn't see anything she could do about it. It was odd, actually, when she considered her position. For

209

the past four months she had not cared especially whether she lived or died – with her mother and Mordecai both dead, what did she want to live for? – but had thought only about vengeance. Now, though, she realized that she wanted very much to live. She wanted to see Charis again, and Ariel. She wanted to help Jean and Sir Kai and the queen. She wanted to see Terence and Gawain well. Life held out more promise than she had thought it ever would again.

But that was the confusing part: the very thing that made life worthwhile again – discovering that she cared about these other people – was what made her go to her death. If she truly cared about Sir Kai and the queen, how could she let Sir Meliagant execute them without trying to stop it? If she cared about Jean and Gawain, then she had to care about their quest, too. They had both been willing to die to free the queen, and so Sarah supposed she would, too. The thing that made life worth continuing was what made it worth ending. This, of course, was stupid, but she couldn't help that, so she practised with her sword until her arms started to feel heavy, and then she removed her helm and fell into bed in full armour.

When she awoke, the sun was already high in the sky and Charis was gone. Sarah blinked at the daylight outside her window, then leaped from bed and pulled on her helm. Slinging her sword over her shoulder, she clattered downstairs to the main floor, wondering why Charis hadn't wakened her. The battle was to take place in the Crimson Room, and though Sarah hadn't been sure where that was, she had no trouble finding it. From the end of a corridor came the sound of loud voices, music (an irritating, whistling instrument), barking dogs, and bleating lambs.

Sarah followed the din, then stopped at the door of the

Crimson Room and stared, open-mouthed, nearly forgetting the battle she faced. King Bagdemagus had evidently indulged to the fullest his twin passions for decorating rooms and for dressing up in shepherd's clothes. Harried serving girls dressed in impractical shepherdess outfits were trying (and failing) to contain a cluster of loudly terrified sheep. As Sarah came near, several sheep bolted, some out the door, and others through the crowd of rustic-clad servants, prompting several crashes and more than one oath. A band of musicians stood on a platform in a far corner, diligently blowing at crude flutes – shepherds' pipes, Sarah supposed. Kitchen lackeys yelled at one another and tried to balance trays of food in one hand while holding shepherds' crooks in the other. They all stepped carefully around a wide semicircular space to the right of the door, where a large ram was tethered to the wall. The ram, obviously not joining in the spirit of the day, was lunging out to the extent of his rope, trying to butt anyone who ventured too close. Two overturned serving trays and some broken crockery within the clear space around the ram testified as to what would happen to the careless servant who came within range. A real and very large haystack dominated the other side of the room, and beside it was a long table covered with an embroidered tablecloth and laden with all sorts of meats and delicacies. Three sheepdogs stood on the table gorging themselves on these refreshments, stopping only to growl menacingly at anyone who tried to move them. The servants were all dressed in leather and coarse sackcloth (probably without the benefit of silk lining), and even the armed guards arrayed along the walls were gaily decked out with wildflowers. From their expressions, Sarah had no trouble guessing the guards' opinion of their pastoral finery.

At the centre of the room was King Bagdemagus in a new shepherd's tunic. He sat on a throne on a high dais, above the melee, clearly delighted by what he perceived to be the success of his decorating efforts. Standing beside him was Sir Meliagant, whose face bespoke murderous rage. Charis's small throne, to King Bagdemagus's left, was empty.

"This is insane!" Sir Meliagant was roaring. "This is a trial to the death, not a public fair! Get this cattle out of here!"

"There, there, son," the king said, wincing visibly, "we do have the field of battle roped off. And don't you think this is festive?"

"No, I do not!"

"Not even a little bit? Lancelot says that shepherds are all the rage just now, and you wouldn't—"

"You old fool! Can't you think of anything for yourself? Your precious Lancelot only said that to explain why his own clothes were so ragged! He was lying to you!"

Bagdemagus's eyes widened, but then he shook his head firmly. "No, I don't believe that. Lancelot is a knight! Knights don't lie to each other. Why, Lancelot would no more deceive me than you would!"

Sir Meliagant opened his mouth to reply, then shut it again, fuming. After a moment, though, he replied, "I think, Father, that it is obvious which of us is to be trusted. Both Lancelot and I promised to be here to face each other in mortal combat. I have kept my promise, but I do not see your precious Lancelot anywhere, do you?"

The king looked around the bustling room. "No, no, I don't. Is it quite time?"

"Past time, Father. No one is here to defend the queen's

honour, after all. By the laws of the trial by combat, that means that my charge has been vindicated."

"No, no, Meliagant," King Bagdemagus said anxiously. "Let us wait another few minutes. Someone *must* show up for the battle. Why, if no one comes, I shall have done all this preparaton for nothing! It would be like having a wedding with no bride!"

"Or a funeral with no corpse," Sir Meliagant replied.

"Yes! Exactly!"

"I'm sorry, Father, but the rules of the trial are very clear. If no one appears—"

Sarah judged it time to make her presence known. Her heart pounding, she pushed past the two courtiers who had blocked her from Sir Meliagant's vision. Once through the crowd, she saw an open area, enclosed by ropes and surrounded by castle servants and courtiers, where the battle was evidently to take place. She saw something else, too: over his armour, Sir Meliagant wore a white tunic emblazoned with a red cross. It was the mark that Jean had described, the mark of the Templar.

Saying not a word, Sarah stepped over the rope into the enclosure, and a hush fell over the human occupants in the room. It might have been dramatic, but in this case human silence only made the animal noise seem louder. From the sound of it, two of the sheepdogs were arguing over some delicacy on the refreshment table.

"Who are you?" Sir Meliagant demanded.

Sarah didn't reply. She had decided that was her best approach, having experimented the night before with lowering her voice. It only made her sound like a girl doing silly voices, she had concluded, so she was going to be

213

mysterious and silent. If she had to say anything, she would speak in a hoarse whisper, as Jean had when they had met him on the dung cart.

"Oh, are you here to fight in Lancelot's place?" King Bagdemagus asked suddenly.

Sir Meliagant gave his father an annoyed glance, then said, "We await Lancelot, not some half-sized proxy."

"Oh, no," the king said blithely. "You've forgotten the rules of the trial, son. Another knight may step in, if he wishes to. Is that why you're here?"

Sarah nodded.

"Oh, delightful!" Bagdemagus exclaimed. "We can have our trial, after all!"

Sir Meliagant stepped carelessly over the rope into the enclosure. "I think not, Father," he said. "It has not been my practice to fight children – or dwarfs."

Sarah stared at the Templar's insignia. "No," she whispered loudly. "You murder women and old men."

Sir Meliagant stiffened, then drew himself up to his full height, which put the top of Sarah's helmet barely above his shoulder. "I beg your pardon?" he said coldly.

"An old Jewish merchant and a woman," Sarah said. "Four months ago at the village of Milrick. I have been looking for you since then."

Sir Meliagant's eyes widened, and Sarah saw in them the confirmation that she needed. He knew exactly what she was talking about. "This boy is mad," Sir Meliagant said, but his eyes searched the front of her helm, trying to see the face behind the visor. "I repeat, I do not fight children." He snapped his fingers, and a servant leaned over the rope and presented a tray, on which were several silver goblets.

"Come, child. Drink and forget your imagined grievances."

Sarah drew her sword and cut through the stems of the goblets. It wasn't a conscious decision on her part. She hadn't planned to do anything of the sort, but her hands moved of their own volition. It was her swiftest unsheathing ever, and her sword cut through the silver stems of the goblets as if they weren't even there. The surprised servant didn't even move, but suddenly he was staring at a tray littered with ruined cups and flooded with wine. Sir Meliagant, who had also frozen for a moment, stepped lightly backwards and drew his own sword.

"Oh, very well done!" declared King Bagdemagus, clapping. "Did you see that, everyone? The challenger cut right through the cups."

"It should have been your neck," Sarah said hoarsely to Sir Meliagant, and in truth she was wishing that it had been. Her only hope in this fight had been the swiftness with which she drew her sword and the chance that Sir Meliagant would take her lightly. Both possibilities had been ruined now by her thoughtless action.

"Who are you?" Sir Meliagant said softly.

But Sarah didn't reply. She held her sword in both hands and assumed the ready position that Sir Kai had taught her.

"Very well," Sir Meliagant said. "Just a moment, my silent friend. Allow me to put on the rest of my armour." He backed off, keeping his eyes on Sarah's sword, making his way to a small table set up at the other end of the closed-off area, where his helm rested. He cautiously laid down his sword and reached for his helm, but before he took it up he reached beneath it and withdrew a small crystal flask, which he raised to his lips and drained. It was Sarah's bottle. She must have made Sir Meliagant more wary than she had known, Sarah thought, if he was taking the potion that he believed would double his swordsmanship. Sir Meliagant threw the crystal bottle to the floor, smashing it, then smiled smugly, put on his helm, and attacked.

Sarah survived Sir Meliagant's surprise charge purely by luck, and by the power of her sword. Sir Meliagant leaped forwards, swinging his sword so quickly that had she not already had her sword up in defensive position he would have killed her then and there. As it was, his blow struck Sarah's sword with enough force that it flew from her hand. Reeling backwards from the blow, she bent over to grab her fallen sword and heard the sound of Sir Meliagant's second swing passing over her. Snatching up her blade, Sarah leaped to one side, hoping to evade a third blow, and unwittingly bounced her sword against Sir Meliagant's leg in the process. Had it been an ordinary weapon, Sir Meliagant might hardly have noticed the tap, but Sarah's sword struck with enough force to knock the knight staggering away. Sarah took her defensive position again, and as she set herself she heard Sir Meliagant talking.

"How the devil did he do that? Is he a wizard? No, no, that's impossible. Lady Morgause promised that no one from the faery realm could enter this land."

Sarah realized that the magic cordial was already taking effect, and Sir Meliagant was speaking his thoughts aloud. "And do you trust your fine Lady?" Sarah whispered. "After all, she promised no one would cross the Sword Bridge, either, and Lancelot did."

"What?" gasped Sir Meliagant. Then he added, "How did he know what I was thinking?"

"I know all your thoughts, little man!" Sarah rasped.

"Can't you see? I'm a wizard! You've been betrayed! You've served your purpose now, and the Lady has sent me to finish you off."

"You lie!" Sir Meliagant screamed, but immediately he added, "Is it true? Is that what she meant when she said she was angry with me? But I've done so much for her!" With a scream, Sir Meliagant attacked again.

This time Sarah was ready, and she was able to grip her sword tightly and parry Sir Meliagant's blow. The force of the two swords striking sent both combatants staggering away. Sarah was thinking rapidly but, oddly enough, felt very calm. He was too fast for her. She would never be able to land a blow. Her best hope was to stay on the defensive and, now that she could hear Sir Meliagant's thoughts, use that knowledge to persuade him to give up the fight.

Sir Meliagant's voice began again. "He must be from the Lady. How else would he know about that Jew and that witch?"

"She wasn't a witch," Sarah snapped.

"Who are you!" Sir Meliagant screamed furiously.

"Remember the knight that you sent to supervise the burning that night? The knight with the black beard and the loud voice?"

"Who told him about Sir Corbon?"

"I've already killed him. Sir Corbon's head lies in the fields beyond the Sword Bridge."

"But why?" Sir Meliagant was speaking in his normal voice now. "The Lady herself sent me to do it! I was only obeying her orders!"

Sarah blinked with surprise and exclaimed, "The enchantress sent you to kill them?"

"No, no, of course not. She sent me to incite unrest, to

show that Arthur's peace was weakening, but she never said *not* to kill those two."

Sarah heard fear in Sir Meliagant's voice, and she swiftly followed up her advantage. "But she didn't mean you to, all the same! Now she's very angry with you! You shouldn't have chosen them for your crime!"

"But I didn't choose them!" Sir Meliagant said, his voice cracking. "It was the priest!"

"Priest?" Sarah repeated, and nearly lost her head. The introduction of yet another participant in the incident had taken her by surprise, and Sir Meliagant's third attack almost broke through her defences. She deflected his blow upwards slightly, but his sword struck her in the temple. She saw lights and heard a roaring in her head as she staggered to one side and fell. Her helm flew from her head, and without it there seemed to be light everywhere, except that her right eye didn't seem to work. Miraculously, she still held her sword, and though she couldn't see clearly, she flailed frantically around her, desperate to keep Sir Meliagant from finishing her.

She heard Sir Meliagant scream with pain, and she scrambled to her feet and scurried to the rear. Slowly her vision cleared, though her right eye was still blocked, and she could see Sir Meliagant again. He stood in the centre of the battle enclosure, blood welling from a long scratch across his chest.

"You cut right through my armour," he said. Then he looked up at Sarah again and said, "You!"

"That's right," Sarah said. "Me. A girl."

"Well done! Well done!" announced a cheerful voice. King Bagdemagus was climbing over the rope into the enclosure. "I don't know when I've had so much fun! Shall we all have a spot of wine to refresh ourselves? I say! What happened to the refreshment table? Have the servants been at the sweetmeats! Goodness, what a mess they've made!"

"Get out of my way, Father," Sir Meliagant said. He added immediately, "Old fool! I don't think I can bear him any longer. Tonight I shall have his throat cut while he sleeps."

"What, son?" King Bagdemagus said, his face blank.

"I said to get out of my way!" With his left arm, Sir Meliagant gave his father a shove that sent him reeling towards the wall where the ram was tied. Sarah heard a bellow from the ram and a shout from King Bagdemagus and was vaguely aware of a commotion, but her eyes were on Sir Meliagant.

"Lady Sarah," Sir Meliagant said, his lips curling in a sneer. He seemed to have lost his superstitious dread now that he could see her face.

"What priest?" Sarah asked.

"A travelling priest. It was he who told the village that a Jew had poisoned their well," Sir Meliagant said. "All I did was provide the Jew – the pedlar I had seen camped nearby. A lucky coincidence, no? I didn't even take part in the execution. I let my vassal, Sir Corbon, lead the villagers in that while I watched from the crowd."

"Mordecai hadn't poisoned anything!" Sarah said.

"Do you think I cared? All I wanted was a disturbance. If I hadn't killed the Jew and his wench, I would have just burned the village. This seemed easier." Then he nodded slowly to himself. "She was lying. She's not from the Lady. I'll kill her now and then all will be well."

"No, Meliagant, all will not be well." This was a new voice, familiar but out of place. Sarah stepped back and glanced quickly around. There, standing at the end of the enclosure, was Gawain. He was leaning on Terence and was obviously trying to appear fit and strong, but both of them looked very ill indeed. The sword in Gawain's hand looked well enough, though.

"Gawain," Sir Meliagant said slowly. "Dear me, I see you've been wounded."

"I see you have, too," Gawain replied.

Sir Meliagant looked struck, and he said, "Good God, I hadn't thought of that. I wonder if my own wound won't heal, either."

"Of course it won't heal," Sarah said, interrupting Sir Meliagant's thoughts. "I told you: the Lady has finished with you."

"If you mean my mother," Gawain said, "then you need to know that she never keeps her men after they've stopped being useful. It's what happened to my father. No, I wouldn't be in your shoes now for anything."

"You see," Sarah said, "you're doomed. Why don't you just lay your sword down and surrender. You don't have a chance against both of us, but if you yield to us now, we won't kill you."

Sir Meliagant hesitated, then to Sarah's surprise, nodded. "Very well," he said. "I will yield. Here is my sword." He removed his helm, knelt, laid his sword on the floor between him and Sarah, then bowed his head.

Startled but pleased, Sarah took a step forwards as Sir Meliagant added, "Two more steps, and then I'll snatch up the sword and cut her legs out from under her."

Sarah hesitated, then almost smiled. The magic potion had finally given her a real edge, letting her know the treachery Sir Meliagant intended. He would grab the sword with his right hand and she would be ready with her own blade. By the time he had seized his sword, she would have his head off. Then she stopped in her tracks. To her surprise, she found that she didn't want to kill Sir Meliagant. No one deserved death more than he, but she didn't want to do it. She set her jaw, took a step forwards, and made a decision: she would cut at his sword hand, as Jean had done to Sir Corbon.

Then all plans fell apart. Throughout the exchange between Sir Meliagant and Gawain and Sarah, there had been a great bustle from the far end of the enclosure, where King Bagdemagus had fallen towards the ram, and now there came a sharp cry of alarm, and the ram appeared in the enclosure, a broken rope trailing behind him, his head lowered and aimed directly at Sir Meliagant's hindquarters. Hearing hooves behind him, Sir Meliagant grabbed his sword and began to rise, and the ram struck him square on the buttocks and drove him forwards into Sarah. Both went tumbling backwards, and Sarah, to her horror, lost her sword. Sir Meliagant stood up quickly, towering over her, gave a shout of triumph, and raised his own sword for the killing blow. Then his head disappeared from his shoulders, and his body crumpled and fell heavily onto Sarah.

Dazed, covered with blood, and uncomprehending, Sarah frantically pushed the body away, then felt strong hands lift her to her feet. She began to flail against whoever held her, but then she heard a gentle voice.

"Sarah, my child, it is I. It is I."

It was Jean, and beside him stood Charis, covered with dirt. "Jean?" Sarah said. "Charis?"

"I found him, Sarah," Charis said. Tears were making

221

lines in the dirt on her cheeks. "I found him."

Sarah looked down at the ground at her feet, where the headless remains of Sir Meliagant lay, looking curiously insignificant. Beside him lay her own sword, the bright blade covered with blood. "Did you … kill him with my sword?" she asked Jean.

"You threw it at my feet," he said. "Just as we arrived."

Now a new voice interrupted them. "Capital! Capital! A splendid trial!" It was King Bagdemagus, looking ruffled and dazed but clapping enthusiastically. "Bless me if I've ever had such a time. A bit tiring, though." His eyes were glazed and unfocussed, and he nearly fell over the rope of the enclosure.

Charis left Jean and hurried to the king's side. "Father, you've had too much excitement for one day. You should go and rest now."

King Bagdemagus looked at her vaguely, showing no sign of recognition. "Yes, my dear, I'm sure you're right. Really, I don't know how real shepherds manage to do it all. Most fatiguing, let me tell you." Charis beckoned to a servant, who hurried forwards to take the king's other arm. Together they led him towards the door, and as they walked, the king said to Charis, "I say, dear girl, would you have my son, Meliagant, trot up to my room later? I have to consult him on something."

Charis took a deep breath and said, "Father, Meliagant can't. He lost the battle. He's dead."

"Yes, yes. When he feels better, of course," the king said, as they left the room.

"It was something you said last night," Charis explained to Sarah. Sarah was sitting up in Charis's bed, her head swathed in bandages. It turned out that the blow that had knocked

222

away her helm had also cut a deep gash in her temple. It had been her own blood that had been blocking her right eye.

"Something *I* said? What do you mean?" Sarah asked. It hurt to move her jaw.

"You said that Lancelot had been hidden by an enchantress and was probably in the one place where we couldn't see him."

"Oh, yes, I remember that. But all I meant was that we had no hope of finding Jean."

"I know. But in the middle of the night, as I was lying awake, it suddenly struck me that that was exactly what she would have done. So I got up and went out in the dark."

"Where?"

"To the empty field west of the castle. You see, I realized that all our searching had been in hidden places, places where Lancelot would have been out of sight, but we never looked at the field, because we could see that there was nothing there."

"But there was?" Sarah asked, impressed with Charis's reasoning.

"A round building of stone, with no doors or windows. It was there all along, but you couldn't see it. I just started walking until I ran into it, then I called out, and Lancelot replied."

"How did you get him out if there weren't any doors or windows?"

"I dug. Lancelot had been digging for three days already, you see, with his hands – or rather with just one hand, because I don't think his wounded hand was much use. He directed me to the spot where he had been working, and I came back to the castle for a shovel and started working

223

from my side. The stone walls went about five or six feet deep, but they weren't mortared together, and once we got deep enough, Lancelot was able to work a few stones free and crawl through. It was already daylight by then, and we came at once to the trial."

Sarah reached out and took Charis's hand. "Thank you." Charis smiled and held the hand for a minute, and Sarah added, "And where's Jean now?"

"Resting and eating. He had no food or water while he was in the stone chamber, and digging out last night took nearly all his strength. I've sent the court physician to see to his hand, too, as soon as he's finished with Sir Kai and Sir Gawain."

"Will a doctor do any good? What about the spell that keeps wounds from healing?"

"You never know," Charis replied. "Terence says that he began to feel better as soon as Meliagant was killed, and he doesn't need to hold on to Gawain any more."

"Good thing, too," came a mild voice from the door to the bedchamber. Terence himself stood there, leaning against the door jamb. "I love Gawain as a brother and more, but four days of touching someone constantly is more than enough." He frowned reflectively and added, "Especially in summertime."

"You look amazingly better, Terence!" Sarah exclaimed, smiling at the squire.

"And so do you," Terence replied.

"With this bandage over half my face?"

Terence grinned. "It's a handicap, surely, but the part of your face that I can see is smiling. I had not seen that before from you, but you should do it often; truly, it suits you."

Sarah felt herself blushing, and, to change the subject,

said, "But how did you come to be at the trial? You looked like a death's head on a stick."

"Gawain and I had been walking, hobbling, or crawling most of the night, I think," Terence said. "We still arrived too late. If you hadn't taken Lancelot's place in the trial and held Meliagant off, I suppose we'd be dead now. Meliagant would have had no trouble dispatching us, as weak as we were."

"You seem to be back to normal now," Sarah said.

"As you will be soon. I thought at first that your wound was mortal, but I gather that you will survive, after all."

"Yes," Charis said. "Sarah cannot be defeated so easily."

"No, indeed. I'll tell the others so," Terence said. "That's why I'm here. All of your wounded friends are inquiring after you, and since I'm the only one who's well, they sent me." He smiled. "With all sorts of messages of gratitude and praise for your courage and so on. I won't bore you with them all, but allow me to say that it has been an honour too great for words to ride beside you." The squire bowed deeply and reverently to her, and then he was gone.

Charis squeezed Sarah's hand, which she was still holding, and said, "Can I bring you anything, Sarah?"

Sarah smiled back and shook her head. "I think I'd just like to rest again." Then, warmed with the unfamiliar feeling of having completed something, Sarah went back to sleep, and when she awoke the next morning, Ariel was there.

XII

HER OWN PRINCESS

For the next week, Sarah remained in bed. The cut in her head was healing nicely, a sure sign that Morgause's enchantment had been broken, but every time she tried to stand she grew dizzy and her head throbbed painfully. At last, though, even the pain and dizziness began to fade, and she was free to enjoy resting and being treated like a hero.

Ariel was at Sarah's bedside constantly, and Charis spent as much time as she could with them, but Charis had other concerns to deal with, such as her father. King Bagdemagus had taken to his bed immediately after the trial, and while none of the physicians could find anything wrong with him, he still acted as though he were near death. "Sometimes I just have to leave the room," Charis admitted to Sarah. "For him to be calling for a priest every hour and patting my hand and telling me I've always been a good daughter and burping out huge mournful sighs every few minutes – it puts me all out of patience with him! And with so many people in the castle who really *are* injured, too!"

She made a sharp, dismissive motion with her hand, then after a moment added contritely, "But then I remember that he *has* lost his son. I suppose I should be grateful that at least he's stopped asking for Meliagant quite so often."

"He still doesn't believe Sir Meliagant's dead?" Sarah asked.

"I think I told you once: Father's only good at believing what's comfortable for him."

"I'm not sure that can be called believing," commented Ariel.

The three were silent for a moment. Then Sarah asked, "What about all the other invalids, then? How are Sir Kai and Gawain and Jean and Terence?"

Charis said, "The knights are all improving. As for Terence, he's been gone two days now."

"I wondered why he hadn't been in to visit," Sarah said. "Where did he go?"

"To Camelot, of course. He stayed long enough to be sure that everyone was mending, then hurried off to tell King Arthur that the queen and Sir Kai were safe. He invited Guinevere to go with him, but she wouldn't leave the wounded knights. She's been tireless, caring for Sir Kai and Sir Gawain. Lancelot's nearly well. In fact, he's been helping me with the guards."

"Helping you with the guards?" Sarah asked.

"Yes," Charis replied. "Remember you told me about those guards who refused to beat you? Well, I found those two, Clem and Coll – that's the other one's name – and they've been helping me separate the men that are faithful to my father from the ones that were my brother's men."

"What do you do with them? Your brother's men, I mean."

"Meliagant's right-hand man, Captain Raven, is in the dungeon. The others I'm expelling from Logres."

Sarah blinked at Charis and was silent. It hadn't occurred to her until that moment that with Sir Meliagant dead and King Bagdemagus in bed, someone else would have to rule the land of Logres. "Don't some of the guards object to being sent away?" she asked at last. "Especially by a girl?"

"A few did at first, but not any more." Charis smiled. "That's how Lancelot's been helping me."

Sarah remembered again the girl with the empty face that she had seen on the little throne beside King Bagdemagus that first day and the timid, indecisive child who had opened Sarah's door later that night. It was hard to imagine that Charis had ever been those people. She was like a tightly coiled flower bud encased in ice that had burst into bloom as soon as the ice had melted.

"As for the guards who've stayed," Charis added, "I haven't had any trouble with them. I give my orders directly to Captain Clem, and he gives them to the men. They think that it's all coming from him, and as for Clem, he says he's used to taking orders from girls. He has three at home."

Sarah grinned, a little ruefully. "You sound very fine and royal. I just hope you don't get too grand for me. I'm from simple folk, after all."

Charis's smile disappeared. "Don't ever say such a thing again, Sarah! If you hadn't come along and showed me how to be brave . . . when all's said, I'm just trying to be like you. I only hope that one day I can be nearly as grand as you are!"

Startled, Sarah murmured a hasty apology, and Charis rose from her chair. "Just don't do it again," she said sternly, but her eyes were gentle. "Now, if you'll excuse me, I must go and see Sir Kai. He told me that today he thought he would be well enough to teach me how to keep castle accounts."

When she was gone, Ariel said thoughtfully, "You know, Sarah, I rather think our friend will make a fine ruler."

Charis's ruling abilities were put to the test the very next day. That morning Sarah left her room for the first time, and although she still felt some dizziness, with Ariel's arm to lean on she was able to visit all of her friends for a few minutes and was talking with Charis and Jean when a messenger came from the front gate, announcing that Sir Hugh the Vavasour had arrived to speak with Sir Meliagant.

Ariel, Jean, and Sarah looked quickly at one another. Charis said, "This will be the one who was going to poison you."

"I assume so, my lady. He never told us his name," Jean replied. "Should you turn him away?"

"No," Charis said, with decision. She turned to the guard. "I will receive him in the green hall in fifteen minutes."

"Yes, your highness," the guard said. Sarah noted the depth of the guard's bow and smiled. Charis had said that the men took their orders from her captain, but this guard seemed to have no doubt who was in command.

"May we come with you, Lady Charis?" Jean asked.

Charis nodded. "Yes, but stay in the back, out of the Vavasour's sight, until I say otherwise. Go ahead of me now; I must see Sir Kai."

"Yes, my lady," Jean said, bowing with almost as much deference as the guard. Sarah and Ariel grinned at each other.

Fifteen minutes later, the doors to the receiving hall opened, and Sarah, standing in a corner with Jean and

Ariel, watched the Vavasour stride impatiently into the hall. "My lord!" he said gruffly, "why have I been kept kicking my heels in the hall when—" The Vavasour broke off abruptly. "Where is Sir Meliagant?"

Charis did not answer at once. Her face was pale, but when she spoke, her voice was steady. "Are you sure you wished to speak to my brother?" Charis asked. "After all, you are not Sir Meliagant's vassal. You are the vassal of my father, King Bagdemagus, are you not?"

The Vavasour scowled at Charis. "Yes, of course, but I see no need to disturb the king today. I am quite content to present my business to his representative."

Charis nodded. "Very well, then. How may I serve you, Sir Hugh? I am Princess Charis, and I am acting for King Bagdemagus now."

"You?" the Vavasour demanded scornfully. "Don't be ridiculous, child! I meant Sir Meliagant."

"I'm afraid that will be impossible," Charis replied. "It grieves me to tell you this, but my brother is dead."

"Dead?" the Vavasour repeated incredulously.

"Yes, it has been a great shock to my father – and to all of us, of course – and I'm afraid the king is still not recovered enough to conduct his own affairs. You shall have to speak to me instead."

"I think not," the Vavasour replied with a growl.

"You must do as you feel best," Charis replied. "As it happens, though, I have a few matters to discuss with you while you are—"

"Look here, child, can I speak to the captain of the guard?"

"If you wish," Charis replied coolly. She spoke to a guard

at the door. "Go and fetch Captain Clem, if you please."

"Captain Clem? No, no, I meant Raven!"

"I'm afraid Raven is not available, either. Do you still wish to speak to Clem?"

The Vavasour stamped his foot angrily. "Then who *can* I talk to?" he snapped, more to himself than to Charis.

"You sound as if you have a complaint," Charis said. "Would it have to do with the spell of protection that my brother promised for your castle?"

The Vavasour looked sharply at Charis. "You know about the spell?"

"The one that was to keep out faeries and wizards?"

"That's the one! Well, you're right. I've come to ask what's wrong with it!"

"Have you had difficulties with faeries or wizards?"

"That I have! Just three days ago! It was an old crone who came in looking for shelter! I sent the guards to throw her out, of course, but how did she get in to begin with is what I want to know! Meliagant said that his Lady's protection spell would be the death of any faery or witch who tried to enter!"

"But how do you know this old woman was—" Charis began.

"A witch? She turned half my guards into badgers, is how I know! Right in my own courtyard, too!"

"Half?" Charis asked demurely. "And the others obeyed your orders and threw her out?"

"I should say not! Dashed cowards are probably still running. I haven't seen any of them since. Now do you deny that the spell has failed?"

"Of course not," Charis replied. "In fact, the spell was

231

broken last week when my brother was killed. I'm afraid that I couldn't restore it, even if I wished to."

"Even if you—" the Vavasour repeated slowly.

"Indeed, it was about that spell that I wanted to speak to you. Am I correct that my brother's orders to you were to stop and to kill any knight who came to you looking for Logres?"

"Yes, of course."

"And this was why, some three or four weeks ago, you attempted to kill a knight and two ladies who stopped at your castle?" The Vavasour stared at Charis, suddenly wary, and Charis added impatiently, "Come, come, Sir Hugh. You meant to put poison in their water bags, I believe."

The Vavasour gasped. "How did you know that?"

Charis ignored the question. "Sir Hugh, your behaviour is unworthy of a knight. Logres needs loyal vassals, but we need honourable vassals still more. I remove you from your position. Your castle and lands are forfeit to the throne. My father and I shall give them to a worthier subject."

The Vavasour gaped at her. "You can't do that!"

"Actually, she can," came a new voice from the other side of the room. Sarah saw with surprise that Sir Kai was approaching, leaning on a crutch and supported by Queen Guinevere. "By the laws of fealty, you hold your lands at the pleasure of your liege lord."

"This is outrageous!"

"If you doubt my own word, I would be happy to ask my brother about the specifics of feudal law," Sir Kai said calmly.

"Why should I care what your brother thinks? Who is your brother, anyway?"

"His name is Arthur Pendragon," Sir Kai replied.

"Sir Kai," Charis interjected. "I thank you for your assistance, but I will handle this matter."

At the names of Arthur and Sir Kai, the Vavasour's bluster faded. "My lady," he stammered. "I'm very sorry. I was doing only what your brother told me to do. What else could I do? I didn't like my orders, but I had to obey!"

Charis said, "It is why I have not thrown you in the dungeon with Raven. But your lands and your title are most certainly forfeit. And" – Charis smiled widely – "I believe that I shall grant them – with my father's approval, of course – to the hero who defeated my brother's plots." Charis looked behind the Vavasour and smiled, looking suddenly like a child again. "I grant them to Lady Sarah of Milrick, to rule with her wisdom and in fealty to my father."

Sarah gawped at Charis. Ariel smiled broadly, and Jean laughed aloud. The Vavasour trembled with fury. "No! Not to a woman! Not my lands! Who do you think you are? You, a little girl, stripping me of my fief? You may be a princess, but you can't do this! Have you no loyalty to your brother? To your father? Whose princess are you, anyway?"

Charis rose to her feet, her face white with anger. When she spoke, her voice shook with suppressed rage. "I can do this. I have done this. And, Sir Hugh, I am my own princess!"

The Vavasour stared at her, then grasped the hilt of his sword. Before he could draw it, though, Charis spoke again, this time in a ringing voice. "Sir Lancelot! Will you escort Sir Hugh from the castle, please?"

The Vavasour turned slowly to face Jean, who stepped forwards. When the Vavasour looked into the eyes of the

233

man he had intended to poison and realized that he looked at the great Sir Lancelot, his face turned a sickly, greenish grey.

"See that you never again enter the land of Logres," Charis said, "or your life will be forfeit as well as your lands."

Defeated, the Vavasour left the room, and Charis sank exhaustedly back onto the throne. The room was still for a long moment, but at last Sir Kai said quietly, "Splendidly done, child."

Queen Guinevere added, "I would that I could summon such queenliness, my dear."

Charis took a deep breath, let it out slowly, then grinned at Sarah. "Good thing he told me all his guards had run away, isn't it? You don't mind that I've given you a castle, do you, Sarah? They're a horrible bother to keep up."

"Especially when they've got a badger problem," added Sir Kai, hobbling up to Sarah's side. Sarah could not speak. Sir Kai rested a huge hand on her shoulder. "You'll do fine. I'll help, if you like."

"And Arthur will send a new troop of guards for you," Queen Guinevere added. "I'll see to it."

Charis's grin grew to a broad smile. "And we shall be neighbours!"

The next day brought more visitors. Sarah was eating a simple luncheon with Charis, Ariel, and Guinevere and was experiencing for the first time in her life the pleasure of talking freely with other girls she trusted. It wasn't that they talked about anything of importance. Indeed, most of their conversation was hopelessly trivial – Mordecai would have shaken his head sadly over such

234

frivolity, Sarah reflected with an inwards smile. But to talk so openly, and to laugh so unrestrainedly, was somehow far more significant than any single thing that was said.

The four had been made curiously equal in their tête-à-tête. The queen had long since begged the others to stop calling her "your highness" and bowing to her, and now, laughing with the others, she seemed much younger than she ever had. Charis and Ariel, on the other hand, seemed to have grown much older since Sarah had first met them. Sarah could hardly remember the innocent and artless prattle that had betrayed Ariel's youth back at the Dividing of the Ways. Now, although Ariel talked as brightly and laughed as easily as ever, her smile was oddly grave, and her eyes were as unfathomably black as the deepest well. Sarah herself felt older. It was as if, in this moment together, away from the world that men inhabited and made in their own image, the four women were all the same age, or rather had no age at all.

The moment passed, though. A guard, having knocked tentatively on the door, entered and informed Charis that a blacksmith and a lady had come to the castle and had requested an audience with her.

"With me?" Charis asked. "Or with my father?"

"The lady said 'Princess Charis', your highness."

Charis pondered this briefly, then looked back at the guard. "Your name is Daw, isn't it?"

"Yes, your highness."

"What do you think, Daw? Is there any danger?"

The guard flushed, clearly gratified at being consulted. He responded promptly, "No, your highness. I can't say why, but when you've seen the lady, you'll know."

"Thank you, Daw. You may admit them. Will you show them to the green hall, please? And, Daw, just in case, would you ask Sir Lancelot to join us?"

Daw bowed. "I've already done so, your highness. Just in case, as you say."

The guard left, and Guinevere said, half-laughing, "You know, Charis, you are in a fair way to having some of the most loyal guards in all the land. I predict you will find more protectors than just Lancelot waiting for you."

She was right. When the four arrived in the hall, they found with Lancelot a dozen armed guards, under the command of Captain Clem, stationed along the wall. "Oh dear," Charis murmured to the others, "I'm afraid that our guests will think me very pompous."

Then the doors opened, and into the hall strode Piers. He smiled at Sarah, then, upon seeing Ariel, smiled more brightly still. After him came the most majestic woman Sarah had ever seen. She wore a green dress that glimmered with its own light as she walked, and her long black hair hung to her waist. Sarah caught her breath and knew exactly what the guard Daw had meant. This woman was good and kind and generous, or else no one was. The woman swept a curtsy to Charis – who was staring at her as rapturously as was Sarah – and said, "Good day, Princess Charis. I have come to bring you greetings from the Seelie Court."

"My lady," Charis managed to stammer. "I think I should be bowing to you, not you to me."

The woman laughed, and Sarah felt a thrill run up her spine at the sound. "I beg you not to, my dear," the lady said, turning to Sarah. "And you are Sarah, are you not?"

Sarah swallowed and nodded.

"Well done, my dear. Oh, very well done, indeed." Then the lady looked at Ariel and smiled affectionately. "But who is this? I hardly recognize this grave and quiet lady here. You have changed, child."

Ariel nodded. "I found that quests are not so simple as I had thought, that the right paths are not always easy to recognize. But you told me that before I came, didn't you, Mother?"

Sarah caught her breath and understood. This grand lady before her was Ariel's mother, the Lady of the Lake, of whom Sarah had heard only in the wildest of faery tales. A strangled sound came from Sarah's left, and she saw Jean step forwards, his face stricken.

"It is you!" he said hoarsely. "I thought you were only a dream!"

The Lady of the Lake walked across the hall and took Jean's hands in her own. "You were very young when last you saw me," she said. "Your father's kingdom was embroiled in civil war. His wife, your mother, had been assassinated by his enemies, and he feared for your life as well. So I took you away and hid you, for three years, until King Ban had put down the revolt. You see, I knew that you had a great part to play in the deliverance of this land one day."

"You mean, to help Sarah and Ariel and Charis?" Jean whispered, dazedly.

"You have indeed done great deeds here, but you have still more to do for England, Sir Lancelot."

These words sounded oddly familiar to Sarah, and she remembered that the Hermit of the Tomb had said something similar back on their travels.

The Lady of the Lake continued, "And so I became your

237

nursemaid and your mother and your sister for a time."
Jean still looked thunderstruck, and the Lady of the Lake
laughed softly. "Have you never wondered why you are
called 'Sir Lancelot *du Lac*' – of the Lake? It was your
father's gift, a remembrance of me. But indeed, you have
more than repaid me yourself, by your own care for my
daughter Ariel in her quest."

The hall was silent for a long and thoughtful minute,
but at last Piers commented wryly, "Well! When I went off
to fetch Lancelot from his woodcutter's cottage, I had no
idea I was fulfilling a lofty destiny! I thought I was just
doing the best thing I could think of at the time." The air
seemed to lighten, and Piers added, "I don't suppose
you've already eaten here, have you? We've been on the
road, you see."

Charis rose to her feet. "But of course! A meal shall be
prepared for you at once. You are welcome, both of you, to
Logres. I gather, sir, that you are the blacksmith who
escorted Lady Sarah to Camelot?"

"Just an apprentice, really," Piers said pleasantly. "But
yes. And I've come to ride back with Sarah, too. Word from
Camelot is that King Arthur is preparing a great feast in her
honour – and to welcome the others home, of course."

"And you've come as my escort?" Sarah asked.

"Heavens, no!" Piers replied promptly. "My Lady
Nimue here's been telling me all you've been up to. I
thought maybe you would escort me this time."

The invitation from King Arthur to which Piers had
alluded came officially that very afternoon, by the hand of
Squire Terence himself. Sarah and Charis were sitting with Sir

Kai, asking him about running a castle, when Terence strolled into the room. He nodded to Sir Kai. "Hello, Kai," he said cheerfully. "My lady" – here he bowed slightly to Charis, before turning to Sarah – "Gawain told me I'd find you here."

"Oh," Sarah said, guiltily, "I haven't been by to see him yet today. I hope he's all right."

"Doing better every day," Terence said, "and I suppose you have to know what it's like not to heal at all to really appreciate getting better."

"Ay," Sir Kai said, with feeling. "Have you come from Arthur? Is all well in the kingdom?"

"He's been busy enough, it seems. He and Bedivere and the rest have had their hands full putting down a series of small revolts, all timed to begin at just about the time the queen was captured. All should be in order soon, though. It seems that the spirit went out of the rebels about – as near as I can tell, about the time Lady Sarah here defeated Meliagant."

"You mean Jean, don't you? I didn't kill him," Sarah said.

"I didn't say you killed him, only that you defeated him," Terence said.

"Don't argue, child," Sir Kai added.

Terence grinned briefly, then put on a formal expression and bowed deeply to Sarah. "In sooth, I come as the king's deputy, to express King Arthur's deepest gratitude to the Lady Sarah of Milrick and to extend to her his personal invitation—"

"If this is about the grand banquet in her honour," Sir Kai said, "you can save the frills and foofaraws. Piers was by earlier today and told her about it."

Terence sighed. "And I had a speech all prepared, too," he said. "And will the Lady Sarah accept the king's invitation?"

"Of course she will!" Sir Kai exclaimed.

Terence ignored him, his eyes on Sarah's face. "I ... I don't know ..." she said. "I'm not a fine lady, like ..."

"Sarah?" Charis said sternly. "What did I tell you the other day?"

"But I'm a nobody, of lowly birth!" Sarah said.

Terence knelt on the floor beside her chair and took her hand. "My lady, I for one am not at all sure about that. But even if it were true, you have saved England by your courage, and that sort of thing is, after all, how nobodies become somebodies."

"Listen to me, princess," Sir Kai said. "If you're worried about your upbringing, I can reassure you. I don't know about your mother's family, but the man who raised you was a great man indeed."

"What? Who do you mean?"

"The merchant Mordecai, of course," Sir Kai said.

"You knew Mordecai?" Sarah asked faintly.

"He and I were, ah, very close indeed for some six months. You might say that we shared everything. Such as lice. That was when he told me about the young lady and her daughter – Esther and Sarah – whom he had taken under his protection. He even told me what your name meant in his own language: princess. It was one reason I helped you on the road, when you tried to steal my sword. You had the right name – an unusual name, you know – and you were about the right age. I was sure you were the one."

Sarah's mind reeled, but in her whirl of confusion, bits

240

of the past and scraps of information began to fit together. Brother Constans, the Hermit of the Tomb, had told her how Sir Kai had been imprisoned by that knight – Sir Turquin – for six months, and how as a part of his humiliation he had been forced to live with all sorts of outcasts, including a Jew. That, along with the vague memory from her early years of the period when Mordecai had gone away for a time, suddenly explained everything. "They killed Mordecai, you know," she said to Sir Kai.

Sir Kai nodded. "I wondered. Who did it?"

Sarah took a long slow breath. "Nearly everyone, it seems. The villagers of Milrick believed that he had poisoned their well – just because he was a Jew. I saw them drag him away along with my mother. There was a knight who was egging them on."

"That's why you wanted a sword, then. To find this knight," Sir Kai said. Sarah nodded. "And you found him, didn't you?"

"Yes," Sarah said, looking at the floor. "But before . . . but he said that he had only been following the command of the Templar."

"The Templar?" asked Sir Kai.

"Sir Meliagant," Sarah explained. "But it wasn't all Sir Meliagant, either. He was only following orders, too. The sorceress who was using him had sent him to stir up trouble."

"How do you know this?" Terence asked, one eyebrow arched high.

"Sir Meliagant told me, during the fight. Just before you and Gawain arrived, I imagine. He said he'd heard a priest telling the village that the Jews had poisoned their well, and he used the priest's sermon as an excuse to stir up a mob. He had already seen Mordecai camped nearby, you see."

"What priest?" came an imperious female voice from the doorway. Terence, who had been leaning against the door jamb, frowned slightly, then shrugged apologetically at Sarah and stepped aside. Into the room swept a tall, breathtakingly beautiful woman in a shimmering golden gown. "Did Meliagant tell you which priest, child?"

"Who are you?" asked Sarah.

"Oh, Good Gog!" muttered Sir Kai.

"I should have told you earlier," Terence said. "I came upon Lady Morgan on my way back here, and she came with me. She, ah, claims an acquaintance with you."

"Look at me, child," the woman said. "Do you not know me?"

"Yes," Sarah said. "Now I do. You're the woman who pulled me away the night of the fires."

"And?" the woman said. "Look again."

Sarah nodded slowly. "And you were the crone who helped me on the way. I can just see it in your eyes and chin."

"That's right," the woman said. "My name is Morgan Le Fay, little Alcina."

Sarah's eyes widened. "What did you call me?"

"Alcina, my dear. It is your name, after all. You are the daughter of my sister Dioneta."

A long and profound silence greeted this announcement. It was Charis who finally spoke. "I welcome you to Logres, Lady Morgan. Do come in. I suppose we are all agog to hear more of this." Then Charis frowned suddenly. "If that's all right with Sarah, I mean. Or rather with Al— what is that name?"

"My name is Sarah," Sarah said.

"Do not deny it, my dear," said Lady Morgan, settling herself in a chair.

"I don't deny it," Sarah said. "My mother told me that I had been christened Alcina, but she herself called me Sarah. So did the man who loved me enough to care for me all my childhood. My name is Sarah."

"Good girl!" said Sir Kai.

"As you wish," Lady Morgan said. "I never interfere with other people's choices."

Terence laughed softly. "That much is true anyway. It's both the best and the worst thing I know of you, Lady Morgan."

Lady Morgan ignored him. "If your mother told you your real name, did she also tell you about your real family?" Sarah started to say that Mordecai and her mother had been her real family but decided it would sound churlish and so only shook her head. "Then allow me to tell you. Your mother, Dioneta, was the youngest daughter of the Duke of Gorlois and the Lady Igraine."

"By all that's holy … !" Sir Kai muttered sharply.

"She alone of all the daughters of Lady Igraine was not an enchantress." Lady Morgan shrugged slightly. "It sometimes happens that way, I believe. For all that, she was beloved by her mother and her next oldest sister – me. Our eldest sister, however, had little use for her. Indeed, she despised Dioneta and persecuted her ruthlessly, especially once our mother died. In the end, it was too much. Dioneta ran away with a passing knight.

"I do not know why, but this infuriated my sister. She set out to find Dioneta and the knight. Eventually, she found the knight, but Dioneta disappeared, taking with her a newborn girl."

"Me," Sarah said.

"Just so."

"What happened to the knight – my father?"

"She killed him, I believe." Lady Morgan's eyebrows raised. "My dear, surely you are not going to grieve over a man you could not possibly remember?"

Sarah swallowed. Her mother must have loved this knight. "What was his name?"

"I haven't any idea," Lady Morgan said calmly. "The rest of the story you know. Dioneta was found by your cloth merchant, who took you both in and did, I suppose, his best with you." Sarah bristled but held her tongue. "All that is left to say is that while my older sister never found you, I did. I have known for some years now where Dioneta was hidden and have even visited you on occasion. Dioneta claimed to be happy where she was, and, although I cannot imagine why, I never – I say it again – interfere with other people's choices."

Sarah nodded slowly. "Why were you there the night of the fires?"

Lady Morgan's lips set grimly. "It was not by design. I have, shall we say, a fondness for my half-brother, King Arthur, and I had been for some time aware that there was some enchantment brewing against him. By my own arts, I had found that the enchantment centred on a person, and I had begun to suspect that my elder sister Morgause, who was supposed to have died years ago, was alive and brewing evil again."

"Yes," Sarah exclaimed. "She was here! That was the enchantress you told me about when you were a crone?"

"Yes. Gawain's mother. My sister. Your aunt. The one behind Meliagant. The one ultimately behind your mother's death. The one behind it all. I traced the enchantment to the village of Milrick, but there the spell's power was too strong for me. I was able to save you, but I could do nothing for Dioneta."

Terence's quiet voice broke in. "A spell too strong for you, Lady Morgan?"

Lady Morgan's face grew solemn. "Yes. Morgause is stronger than ever. This time, she centred her power in the person of Meliagant – perhaps so as to hide herself. That's why all her spells came apart once Meliagant was dead."

"But next time . . ." Terence murmured.

Lady Morgan lifted her chin. "We shall deal with that when it comes. For now, we must complete what we began. I have hidden behind a haggish crone's face for months in order to bring all to rights. Sarah, I ask you again, what priest was it who told the village that Jews had poisoned their well?"

"Why?"

An implacable light glimmered in Lady Morgan's eyes, and for a moment she looked much more like the crone. "Because he must be informed of his mistake – just as you informed the knight of the fires and Meliagant of theirs."

"No," Sarah said slowly. "I don't know what priest Meliagant meant, and I wouldn't tell you if I did. What are we to do? Kill everyone who had a hand in it? The whole village of Milrick? The farmers who gave Mordecai bad directions so that he got lost and ended up camped there? No. I do not choose to hate any more."

"But, my child, your mother—"

"And you, Lady Morgan," Sarah said, pressing on ruthlessly, "never interfere with other people's choices."

Just over a week later, they set off for Camelot. All of Sarah's friends and companions went but the Lady of the Lake, who had returned to her own world, and Charis, who stayed to care for her father. King Bagdemagus was still keeping to his bed, although he had recently begun to show some interest in living again. Sarah was partly responsible for this improvement. Charis had taken Sarah to see him, to get the king's official approval of giving Sarah the Vavasour's old castle. The king had agreed, somewhat lackadaisically, upon which Sarah – struck either with inspiration or madness, she wasn't quite sure – had suggested that when he felt better he should come help her decorate some of the rooms. Since then, his stream of mournful sighs had been increasingly interrupted with reflections like, "I wonder if she should like puce carpets." Charis predicted that he would be up and around and dressing his servants in embarrassing clothes again in no time.

Leaving Charis had been hard, but Sarah enjoyed being back on the road after the long time of convalescence at Logres Castle. It was a formidable travelling party – Sir Kai and Gawain leading the way, followed by Guinevere, Sarah, Ariel, Lady Morgan, Jean, Piers, and Terence. There was no question of danger on the road. Riding with King Arthur's three greatest knights – not to mention an enchantress – probably made Sarah safer than King Arthur was in his castle at Camelot. Such a guard was suitable, though, since it was escorting royalty: the Queen of All England. And Sarah.

Sarah was royal, too. It still felt unreal, but Sarah was gradually accepting the fact. Her grandmother, Lady Igraine, was not only the mother of Morgause, Morgan, and her own mother, but also of King Arthur himself. Sarah was, in fact, the king's niece. As she had said in wonder to Sir Kai the day after Lady Morgan's revelations, "Then I really am a princess!"

"Of course you are," Sir Kai had growled. "Haven't I been calling you that since I first met you?"

"Yes, of course," Sarah had admitted. "But you didn't know then who my relatives were."

"Didn't need to," Sir Kai had replied.

They travelled slowly and stopped often, so as to rest Sir Kai's hip, which was still irritated by riding, but Sarah enjoyed the ride as she had not enjoyed anything since her mother and Mordecai had been killed. She was liked and treated as an equal by all her companions, whom she liked in her turn. Even Lady Morgan, who could seem so distant and inaccessible when she wished, was a gracious companion. Lady Morgan and Gawain took turns riding with Sarah and telling her about the alarming number of relations she had acquired. Some of these sounded wonderful. For instance, Sarah found herself eager to meet her cousin Gaheris, Gawain's favourite brother. Other relatives sounded less interesting, though. "Sorry, Sarah, but that's the way it is," Gawain said. "You're family now, and that means you're stuck with the lot of us."

Less than a day's journey from Logres, they stopped for a brief visit at Sarah's new home, the castle of the deposed Vavasour. Queen Guinevere, with an awe-inspiring display of royal hauteur, introduced Sarah to the remaining castle servants as their new mistress. No one expressed any objection, especially after Gawain presented himself and said that he himself would be bringing a new troop of soldiers for his cousin's castle. This information was well received. The lack of armed men in the castle had been acutely felt, as none of the servants remaining felt up to dealing with an infestation of badgers. "I must beg your pardon for that," Lady Morgan told Sarah. "Had I known this castle would become yours I would have turned the Vavasour's guards into less troublesome creatures."

On the fourth day, they came to the village of Milrick, or what was left of it. Every house was deserted. Only a few scrawny chickens pecking vainly at the barren dirt of the street indicated that anyone had ever lived in these desolate buildings. "What happened here?" Sarah asked. "The village was full and bustling when I was here last – just a month or so ago."

"Look over there," Terence said, pointing to a patch of earth beside one of the nearest houses. There in the dirt were four small mounds of earth and one larger mound.

"Graves," Lady Morgan said, satisfaction in her voice. "It can only have been the plague. How appropriate, that the village that killed my innocent Dioneta for causing a plague should be stricken with the disease after all. How fitting!"

Sarah looked at the spot in the village green where her mother and Mordecai had died, then back at the house. She remembered the house. She had stolen food from it more than once, and had rejoiced to do so, but that had been a long time ago. She looked again at the children's graves. She saw nothing appropriate, nothing fitting. "Let's go," she said.

On the last day before they were to arrive at Camelot, the

cavalcade came upon a fair in a town. Sarah smiled reminiscently at the booths and tents and wagons set up on the town green. Once she would have been there, helping Mordecai show his cloth to the crowds. There was a juggler, a very bad minstrel, a man sharpening knives, another mending shoes, and assorted other typical fair denizens. Gawain parted from the rest to listen to a travelling preacher, a man in a coarse woollen cloak who wailed and waved his arms over his head, but after a few minutes Gawain came back. "I was just checking," he explained. "All this began with a fortuneteller promising that Arthur would be overthrown, but this one is just promising the end of the world. The usual stuff, in fact."

Suddenly, a familiar, whining voice reached Sarah's ears. "Gawain? Terence?" she said. "Isn't that—?"

"It is! Our old friend Adrian the Pardoner!" Gawain exclaimed.

Sarah turned, and there he was, as fresh-faced and unctuous as ever, standing on a stump and addressing a crowd of women. "This water," he was declaring, "comes straight from Canterbury itself, where it wells up on moonlit nights from the grave of our holy, blissful martyr Saint Thomas himself! Use it on your face, and it will clear freckles! Use it to reduce the swelling on your piles! But I must warn you! If you have been unfaithful to your husband, do not buy this miraculous water from me! It will make you grievously ill, for it cannot endure such baseness! There, I see several of you women to the left holding back. I beg of you, ladies, if you have betrayed your husbands, have naught to do with this water!"

Sarah nodded slowly and said to Gawain, "He's actually

very good at what he does, isn't he? Look at those women, pushing up to buy his worthless water, if only to prove to their husbands that they have nothing to hide."

"He deserves no such respect, my lady," said Terence sternly. "Come away."

They started to turn, but just then Adrian's voice rose again over the crowd. "Yes, yes, ladies! There is enough for all! And I haven't even told you the most powerful effect of this water! It is an infallible remedy for poisoned wells! As everyone knows, the despicable Christ-killers, the Jews, have come from distant lands with poison to put in all good Christian wells! But drink this water, and you cannot be harmed! Saint Thomas will not permit it!"

Sarah caught her breath, and her heart faltered. Slowly she looked back at Adrian. As before, he was wearing black robes of a clerical cut. "Not a priest at all," Sarah murmured slowly. "Just a man pretending to be one."

Lady Morgan caught her breath. "This is the one? The priest who started it all?"

Sarah nodded. Without knowing exactly why, she was certain of it. "Yes," she said. "But he didn't start it. Your sister did."

"He played a part, though," Lady Morgan said. "That's enough for me."

Sarah placed her hand on Lady Morgan's arm. "Let me."

Together the knights and ladies rode their horses through the gathered crowd, right up to the stump where Adrian stood. The pardoner squinted at them, then smiled in bright, fawning welcome. "My lady! So good to see you again!"

"It isn't so for me, fellow," Sarah said. "I have not missed your lies."

"Lies? But my lady, by the collarbone of Saint—"

"I just heard you say that Jews poison the wells of Christians. I say it is a lie, and a lie that has caused great harm. Not two days' journey from here is the village of Milrick, where an honoured Jewish man and a noble princess of the family of King Arthur were both murdered because of this lie of yours."

Adrian's mouth gaped, but he knew what Sarah was talking about. She saw the memory flicker in his eyes.

"That noble lady," Sarah continued, "was my mother. You did not kill her, but if it had not been for your lies, she would be alive today."

Adrian's eyes flickered from Sarah's face to the faces of her companions. What he saw in them made him turn pale. "My lady, I assure you that I meant no harm to anyone!" he bleated.

Sarah looked away, at the wide-eyed villagers who stood near her. "The man is a fraud," she said. "His bones are sheep bones, his pardons are useless, and his miracles do nothing. Take his wares and destroy them! Take his money and keep it for yourselves!" She gestured at the shivering pardoner. "Go on!"

Five minutes later, the newly impoverished Adrian stood in his underclothes, nearly fainting with fear, before Sarah. Everything he owned of value had been torn from him by the eager villagers. "See that you never again make your living with lies," Sarah said. "Go!"

"What?" demanded Lady Morgan. "You're not letting him go! He must die!"

Adrian cringed, and Sarah was silent. After a moment, Gawain said, "As much as I hate to agree with my heartless auntie, I think she's right. I once thought this pardoner was a vile but harmless creature who hurt only those foolish enough to believe his lies. But no more. He is a murderer. What say you, Terence?"

"I never thought his lies harmless, milord," Terence said.

Sarah didn't wait to hear the others' judgments. Leaning forwards in her saddle, Sarah withdrew her sword and held it over her head. Adrian swallowed several times, his Adam's apple bouncing spasmodically about his throat, as his eyes followed every movement of the sword. "By bloodright, this man's life is forfeit to me!" Sarah said. "I took up this sword for no other purpose than to avenge my mother's death!"

Sarah paused, still holding the sword high, then deliberately returned it to its scabbard and handed it to Piers. "I renounce that purpose today," she said. "Piers, please give this sword back to your father. It has done enough." Then she turned back to Adrian. "Go on, little man! Run!"

And he did. Holding his linen under-breeches in both hands, he fairly flew across the green. When he was out of sight, Sarah turned back to the others. Ariel's eyes were misty, and Terence was smiling, but Lady Morgan's face was suffused with rage.

"And this is how you honour your royal mother's memory, little Sarah? By letting her killer go free? What kind of a daughter would do that? What kind of a princess are you?"

Sarah met her blazing eyes without flinching. "Like my friend," she said, "I am my own princess."

Then she turned her horse back to the trail and kicked it into a canter, leading the rest down the road towards Camelot.

AUTHOR'S NOTE

One of the earliest, and certainly one of the best, of the Arthurian storytellers was a French poet named Chrétien de Troyes. His romances (that's what they're called, even though they're not all about love) started a new style and inspired a generation of imitators. He was a great artist, but like all artists could still drop the occasional clinker. His romance *Le chevalier de la charrette* (*The Knight of the Cart*) was one of those clinkers.

The story itself isn't that bad. It begins with the abduction of Guinevere and the wounding of Kai by the evil Sir Meliagant and continues through the parallel quests of Gawain and Lancelot, focussing on Lancelot. Chrétien tells of the shameful cart ride, the knight at the ford, the Vavasour, the Hermit of the Tomb, the Underwater and Sword Bridges, the false accusation of Guinevere, and the trial by combat. All of that seems to me to hold together pretty well, which is why I decided to retell this story. It's just that Chrétien also packs his story full of weird extra details that don't fit the plot – don't fit any plot, really. For instance, in Chrétien's tale, while Lancelot is imprisoned in the tower and left there to die, he gets special permission to leave for a while to fight in a tournament. Sort of a weekend pass. Then he goes back to his cell to die. Well, you see what I mean. I just get the feeling that Chrétien wasn't concentrating on this one.

But as I say, once you get past the silliness, it's a pretty good story, and I've followed the original plot pretty closely. To fill it out, though, I've also borrowed from other Arthurian tales when it suited me. For instance, from Sir Thomas Malory's *Morte d'Arthur*, I've taken the stories of Lancelot and Sir Turquin, Lancelot and the falcon in the tree, and Lancelot and Sir Pedivere (whom I call Sir Pedwyr). Finally, to spice it up and make it my own, I've put it all in the context of my primary hero, Sarah, and my secondary hero, Charis, along with some other people I invented in earlier books, such as Terence, Piers, and Ariel.

Sometimes it can be difficult to piece together the relationships of Arthurian characters, partly because there never really was a standard genealogy that the original tellers had to follow. For instance, when a fourteenth-century Welsh storyteller, author of *The Birth of Arthur*, needed the famous enchantress Morgan Le Fay to have a sister, that artist just invented one and named her Dioneta. I've done the same sort of thing, borrowing this Dioneta, giving her a daughter, and adding her to Arthur's family, not because it's accurate but because I felt like it. But, just in case it gets confusing, here is Arthur and Gawain's family tree, borrowed mostly from Sir Thomas Malory, then adapted for my own purposes.

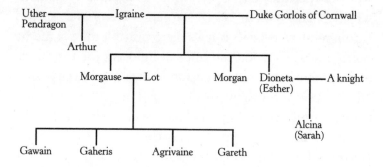

One more thing. The medieval stories of Arthur are not historically accurate. What I mean is that while there may have been a leader named Arthur, he would have lived long before the time of armoured knights on horseback and jousts and so on. The Arthurian legends are a gleeful mix and match of characters and customs from nearly a millennium of history. Knowing that, I've never made too much effort to be historically accurate. In fact, it always makes me squirm a bit when people tell me that I do a good job of presenting the *real* Middle Ages, because I've never tried to do anything of the sort. I tell stories about an imaginary world, and the only historical side to my work is that historical people told tales about the same world. In this story, though, I did introduce one piece of historical realism: the brutal murder of a Jew.

In 1348, the year that the Black Death swept through Europe, terrified villagers who were looking for someone to blame settled, as people usually do, on a group they didn't understand. The Jews lived apart, followed their own rules, didn't worship in the same way, and (maybe most important) didn't have equal protection under the law. Jews were not permitted to file complaints against Christians, which made them easy targets. Rumours spread throughout Europe that Jews were causing the plague by poisoning wells, and thousands of innocent men, women, and children were rounded up and burned. In some places, whole communities were destroyed together and, not coincidentally, their property taken over by the local lord.

This addition of grim historical fact may be a bit jarring in the imaginary world about which I write my lighthearted stories, but I can't regret it. It occurs to me that one of the most useful things to do with our imaginations, after having fun, is to imagine how we might deal with the bleak side of reality, which is never too far away.

—Gerald Morris